Praise for *The Lost Mother* by
Mary McGarry Morris

"Morris's nearly flawless prose is mesmerizing."
—*Booklist*

"Never one to shy away from the messy and bleak, Morris unflinchingly illuminates the bitter existence of neglected children and their inspiring resilience, once again proving herself a storyteller of great compassion, insight, and depth."
—*Publishers Weekly*

"*The Lost Mother* paints a nuanced portrait of small-town life. . . . Morris's characters are finely drawn, her dialogue rings true, and the epic sweep of her storytelling draws apt comparison to Dickens and Steinbeck."
—*The Orlando Sentinel*

"Morris tells a sad story and works into it slowly, capturing the feel of a hopeless time." —*Arizona Republic*

"Character-driven stories of such excellence are all too rare. The characters of *The Lost Mother* will stay in readers' minds for a long time." —Bookreporter.com

ABOUT THE AUTHOR

Mary McGarry Morris is the author of *Vanished*, which was a finalist for the National Book Award and the PEN/Faulkner Award; *A Dangerous Woman*, which was chosen by *Time* as one of the five best novels of 1991; *Songs in Ordinary Time*, an Oprah Book Club Selection and national bestseller; and the critically acclaimed *Fiona Range* and *A Hole in the Universe*. She lives in Andover, Massachusetts.

THE LOST MOTHER

Mary McGarry Morris

PENGUIN BOOKS

PENGUIN BOOKS

Published by the Penguin Group
Penguin Group (USA) Inc., 375 Hudson Street, New York, New York 10014, U.S.A.
Penguin Group (Canada), 90 Eglinton Avenue East, Suite 700, Toronto,
Ontario, Canada M4P 2Y3 (a division of Pearson Penguin Canada Inc.)
Penguin Books Ltd, 80 Strand, London WC2R 0RL, England
Penguin Ireland, 25 St Stephen's Green, Dublin 2, Ireland (a division of Penguin Books Ltd)
Penguin Group (Australia), 250 Camberwell Road, Camberwell,
Victoria 3124, Australia (a division of Pearson Australia Group Pty Ltd)
Penguin Books India Pvt Ltd, 11 Community Centre,
Panchsheel Park, New Delhi – 110 017, India
Penguin Group (NZ), cnr Airborne and Rosedale Roads, Albany,
Auckland 1310, New Zealand (a division of Pearson New Zealand Ltd)
Penguin Books (South Africa) (Pty) Ltd, 24 Sturdee Avenue,
Rosebank, Johannesburg 2196, South Africa

Penguin Books Ltd, Registered Offices:
80 Strand, London WC2R 0RL, England

First published in the United States of America by Viking Penguin,
a member of Penguin Group (USA) Inc. 2005
Published in Penguin Books 2006

1 3 5 7 9 10 8 6 4 2

PUBLISHER'S NOTE

This is a work of fiction. Names, characters, places, and incidents either are the product of the author's imagination or are used ficticiously, and any resemblance to actual persons, living or dead, business establishments, events, or locales is entirely coincidental.

THE LIBRARY OF CONGRESS HAS CATALOGED THE HARDCOVER EDITION AS FOLLOWS:
Morris, Mary McGarry.
The lost mother / Mary McGarry Morris.
p. cm.
ISBN 0-670-03389-8 (hc.)
ISBN 0 14 30.3645 9 (pbk.)
1. Motherless families—Fiction. 2. Abandoned children—Fiction.
3. Depressions—Fiction. 4. Vermont—Fiction. I. Title.
PS3563.O874454L67 2005
813'.54—dc22 2004057170

Printed in the United States of America
Designed by Carla Bolte

For the children—
Past, present, and yet to come

THE LOST MOTHER

1

THEY SAID IT WAS BAD FOR EVERYONE, BUT NOBODY ELSE the boy knew had to live in the woods. Even all these years later, with histories aligned—his own, the country's—his dreams can still erupt in this welter of buggy heat, the leaf-rustling prowl of dark creatures a canvas thinness away, and stars, millions of stars so brilliant through the slant of the flap that with all the night sounds and sourceless shadows in wait the stars crackle around them as if the tent is an enormous boiling cauldron. And yet, they sleep, his father and sister on cots across the way. Everything they own is in this tent, most important the knives, cleavers, and saws. Without his slaughtering tools, his father says he has nothing.

Supposedly the bad times came from New York City when the stock market crashed. But it seemed to Thomas that everything really started a few years later on the wintry morning his mother left them at her sister's house in town. Irene was awfully dressed up just to run a few errands, Aunt Lena sputtered that night to his father, Henry—as if she hadn't known, when she'd been the one who'd called the taxicab to take her sister down to the bus depot.

So here it was summer and his mother still wasn't back.

His father said she'd ridden the bus from Vermont down to Massachusetts to get a job in one of the big mills there. Why? Margaret kept asking. You work, why'd she get a job? Well, for extra, to help out the family, his father explained. Some ladies do that. Not any she knew, Margaret said. Not mothers anyhow.

She won't be gone long, was the most his father said in the beginning. Thomas heard his father tell his friend, Gladys Bibeau, that she was working temporary—just long enough to help get the farm back. That was a waste of time, Gladys's father couldn't wait to tell them the next day. Old Bibeau said he knew for a fact the bank was selling the mortgage to their neighbor, Fred Farley, who'd been after the land for years. Thomas understood his father might have to twist the truth and dress it up for others, but Henry Talcott wouldn't lie to his children. Never had, anyway. Soon, all talk of their mother ceased.

Once morning came living in the tent was swell again. They had set up camp in old Bibeau's woods out by Black Pond. Some days Thomas and Margaret rowed to the middle and just floated in the rippling stillness while he caught sunfish with his father's pole. His sister didn't care much about fishing. She'd end up either crying or inventing wild stories of how they should just hitch a ride down to Collerton, Massachusetts, and bring their mother back whether she had enough money saved or not—it didn't matter to Margaret. She didn't care if they stayed poor and had to live in a tent forever so long as they could be together again. It was important for Thomas not to get too caught up in her fantasies. More and more lately, it seemed he was the only reasonable one in the family. His father had always been a quiet man, only now his intractable silences were fueled by sadness and anger.

Henry Talcott butchered livestock, some cows and lambs, usually pigs from farm to farm. The work (mostly now, the looking for work) took him all over the county. He'd rattle off in his old truck before the sun was up and wouldn't get back until nine or ten at night. Gladys Bibeau came by the tent most days to see how things were going. If Henry hadn't returned by suppertime she'd drag the boy and his sister back to eat with her and her father. Margaret didn't like old Bibeau with all his grunting, belching, and gassing, but every now and again she needed to be near Gladys. That's when Thomas missed his old life most, sitting at the table with pea soup simmering on the stove while the plain, gaunt woman whistled through the gap in her teeth and pressed bowls of buttery mashed potatoes and stewed tomatoes on them. His mother might have been a terrible cook, but she was the most beautiful lady he'd ever seen, with the softest hands and a voice so sweet when she talked it came like singing.

Everyone agreed Irene Jalley was the prettiest girl in town. Her attraction to taciturn Henry Talcott had caught a lot of people off guard, especially Gladys Bibeau. Gladys and Henry had been childhood friends; then when Henry was fifteen his mother died and his father just kept on walking out of the cemetery, never to be seen again. Old Bibeau took Henry in, not from any kindness of heart, he liked to say, but to keep the damn dogs from barking every night the boy snuck into his barn to sleep. Grateful as Henry was, he hadn't been raised to be anyone's burden. The War came and, soon as he could, he joined the Army.

Henry and Gladys got engaged after he returned from

France, nothing but gray skin and lanky bones, his lungs seared by mustard gas. He tried to get right back to slaughtering work, but couldn't walk more than a few feet before he'd be so winded he'd have to sit down. Most days were spent on Bibeau's porch in worn army pants, whittling as he stared out at the dirt mountain road. It was old Bibeau who took the wheezing ex-soldier aside and pressed Gladys's mother's yellowing pearl engagement ring into his hand. After months of Gladys's care, Henry was strong enough to start back to work. It took a couple years but soon Henry had his own truck and tools and a house he was building on land he bought from old Bibeau with a bank loan. Those were twenty choice acres because they cut between Farley's dairy pastures and the main road up to Burlington. Someday that land would be worth a hell of a lot of money, old Bibeau predicted. As soon as the house was finished, Henry and Gladys were going to have a church wedding and a honeymoon to Niagara Falls.

Then one spring day Henry Talcott butchered Irene Jalley's father's three lambs. In spite of his gory mission Irene must have known instantly that this plain, rugged man would never fail her the way her own father had constantly failed her bitter mother with all his whoring and gambling, driving her to an early grave. Irene had had just one more course to go for the business college correspondence certificate that would deliver her from under her father's thumb. But her father refused to give her the seven dollars he owed her; then when she announced she was moving out he piled her books and clothes in the front yard and burned them for everyone to see.

Aunt Lena said the reason her baby sister Irene set her sail for Henry Talcott was that she wasn't used to being so completely ignored. Especially by a man.

"He climbed down from his truck and walked right by me on into the barn without a word or even a tip of his hat, like I wasn't even there," she would tell her children later, always with a note of surprise, of wonder almost, as if she too were still trying to figure out how it had all come to pass. He was a good man, respectful and hardworking, she would continue, as if testifying to them and herself what everyone already knew. If he had any faults they were just the result of who he was, a man's man who often ended a job with a drink after a long day, made longer still by his appreciation of the farmhands' bawdy tales and corny jokes. It was the life he knew best, having worked from the time he was twelve.

Irene was lonely on the little farm in rural Belton miles from Atkinson, the bigger, busier town, where she longed to live. She wanted to walk down sidewalks, on paved streets where she could talk to people on their front porches. She wanted to go to her sister Lena's beauty parlor and have her hair done and shop whenever she felt like it, instead of waiting until Henry could bring her into town, which was usually on Sunday when everything was closed. And that was another thing, she wanted to learn how to drive like Lena and work in an office where she could put her business skills to profitable use.

But she had fallen in love with Henry, who loved her back so much he couldn't think straight sometimes, much less understand her skittish ways. A few months after they married, Thomas was born. Margaret came almost four years later. Then, Jamie. He was the last, the difficult pregnancy Dr. Creel refused to help her end. It was ten thirty at night. Crying all day, the baby grew sicker as night came on. Nothing would bring his fever down. He vomited and convulsed. She couldn't get help. The nearest phone was Farley's, three miles away. And Henry had stopped in at the Dellicote farm on his way home from Bennington to see if they had any work, which they did. Then came supper and a few beers with his old friend Bob. Before he knew it, midnight was long gone and Jamie was already cold in Irene's arms.

She never got over it, Aunt Lena said. She never forgave him. After that she didn't want any more babies to bring into this world and then lose. Henry understood. His own pain was all the more unbearable because he had loved that blue-eyed boy more than life itself. And he had only himself to blame. From then on Henry slept in the little sewing room/nursery off the kitchen and watched his wife turn into someone else.

. . .

Margaret's kitten was the start of all the trouble that summer after his mother left. It was the day Thomas and Margaret had been playing Indians, tracking the men who were putting up poles that would bring new electric lines farther up the mountain. The crew had no idea the children stalked them through the woods. Suddenly one man ran behind a thicket of birch. The minute he undid his pants, Thomas leaped on top of his sister and pushed her face into the ground. Margaret hollered and the man yelped, and then, soon as he was able, began to look for them. His search, if even there was one, proved useless. By that point in the long summer the children ran those woods, every gully, rill, and copse as if it were their own backyard, which of course it had become. Panting, they galloped down the last hill and darted past the tail-switching cows in the hot, hummocky pasture behind Farley's rambling red barn. Fred Farley was the biggest dairy farmer around. He had five hired hands, a truck with his name on the door, and a shiny black sedan his wife usually drove. Round little woman that she was, she'd back the car right up over the curb in front of the movie theater, then haul their sickly son's big wheelchair out of the trunk to get Jesse-boy inside. Afterward she'd push him down to the drugstore for lemon phosphates from Leamings soda fountain.

Last week Thomas had seen them through the drugstore window after he and Margaret had walked all the way into Atkinson. Margaret's feet hurt. She wanted to go in and sit at the next table. She thought if they looked thirsty enough Mrs. Farley might buy them a soda. Margaret was like that then, not minding a bit if someone wanted to give her something for free. She kept trying to pull open the door, but he held it shut. All he had to do was say Aunt Lena's name to get her to mind. Neither of them wanted to end up in that messy house with beery Aunt Lena and her creepy husband, Max.

Anyway, in their flight from the lineman, Thomas and Margaret were hurrying alongside the barn when Mrs. Farley came down the ramp carrying a cardboard box. She called to Thomas. She knew him from the brief time Jesse-boy had gone to their one-room schoolhouse. At first the Talcott children thought she was angry they were on her property, but she only wanted to know if they'd like a kitten. There were three in the litter and they could have first pick. Before he could say no, Margaret scooped up the gray and white one. It had black-tipped ears and a black M over its nose.

"M for Margaret," his sister said, nuzzling the kitten's neck.

"Thank you, but we can't take it." Thomas dug his elbow into Margaret's dusty brown arm.

"Yes we can," Margaret countered, moving away so as not to be nudged again. The kitten perched on her shoulder, its big eyes like hers, bluely defiant.

"You know we can't," he said, narrowing his hard stare. Backing Margaret into any kind of corner could be dangerous.

"Is it your father, Thomas? Doesn't he like cats?" Mrs. Farley asked.

"He likes them all right." He tried not to squirm. "We just can't right now."

"Oh," Mrs. Farley said as if she were beginning to understand. "Well, with the barn cats there's always a new litter, so when you can have one just let me know and I'll be sure and save you one." She reached for the kitten.

"No! She's mine now and I'm keeping her."

"Margaret!" Mrs. Farley seemed amused.

That was the way people often reacted to his sister. Small for her age she made up for it in spunk. Even old Bibeau, crank that he was, knew not to push her too hard. Instead he'd address his complaints to whoever else was present: "Gladys, tell the girl to stop thumping the table." Or to him,

"Tell your sister she's had enough chicken. That wing's mine."

Mrs. Farley was telling Margaret in the cautious tone people used around kids stranded on broken ice that she should listen to her big brother: Thomas was just trying to do what his father would want. She should go home and ask permission. If her father said yes Mrs. Farley would bring the kitten by herself. She asked where they were living. And the minute she said it her face clouded. Stammering, she inquired if they were staying at their Aunt Lena's. That was the thing about backing Margaret into corners—she sucked you right in with her.

"No. We're out at Black Pond. In a tent," Margaret added, sending flares of color into Mrs. Farley's cheery, round cheeks.

"Oh, well then." Mrs. Farley plucked the purring kitten away by its scruff and returned it to the box. "When you're more settled then," she sniffed, as if she couldn't send one of her cats to go live in a leaky tent with dangling spiders and quick green snakes slithering along the damp dirt floor.

"We are settled." Just as surely, Margaret plucked the kitten from the box. "That's where we live." Hugging the purring curl of fur, she headed toward the road with Thomas swept along once again in his little sister's wake.

. . .

Because the kitten followed Margaret everywhere, they had to be careful not to go too far. Once, after hours fishing in the boat, they returned to the tent, but the kitten was gone.

"Kitty! Please come back. Please, kitty, kitty, kitty!" Margaret screamed, thrashing through bushes and trees.

They dragged back to find the curled-up kitten hidden in the blanket-tangled mess that was Margaret's cot.

Henry Talcott didn't mind the cat one way or another. If anything, he seemed glad Margaret had found something to take her mind off missing her mother so much. Neither Thomas nor his father talked about Irene, and whenever Margaret burst into tears demanding to know when she was coming back father and son retreated even further, each into his own cave of loneliness.

The wall of silence grew higher. Because Margaret was afraid to leave her kitten again, she stopped going on adventures with her brother. Thomas was tired of playing by the tent or rowing alone on the pond. The little cat was far more attached to his sister than to him. As the summer days passed, he felt more alone. His father drove even longer distances to find the few farmers left who could afford to raise animals for slaughter. After the cows or hogs were gone, they usually weren't replaced. The price of feed and hay had gone too high.

One sunny morning after a rainy week of sodden confinement, Thomas told Margaret they were going into town. Gladys had paid him ten cents last night for helping clean out her back shed and he knew exactly what he would buy with it: the Palomino, the nickel-plated, double-blade jackknife in the window of Whitby's Hardware. Margaret refused to leave her kitten alone that long. All the way into town he knew he should have made her come. If his father got home early and found her alone there'd be hell to pay. But what harm could possibly come to her? Margaret was sensible enough, and besides, who would bother with her? Especially if she stayed near the tent as he'd told her to.

Creaking toward him along the rutted road was a wagon pulled by a swaybacked, blinkered horse. Gypsies? He froze. Sometimes they crept through the woods looking for children to steal. Or, worse yet, to murder. For a while after his mother disappeared, gypsies were one of the possibilities he and Margaret had considered. At first no one would tell them anything. But now Thomas was realizing it wasn't any great mystery, just his father's deep secret—and theirs. The driver was an old woman in a red-checkered dress. Thomas raised his hand to wave just as she leaned to one side. A long brown gob of tobacco juice hit the dusty road. There weren't any gypsies. Margaret would be fine.

. . .

The minute he came out of the store he sat on the curb and opened the jackknife. Both blades were rusted. He rubbed them on his shirttail, but nothing came off. It took all his courage to go back inside. A dour, hairless man, Mr. Whitby didn't like many people, especially children. Thomas showed him the pitted blades and Whitby made a great show of examining the jackknife at every possible angle under the thin light of the hanging bulb that made his bald pate glow.

"Moisture got at it." He closed the blades and held it out to Thomas. "You got to keep it dry."

"I just bought it!"

"I know you did." He stared down at him.

"Can I have one that's not rusted?"

"You just bought the last one."

"What about that one?" He pointed to the jackknife gleaming in the window.

"That's display. It ain't for sale." He peered over smudged, rimless glasses. "So when's your mother coming back?"

"Pretty soon." As Thomas stared back a smile worked at the little man's mouth. His mother used to do Whitby's books every few months. In fact he'd been with her when he'd first seen the jackknife. She was always different when they came in here. It used to bother him the way she'd act like somebody else, something she wasn't, not his mother but businesslike, as if there were important things for her to do here so he and Margaret had better sit quietly and wait for her to be done.

"Hear she's a mill hand now," Whitby said.

Stung by his own ignorance, Thomas closed the blades. He laid the jackknife on the counter. "This ain't no good. I want my ten cents back, please."

Whitby smiled. "I don't take nothing back that's damaged."

"But I didn't do it."

"It's still a good knife." He smiled again. "And it's better than nothing, now ain't it?"

"Nothing's better than nothing." He had no idea what he meant, but felt strong saying it.

Whitby seemed confused. And mad. "Go on. Take your knife and get the hell outta here."

"It's not mine," Thomas said, leaving the jackknife on the scratched glass countertop. Whitby's eyes followed him to the door. "This one is!" he declared, snatching the jackknife from its silver display case in the window.

"Put that back, you!" Whitby yelled, but Thomas slammed the door and ran up the street. As soon as he got outside of town he picked up a stick from the road. He whittled as he walked. He wasn't very good. He couldn't make the hook-nosed, witchy faces his father used to do, sometimes with wavy lines of hair even. The best he could do after a couple miles was a sharpened tip. He snapped the spear in two, a dagger now, slipping it into his waistband. At the bottom of the gully lay a pile of broken branches, probably from the crew clearing for the electric poles. He skidded down the steep side and found a choice stick, just dry and thick enough, when a car passed above him. A big gold star glittered on the door. The sheriff. He scrambled on all fours up the gravelly rise back onto the road. Last week the bank in Atkinson had been robbed. Old Bibeau said all the crook got was a bag of promissory notes. *Maybe they got yours,* Gladys said to his father. Old Bibeau laughed. *Farley's got it now,* he crowed.

Or maybe gypsies had been spotted. Margaret! Thomas dropped the branch and ran. Suddenly every terror that could befall such a stupid little girl as his sister reared into mind. For a penny candy she'd climb right in beside them and be gone forever. People were always saying what a beautiful child she was, with her mother's delicate face. But then, she had her father's stubborn ways so maybe she wouldn't. Maybe she'd know better. No, she'd probably do what he'd just done with the jackknife, grab the candy and run. But what if she had gotten tired of being alone all afternoon and decided to go out in the boat with her kitten? The only time they'd taken the kitten out it had walked along the rim of the boat. He could just see it falling in and Margaret trying to rescue it from the bottomless water. One winter when his father was a boy, a wagon, horse, and driver broke through the ice never to be found again. Not a bone, thread, or sliver of wood was ever dredged up. She was always leaning over the side. She could dog-paddle some, but what if the boat tipped when she was trying to get the kitten back in and it fell over, right on top of her, trapping her in a watery casket. "Stupid girl," he muttered, running as fast as his cramp-toed shoes would allow, because she'd never think to swim out from under it. No, she'd be banging her head into the dark seat, bobbing up and down while she sobbed and screamed his name, over and over again, so scared and panicky he was sure he could hear her. *Thomas! Thomas! Thomas! Thomas!*

Coming in the opposite direction was the sheriff's faded green car. It stopped dead in his path. The sheriff jumped out. "You Thomas Talcott?"

"Yessir!" He nodded and panted, needing to tell about Margaret.

"Get in the car." So the sheriff already knew. Talk was useless. Speed was everything. He ran around to open the front door. "Backseat!" the sheriff barked. When he was in the sheriff locked the back door, then climbed behind the wheel. He started the powerful engine with a key attached to a rabbit's foot. Good luck. Especially to have the sheriff find him.

"No! You're going the wrong way," Thomas shouted as the car rumbled up the dusty road.

"Oh yeah?" The sheriff glanced back. He seemed amused. "Which way's the right way?" He kept on driving.

"Back there! Out to Black Pond. My sister, she's eight, and I gotta go help her, she's—"

"You got a Palomino, two-blade, nickel-plated jackknife on you, son?"

"Yes, sir."

"Give it here then." The sheriff's wide hand went back over the seat.

"It's new. I just got it."

The big fingers wiggled.

Hesitantly, Thomas held it up and the sheriff snatched it away. "T. C. Whitby's? You took it from the window, right?"

"Yes, sir. But it's mine. I paid for it. I did," he averred in a weakening voice.

"That's not what I heared. I heared you grabbed it and took off running, that's what T. C. Whitby says. And I don't think a busy man like T. C.'s got any reason or time to make up a story like that."

"Well he did. I paid him. Ten cents. Did he tell you that?"

"That's not what I heared."

"It's the truth."

"You Henry's boy? Talcott, the slaughterman?"

"Yessir. But my sister's alone. I'm afraid of her going out in the boat all by herself. She's—"

"Well, we'll get to the bottom of it." He glanced back. "One way t'other."

The sheriff didn't understand about Margaret. Thomas stared down at his stained brown pants, the torn knees and frayed cuffs. Even if he had stolen the knife his father wouldn't be as mad at him as he was going to be for leaving Margaret and her damn kitten alone all this time. And if anything happened to her . . . Oh God, he closed his eyes, unable to bear the thought. What would he do? His poor little sister . . .

"I know your Aunt Lena. Yep, she's a friend of my sister. Your mother's Irene, right?"

Thomas opened his eyes.

"I heared she's gone, right? Someplace down t' Massachusetts. Got herself a job or something there, right? Some friend of hers got it for her. A real good job. Least that's what Lena says. Well, here we go, son." He parked in front of the jail.

T. C. Whitby'd be by soon as the store closed. Bad enough he'd been stolen from, he wasn't about to shut down and lose even more because of the thieving Talcott boy. Thomas perched on the narrow bench by the front window, big as life for every passerby to see.

"Not surprised a bit," a deputy muttered to the sheriff when he came in carrying supper in a tin pail. "Them Talcotts always been a rugged bunch."

"Henry's okay," the sheriff said. "Long as he ain't mad about something."

"Which is just about all the time lately," the deputy snorted.

Paper crinkled. Thomas smelled beef gravy. His empty stomach growled. Hours ago breakfast had been a shared biscuit and the blueberries he and Margaret had picked, covered with some cream his father had brought when he got home late last night and left in the ice chest for them to find as a surprise after he'd left early this morning.

"Can you blame him?"

"I never woulda thought it. Not of Irene Jalley."

"Lena for sure. But Irene, Jesus, no."

"Takes all kinds." The words, thick globules with the deputy's chewing.

The front door opened. T. C. Whitby appeared in rolled-up shirtsleeves and shiny black tie. He smiled triumphantly at the boy. Even though they started off hearing the boy out, the sheriff and deputy were soon kowtowing to the man. If Whitby got his knife back that would be the end of it. Thomas could go home.

"Sounds fair to me." The sheriff handed Whitby the two-blade Palomino.

"Fair's fair, so here's the one you bought." Whitby held out the rusted jackknife.

"No, sir." Thomas wouldn't take it. If fair was really fair he should have been able to buy the jackknife in the window.

"Don't be foolish now," the sheriff warned.

Once again, Thomas explained that that one was rusted.

The sheriff pulled out the blades. "He's right," he told Whitby.

"That's why it's only ten cents," Whitby said. "Now that one," he said pointing, "that one's twenty, being in such pristine condition."

The sheriff glanced at the deputy and Thomas felt better. Whitby was a crook and they both knew it. He hadn't broken the law, but Whitby had, trying to pass off the inferior jackknife on him just because he was a kid. The sheriff said if Thomas wanted the jackknife from the window he'd have to pay a dime more. That wasn't fair, Thomas objected. The deputy eyed his cooling dinner. Rapping his knuckles on the desktop, the sheriff told the boy to make up his mind. This was taking up way too much of everyone's time. Thomas said he wanted his dime back.

"No sirree!" Whitby squealed. "Not for all this trouble, you're not going scot-free plus being paid besides."

"Give the boy his dime. That seems fair. Don't you think?" the sheriff added, and though Thomas couldn't have put it into words then, he understood later, years later, that he had been not just disappointed by the tremor in the sheriff's voice, but ashamed.

"For what? Reward for his brazen thievery? No, sheriff, I'm keeping this dime." Whitby flipped it into the air, then caught it. "That way he'll think twice before stealing from me or anyone else again. The wages of sin," he said, slipping it into his pocket.

"I suppose," the sheriff considered with a look meant to be both appeasing and stern, "it's kinda like a fine then, you could say, son, a lesson learned. I guess that's fair enough." He patted Thomas's shoulder, but the boy would have no part of it.

"Then he better give me the rusted one then!" he cried, with more indignation and anger than he had ever felt for anyone. "Or else he's just stealing from me then, that's what he's doing, and you damn well know it too, don't you, sheriff?"

"Now you just watch your mouth!" The deputy shoved him down onto the bench, so hard his head banged back against the wall. For a moment it felt as if he were struggling to wake from a pressing sleep.

"Mother takes off, that's what happens," Whitby was saying.

Tears came. No way to stop them. Closed his eyes. Held his breath, but they burned down his cheeks with the awful girl-gasping sob that shuddered through him. His mother was gone, his house. His father passed through the days like a dead man. All he had was Margaret and she was probably gone too. And here he sat bawling in their shadows because his whole life had changed and he couldn't do a thing to make it better. He didn't want the stupid jackknife or the dime even. Just for life to be fair, that's all he wanted.

"Give him something. That there, the rusted one," the sheriff said. "Here." The sheriff put the lesser jackknife into his hand. "Now go on. Go on home." He steered him through the doorway.

Thomas wanted to run. His heart and brain raced so much he was short of breath, but he made his feet walk down the street, slowly.

"And you better tell your father what you did, because if you don't, I will!" the sheriff shouted after him.

. . .

At that very moment, a few miles away, Mrs. Farley had just parked her car at the wooded edge of Bibeau's property. She slipped off her driving scarf, patted any mussed waves into place, then slid the wrapped plate of warm cookies from the backseat and followed the old logging trail toward the pond, whistling softly to warn off animals and snakes. This mission required a great deal of courage, for Mrs. Farley was not a born country girl. Her free hand waved in front of her face. Even the bugs scared her. Especially mosquitoes. After all the rain they buzzed in bloodthirsty clouds. Her heel teetered on the bumpy path, but she caught herself in time. Two bites rose on her arm, one swelled on her cheek. Had she known it was this far in she would have worn more sensible shoes. Imagine, she thought, with the sagging black tent in sight now, children having to live like that. Fred said he'd done all that he could under the circumstances: she could ask anyone, and they'd all tell her the same thing. Henry Talcott was a stubborn man. After Fred took over Talcott's note, he'd sent word through the bank that he'd be glad to have Talcott stay on as a tenant. But he'd chosen pride over his family. And now look . . . "Hello? Hello? Hello there!" she called, then paused, certain she'd heard something. A child's voice. Crying! "It's just me! Mrs. Farley . . . Margaret?" She rushed toward the tent.

. . .

When Thomas finally got back, Margaret and the kitten were gone. Shouting to her he ran to the pond, relieved to find the boat docked, the rope knotted exactly as he had left it. Maybe she'd gone into the woods to see if the blackberries they'd found yesterday were ripe yet. The blackberry thicket was at least a mile off. He hollered her name as he went. The sun sagged low in the streaked sky. His stomach twisted with hunger. It was surely past suppertime. Maybe six-thirty by now, seven, he couldn't be sure. "Margaret! Margaret!" The warm thicket hummed with bees, most of the berries hard, still white and green, and there was no sign of her.

He had to find her before dark. Before his father came home. He ran back, not even bothering to stay on the trail. This time he saw the note in the fold of canvas flap.

> *Dear Thomas and Mr. Talcott,*
> *I brought some fresh baked cookies by and found Margaret alone and covered with bee stings. I have taken her to Dr. Creel's. I will bring her to my house after.*
>
> *Sincerely,*
> *Your neighbor*
> *Mrs. Fred Farley*

It was almost dark by the time Thomas arrived at the Farleys'. Mrs. Farley stood just inside the door, whispering how Margaret had fallen asleep on the way home from the doctor's. Her arms and legs were stung the worst. She'd gone out with the kitten and had stepped into a yellow jackets' nest. Dr. Creel had tweezered out the stingers, then made a baking-soda paste to bring down the swelling. But it hadn't done much for the pain. Every now and again she cried out in her sleep.

She'd be all right; Margaret was a brave girl, Thomas said, which was a lie. What she was was a very good actress, though he knew better than say this to Mrs. Farley, who was obviously in the thrall of his sister's drama. He said he'd better take her home now. She asked if his father was there yet. No, but he would be any minute, Thomas said. Well, he'd see her note then and know to come here, she said. She invited him into the kitchen, where Jesse-boy sat on a blanket-covered chair, thin legs stretched out on a leather hassock, nibbling cookies from his lap tray while he listened to the radio. She asked Thomas if he'd had supper. He lied and said yes. She gave him a plate of cookies and a glass of cold creamy milk at the table, then skittered happily, eagerly, nervously up and down the stairs to check on Margaret—poor little thing's sound asleep, she'd whisper, bustling back into the kitchen. With more than a few sentences Jesse-boy's breathing grew labored, so Thomas found himself doing most of the talking, not because he had anything to say, and not even to fill the strange silence, but because, just as his father's did, Jesse-boy's wheezing scared him, made him panicky in that same way. As long as he kept talking, Jesse-boy wouldn't have to.

Jesse-boy was four years older but they had been in school together years back, before Jesse-boy left to be taught at home. Thomas was recalling his way through the grades. Jesse-boy's eyes gleamed with the comeuppance stories. Thomas tried to think of every bad thing that had ever happened to a bully. A few he even made up. This one though was true. It was about Billy Humboldt's terrible accident, falling on his head from his father's tractor. He'd never been right since. But then his fits got so bad last year they had to send him to some place up in Burlington. "Like a crazy house almost—"

"Shh!" Mrs. Farley said, and Thomas realized that Jesse-boy had fallen asleep. She hurried off again, then tiptoed into the room with Mr. Farley, who slipped his arms under his son's limp body and carried him up to bed.

At ten-thirty when Thomas's father still hadn't come, Mrs. Farley made up the daybed for Thomas. He said he wasn't tired. She insisted he at least rest on it. At three in the morning he was awakened by Margaret screaming. Bolting upstairs, he followed her cries to the bedroom, where Mrs. Farley had already arrived. Margaret's cheeks hung in jowly sacs past her chin. Her eyes were swollen to slits. Helpless, he watched Mrs. Farley dab on another coating of the white paste that cracked the minute it dried.

"There, there now," she whispered, holding his sister's puffy hand while she moaned.

She looked like a monster. Like one of the sideshow freaks at the fair. Mrs. Farley kept assuring Margaret that she was going to be all right. Her tongue was so swelled up she could barely speak. When she grunted like that, she sounded like Billy Humboldt. What if she ended up like him? In some crazy-person place? It could happen. Anything could, he was beginning to find out.

At four thirty he sat up on the daybed. His father's rackety old truck had just pulled up to the house. Henry left the motor on and ran onto the porch. His truck had broken down in Montpelier and he'd been most of the night trying to get it fixed and going again. No matter how Mrs. Farley went on about Margaret's dangerous condition, he insisted on taking his children home. Shushing him all the way, Mrs. Farley led him upstairs to look in on the poor little thing. Thomas watched from the doorway. His father bent down and whispered in Margaret's ear. Then, just as Mr. Farley had done earlier to his son, his father lifted her from the bed. She screamed with pain. Easing her back down, he said she could stay if she wanted. Did she want to? he asked through her sobbing. She said yes, Mrs. Farley reported, gently touching the baking-soda poultice to the little girl's neck.

"And Thomas, you can stay too if you'd like. That way Margaret'll have a familiar face here when she wakes up," Mrs. Farley offered.

He didn't want to. He wanted to be with his father, who just stood there like a drained and broken man, grease-streaked arms hanging at his sides. But he also didn't want to have to explain how it had all come to be this way because of him. "Okay," he said with a quick step into the room.

"No! He comes with me. She can sleep here. Until I come back. In the morning at eight."

It was a long, silent ride back. Thomas was relieved. His father had had enough bad things happen for one day. He didn't need to hear how his son had been picked up as a common thief and been hauled into jail by the sheriff, though he'd know soon enough. News traveled fast, especially bad news.

"Listen to me now," his father said, pulling up to the tent. He turned off the lights, but not the engine. "Fred Farley might have my house and land, but he's not taking my kids."

"No, I know!"

"Well it didn't sound like it back there. Seemed to me you were ready to move right in."

"No, I wasn't! I swear!"

His father was silent a moment. "I'm doing my best, Tom, but I don't know, maybe that's not good enough. Maybe one of these days I'll just run down dead like the truck today."

"No! You won't! It's just bad times. Like you said."

"Some people's bad times just seem to get worse and worser, no matter what. And that's what we gotta be ready, prepared for."

"For what?"

"For what to do. If that comes." Here came a longer silence, strained with the rasp of his hard breathing. "What to do with you and Margaret."

"We're doing fine. Just fine, Daddy."

"Yeah?"

"Yeah! I never had so much fun as this. This summer, living in the tent, going fishing every day, just going in the woods all the time. Margaret and me, we're probably the luckiest kids in the whole world!"

His father patted his knee. "You're a good boy, Tom. A real good son."

Thomas's eyes burned with tears. He wasn't a good boy, good son, good brother, good anything. If he had been his mother never would have left.

2

SCHOOL WOULD START SOON. THOMAS WASN'T SURE WHEN exactly, but he could feel it coming. The dry stubble of old Bibeau's hayfields puffed up yellow dust underfoot. In the briefer sunlight the cidery rot of fallen apples drew crows from miles around. Some sugar maples were already tarnished with red. Old Bibeau predicted a hard, early winter; he knew by the squirrels' frenzied nut gathering, and the deer edging nearer the tree line, and by Donald's limp. The ancient setter's arthritis was worse than ever. This morning when Thomas and Margaret came to pick up berrying pails, Donald limped off the porch with a pitiful yelp, dragging his hind legs toward them.

"He's been missing you." Hands on her hips, Gladys scowled down from the front steps. "You haven't come by all week. I made your favorite meat pies. Extra even for your dad, but then you didn't come."

Thomas apologized and left it at that. She knew well as he did why they hadn't been back. Their last supper here old Bibeau had said something bad about their mother. Thomas didn't know exactly what though, because he'd been on the porch having one of Gladys's homemade root beers and playing with Donald. While Margaret helped Gladys wash the dishes, the old man and Henry had a drink at the kitchen table. Usually Henry preferred not to drink in front of his children, but Thomas could always tell when he had by the fullness that warmed his father's voice, not to mention how much more he seemed to talk.

Anyway, the next thing Thomas knew his father stormed onto the porch with Margaret demanding he get into the truck; they were leaving. Gladys ran out with her faded blue apron front stained wet, trying to explain that her father hadn't meant what he'd said about Irene. It was just his way; he was so old-fashioned, especially when it came to women. "Henry! Please don't leave," she called, hurrying alongside the truck. "I'm so sorry."

"It's not your fault," Henry muttered, though Thomas doubted she could have heard over the truck's noise.

"Don't forget about the meat pies," she hollered as they turned onto the road.

So, this was their first time back. Asking how their father was, Gladys gave them the big galvanized buckets she'd offered for blackberrying. Good, Thomas answered. What she really wanted to know was if he was still mad.

"You got any more meat pies?" Margaret asked from her squat next to Donald, whose wagging tail whisked up a cloud of dust. She had left her kitten back at the tent in an overturned peach basket that Thomas had weighted down with rocks.

"No, but I got egg salad and two big fat drumsticks from last night if you want."

"Margaret!" Thomas warned as she ran onto the porch.

She looked back. "Come on, Tom. Please! You want to as much as me, you know you do."

He had to admit he'd envisioned just this scenario on their way here. But now at the moment of testing, he couldn't. "We can't," he said simply. Weakly.

Pressing her face to the screen, Margaret peered inside, looking for the old man. "He's not even in there," she hissed back.

Thomas wouldn't go in, so she had no choice but thump her bitter way down the steps to wait with him, muttering all the while what a stupid brother he was, how he didn't know anything and she didn't see why *she* had to go without. All he was doing was taking it out on her because of what the sheriff had told their father about him trying to steal that knife. His father had just found out the day before yesterday, when he ran into the sheriff at the barbershop. By the time he got home, he was so enraged he demanded Thomas's rusted two-blade Palomino, then threw it hard as he could into the pond. His father yanked off his belt and stood there whipping his own palm to welts while he told him how not having money wasn't any kind of license to steal. Every time Thomas tried to say he hadn't stolen the jackknife his father got madder and yelled at him to shut up! A liar and a thief didn't deserve to speak, much less make excuses. The warning belt whistled through the air while his father grew madder and madder. If Thomas had stayed home that day like he was supposed to, his sister never would have gotten stung. And he wouldn't be feeling so beholden to Mrs. Farley, who had paid the doctor bill, but Henry Talcott wasn't about to owe the Farleys for anything. Nossir!

His father pointed to the tree stump, and Thomas leaned over.

"That's what you get for stealing!" His father whacked Thomas's bottom ten times with his hand, hard. "Next time you get the strap," he wheezed as he hurried away, slipping the unused belt through his pant loops.

When his father was safely inside the tent, Thomas shouted as loud as he could, "There won't be no next time, because there wasn't a last time. I paid a dime for that jackknife and it was rusted . . ." He teetered at the edge of the woods bellowing out the story, every bit of the injustice, fully expecting his father to come charging out from the tent, but he didn't. Outrage spent, Thomas ran crying into the woods, where he stayed until Margaret finally came looking for him.

His father lay on his cot with his arms over his face, pretending to be asleep. Thomas knew he wasn't, knew he didn't know what else to do.

Besides, Margaret was reminding him now, it was their father who had sworn never to step foot inside the old man's house again. He hadn't said *they* couldn't. Thomas told Margaret to shut up and she told him to, back.

"You can come eat if you want." Gladys offered the plate through the doorway.

"We better stay out here," Thomas said, so she set the plate and forks on the oilcloth-covered plant table.

"He's afraid of getting in more trouble," Margaret said, shrugging when he glared at her. Three big bites of the drumstick and she still wasn't chewing.

"Well, that's what happens when men drink," Gladys said. "Things get said that shouldn't."

Thomas busied himself with the egg salad. Because Gladys had known his father for so long, she figured she could say whatever she wanted. She'd better not be criticizing him now, he thought, or else he'd have to grab his sister and take off. Without finishing this delicious food.

"And they snore a lot too," Margaret said, cheeks bulging with chicken.

"Swallow!" he said, but she took another bite to spite him.

Gladys seemed amused. "I hope you don't ever drink, Thomas." She poured him a glass of milk.

"Well, not until I grow up."

"No, not even then you shouldn't."

He didn't say anything. To agree would seem a betrayal of his father, and right then Gladys was too adamant to contradict. As usual, Margaret couldn't stand the silence. Suddenly she was asking Gladys what old Bibeau had meant by saying her mother was a tramp. Her mother wasn't a hobo. She didn't ride boxcars or beg for food or work.

Gladys's high-boned face reddened. "Of course she doesn't. Your mother's got herself a good job down in Massachusetts."

As with much of childhood's enlightenment, right then and there Thomas realized he knew things he did not yet understand. And what did Margaret know? Was this the first time she had innocently repeated something overheard? Or had she already asked her father this very question and been scolded for it? Funny she hadn't said anything to him, he thought. Margaret was not a secret keeper.

. . .

Later that day, as they trudged back to the tent, arms and legs crosshatched with scratches from thorns, their purple-stained hands cramped from carrying pails filled with fat, warm blackberries, Margaret asked the same question he'd been pondering a lot lately. "How come Mommy never writes us a letter?"

"She did. Daddy read it to us."

"Just parts though. Why can't we read it?"

"I don't know."

"That time I asked he got mad. He got so mad he swore. Remember?" She sounded as hurt as she'd been then. She wasn't used to his father's anger the way he was.

"All he said was 'damn.' That's not so bad, Margaret. There's a lot worse words he could've said."

"Why? I didn't do anything."

"I know. But he feels bad. And he doesn't want you to feel bad."

"Well I do." She burst into tears. "I don't know why she had to leave like that."

"She'll be back, you know she will. As soon as she gets enough money saved. It's like Daddy said, she's doing it for us."

"Well, I don't care about money. I hate money. And when I have little kids, I'll never leave them alone. And if I go away even for one day I'll write them letters and I'll tell them how much I love them and the exact minute I'm coming back!"

He would always remember his sister's words, both for their pain and the simple eloquence of their truth. And as well for the promised woman his sister was already determined to be.

. . .

The next day he and Margaret were walking to town. They hadn't gone a half mile before she complained how heavy her pail was. The thin metal handle cut into her hand so he ended up carrying both pails. Door to door they went, street after street, peddling their berries. After an hour and no sales Margaret begged to quit. Instead, he dropped the price to two cents a bowl. At the very next house a lady in pin curls wanted to buy some. She came back out with a big mixing bowl, which she filled.

"That's not fair," Thomas finally said, having mustered his courage.

"You said a bowl."

"But I meant a small one."

"Then you should've said." She had him there. And most of the berries too.

"All right, then give us more money!" Margaret demanded. "You took a whole pail!"

"Don't be so fresh, you little brat!" The woman slammed the door.

Margaret reached into the pail for a handful of the plump berries and flung it at the house. A plop of fleshy seeds and purplish juice ran down the white clapboards.

"You shouldn't've done that!"

"She asked for it," Margaret cried, darting past him.

They skipped the rest of the houses on that street. Even at a penny a bowl now, sales were few. With rounded hands Thomas demonstrated the size bowl he meant. An old woman invited them in for lemonade. Her house reeked of cat pee and camphor, but Thomas was too thirsty to mind. Margaret kept sniffing. He was sure she'd say something.

The old woman said she'd love to buy some berries, but the seeds caught in her teeth and were a devil to get out. She suggested they try at the Metropole, the big hotel downtown. Go around back, she advised. To the red door. The cook was always looking for fresh berries. She said, tell him his Aunt Shirl said they were fresh-picked.

Margaret chattered the whole way, which was mostly downhill. The closer they got to Main Street the more excited she grew. She loved seeing the cars whiz by, all the colorful signs, the store mannequins in pretty dresses and fancy hats. His mother used to act just like this when they came into town: bright-eyed, smiling, chattering in the same breathless voice. The Metropole cook bought all the blackberries. Fifty cents. He said he'd buy more if they brought them to him. It was the most money Thomas had ever earned. He let Margaret buy three cents' worth of rock candy, then bristled when she wouldn't give him any. She asked why he hadn't bought himself any. He was saving for new school pants, he said, but the truth was he wanted to buy a bus ticket. The idea had just come to him when they walked by the depot. Maybe their mother couldn't get a day off from her job to come visit them, but they could take the bus down to see her. If he could earn enough money. He knew better than say anything to his sister.

The next day he made Margaret go blackberrying first thing in the morning. She was tired from the previous two days and reluctant to leave her kitten penned under the peach basket again. When he said they might earn enough to buy her new shoes, she finally gave in. Again, they filled two buckets. This time they went directly to the hotel, where the cook gave them seventy-five cents. Thomas was disappointed. He'd been sure they'd get a dollar, but still, he now had one dollar and twenty-two cents toward a ticket. He told Margaret to wait out here on the bench while he went inside the depot. Only if he'd tell her why, she said. He said he had to use the bathroom. She did too. They only had a men's room, he said.

The stooped-over clerk said a round-trip ticket to Collerton, Massachusetts, cost two dollars and fifty cents. Thomas was crestfallen. How much for one-way then? A dollar thirty. Eight more cents and he'd have enough for himself anyway. Maybe his mother could give him the rest to get home. Or maybe she'd just tell him to stay. After all, he wouldn't be half the worry a little girl would be, his mother would say, so it would probably be best if he went alone. He turned from the counter right into Margaret's squinty stare. She knelt on the bench, watching through the lettered plate glass. He hurried into the men's room. What were you asking that man? she asked when he came outside. Where the bathroom was, he answered without a twinge of guilt. The thought of that bus ride into his mother's arms made him happier than he'd been in a long time.

. . .

Lately, everything his sister did annoyed him. He didn't know it was privacy he wanted, only that he was in great need of something and Margaret had become his obstacle.

"What're you looking for?" her muffled voice asked again from her cot. She was sprawled facedown while the kitten sat purring on her back. A moment ago she had been helpless with laughter as it walked the length of her.

Silently, he continued his hurried search. It was three in

the afternoon. His father wasn't expected back until suppertime, but he'd come home early yesterday when his truck broke down. A flat. Half the blackberrying money had gone toward patching the tire. Last week the fan belt had broken and he had to hitch a ride into town to buy a new one. Things weren't going well. Summer would be ending soon, with winter howling close behind. Thomas couldn't imagine living here then. All it took now was a cold, rainy, windy night to make the mildewy tent so miserable by morning that Margaret wouldn't budge from under her covers.

"Tell me!" She sat up with the kitten clawed to the back of her frayed sweater.

"Nothing."

"Yes, you are. You're looking for Mommy's letter."

"No, I'm not! I'm looking for my school card."

"Why?"

There it was. At the very bottom of the hinged wooden box he had dragged out from under his father's cot. His mother's feathery handwriting on the envelope. "I forget what grades I got." Damn. It was empty. His father probably kept the letter safe in his wallet. Or maybe he'd thrown it out in anger. Lately any mention of his wife turned his moods even blacker. Thomas had asked to read it when his father picked it up at the post office. His father hadn't answered. So Margaret asked if he'd read it to them then. "Leaving out the love parts, please," she'd giggled. His father hunched over the steering wheel and didn't speak the rest of the way home.

Thomas was piling his father's important papers the way they'd been over the envelope when he realized the value of his find. Not a letter to read, but her address on the envelope flap, her exact location, 34 Common Street, Collerton, Massachusetts, the place where he would find her. If he had to. If he wanted to. He sat on his cot and wrote as fast as he could because the words were pouring out of him.

Dear Mommy,

I miss you very much. And Margaret does too. She cries a lot. Her new cat is gray and white. It is a baby kitten. I told her you don't like cats. Margaret says you do. She says I'm being mean, but I remember that. How you said you never wanted a pet because they always die. If that is right will you please tell Margaret. She is getting very naughty and I don't like it. She is fresh as paint is what Gladys says to Daddy.

He paused, rubbing his chin to the pencil. He didn't want to make her glad to be far away from bratty Margaret, so he continued.

But she is mostly a nice little girl just like you want her to be. So please, please come home soon. We miss you. I wish I could see you. Maybe I can come there. Soon, I hope. I can take the bus.

Your loving son, Tom.

Sincerely, Thomas H. Talcott

"What're you writing?" Margaret asked.

He folded the paper and put in his pocket. Now he had

to get an envelope and stamp somewhere. Maybe tonight at Gladys's.

"Tell me what you wrote!" Margaret cried as she dove next to him on the cot. "Show me!" She tried to pull the letter out of his pocket.

"Don't, Margaret!" he warned, slapping away her hands.

"Why not?"

"Because it's private."

"What's that mean?"

"It's like a secret. I can have secrets. I don't have to tell you everything. I'm older than you."

She moved away and sat on the edge of the cot, her back to him.

"Is it a secret like Jesse-boy did?"

"I don't know. How should I know?"

She didn't answer, and didn't move from his side.

"What did Jesse-boy do?"

"I'm not supposed to tell."

"Why?"

"Because he said not to. I can't." She looked frightened.

"But I'm your brother. You have to tell me."

"But you won't tell me your secret."

So he did then. He unfolded the letter and read it aloud, leaving out the part critical of her. But when she would not tell her secret, he realized she'd tricked him. That's how the girls in school were too. Just when he would try and be nice to one, he'd turn around to find her and her friends laughing at him.

"Hello! Hel—lo—oh!" piped a woman's hell-bent, breathless voice.

Startled by the novelty of a visitor, they sprang from the cot. Peering over the little round glasses that hung at the tip of her nose, Mrs. Farley emerged from the line of spindly birches that had snagged her stockings and mussed her hair. She trudged along the path, a basket in each hand. "Hello! Look what I've brought you!"

There were sweet potato muffins, fried chicken, even buttery corn on the cob fresh from Mr. Farley's garden. He only grew enough for the family, she was explaining as she set everything out on their rickety camp table. Dairy, that's what Mr. Farley grew up doing. "I, myself, am from an educational background." Their blank stares caused her to explain. Until her marriage she had been a schoolteacher, like her father and grandfather before her. But then one fine day she met Mr. Farley at a Lenten service, with her sister. Six months later they were married, so she had to leave teaching. Only single ladies taught school, but then she and Mr. Farley had to wait twelve, almost thirteen years before Jesse-boy came along.

"So here, dear. Start in now." She patted one of the wobbly stools for Margaret to come sit next to her. Thomas moved quickly onto his. Passing out pink linen napkins and flowery china tea plates she presided over the tent as if it were her home and not theirs. His mother was always pleasant to Mrs. Farley when they met in town, but as soon as she was gone his mother would berate herself for being too nice and falling all over the woman just because of who she was. Out of loyalty Thomas tried to look stern.

Once he and Margaret started eating neither spoke. His eyes sagged heavily with pleasure. Everything was delicious. Maybe even better than Gladys's cooking. Of course that was probably more the result of being able to eat in their own place and not under old Bibeau's caustic stare. Old Bibeau liked their father and hated them. Mrs. Farley liked them, but not their father. She kept glancing toward the path now. Thomas hated to do it, because he wanted it to last, but he began to eat as fast as he could. Mrs. Farley was surely thinking the same thing he was. If Henry Talcott came home now and found her with them, there'd be hell to pay.

Mrs. Farley had resumed her strange narrative. Strange to Thomas who had never heard his own mother tell about lady things. Aunt Lena did, but her tales were different, vulgar, some too wild to be believed. Mrs. Farley was telling a very personal and, to her, thrilling story. She grew more breathless. Forty-three years old, and when she found out she fainted—just fainted dead away in Dr. Creel's office from the shock of it. Thomas gnawed his drumstick clean to the bone. What a creepy baby Jesse-boy must have been to make his mother faint. Born the day after Christmas, he was the most beautiful baby she had ever laid eyes on. God had answered her prayers. When he was almost a year old they realized their sweet, weak child had a heart condition. They brought him to the best doctors in Boston and New York, who all said the same thing. There was no cure, nothing for them to do, but keep him as healthy and happy as they could in the short time he had. Probably not much past his third birthday the doctors said. And here he was fifteen—all because of one thing. Mrs. Farley's voice hushed to a whisper. A mother's love, she said. That's what was keeping her Jesse-boy alive. Love. It was her life's work, she declared in a surge of passion. "He's a happy boy in spite of everything." Her voice trembled and behind her thick lenses her eyes were bright and wet. "But he gets so lonely," she gasped, then looked away.

Please don't cry, Thomas thought. He didn't know what he'd do if she did.

Margaret was also staring at her. "Excuse me, Mrs. Farley," she said in a small voice. "Is there any more ginger beer, please?"

Mrs. Farley grunted as her short, plump fingers struggled to wrench out the cork. She gave Margaret the bottle. Margaret slurped at the amber bubbles fizzing down the neck.

"And so that's why I thought I would speak to you children first. Maybe if it comes from you, your father would be more receptive to the idea. I bake almost every day. You could each have your own bedrooms. And you wouldn't have to go to regular school anymore. Mr. Wentworth said he'd welcome two more pupils in our front parlor classroom. It would be so much better, so much more normal if Jesse-boy had little classmates. You could visit with your father any time you wanted, of course." Seeing the panic on Thomas's face she waved, as if erasing a chalkboard. "You don't have to say anything now. In fact, it's better if you don't. I wouldn't want to get Jesse-boy's hopes up. So just think about it." With one of the pink napkins she wiped Margaret's greasy chin, her hands, then each finger. "Think how happy you'd be. How much fun we'd all have together," she said softly. To Margaret, who smiled up at her. She leaned closer and whispered in Margaret's ear. Then she packed up the bones, gleaned cobs, empty bottles, and, as quickly as she'd come, bustled her way down the path again.

Thomas and Margaret sprawled on their cots, dazed with gluttony. They had even eaten the molasses cookies she'd left. He asked what Mrs. Farley had whispered.

"That she loved me. And that Jesse-boy did too." Margaret sat up and looked over at him. "She said she asked him what he wanted most in the whole world and he said for me to be his sister."

"You're my sister!" Thomas snapped with the fire of his father's quick anger.

"I know, but you could be his brother too."

"Margaret! We're *this* family," he said, gesturing around as if the shadowy tent teemed with relatives. "You don't want to leave Daddy, do you?"

"No. But I don't like it here anymore. I don't!"

He told her not to worry, as soon as their mother read his letter she'd see how badly they needed her back. In fact, he took it out and in front of Margaret wrote exactly that in a boldly underlined postscript. PLEASE COME RIGHT AWAY, he printed. The blunt force of the capitalized letters filled him with an urgency he had not felt until that moment, with Margaret so close at his side that her breath raised not just the hairs on his arm but the realization that it was up to him. He had to get his mother back before something terrible happened. He thought of Mrs. Farley's mother-love keeping Jesse-boy alive all this time. He printed, I HAVE BEEN VERY SICK. SOME DAYS I CAN'T BREATHE TOO GOOD. What else was wrong with Jesse-boy? I GET TERRIBLE HEADACHES AND HAVE TO BE IN THE DARK A LOT. Jesse-boy's legs and feet twitched, but he was afraid to go that far, afraid to tempt fate. This was for Margaret's sake. She was so easily swayed. It was a good thing Mrs. Farley didn't know how much she loved black licorice. That's all it might take, a few whips in the next basket and Margaret would be gone.

. . .

For three drizzly days the truck was parked dead in the clearing off the old logging road that led to the pond. Even if Henry Talcott could get into town there was no money for new spark plugs. From time to time Thomas and Margaret pretended to be sad for their father. Having him with them all this time was wonderful even as he sank deeper into his bitter malaise. "Poor Daddy," Margaret sighed as she trimmed the hair above his collar. "I'm going to make you look like a movie star." She blew cut hairs off his neck, then peeked around at him. "Which one you wanna be?" Usually when he got this gloomy only Margaret could make him smile, but now even she wasn't succeeding. Thomas knew to keep out of his way best as he could, but the tent seemed to shrink up even smaller with his father here. Hands behind his head his father would lay on his cot with his eyes closed. Just when they thought he was asleep there'd come a rubbly groan, like rocks being scraped up from deep in his chest. There was plenty to worry about, Thomas knew that, but lately his father acted as if it was the end of the road for them. Thomas was sure his mother wouldn't be gone much longer. He had mailed his letter two weeks ago. At first he'd been disappointed when she didn't write right back. But now he understood. She was probably preparing for her return. A trip like that would take time. Collerton, Massachusetts, was a long ways away. He pictured her riding the bus back, which was how she'd gotten down there in the first place. She had probably saved every cent she'd earned, so he'd have to warn Margaret not to expect a present. Having her back would be the best gift of all, he'd tell his sister.

Henry Talcott had gone outside to shake the hair from his shirt. Margaret was trying to bundle the kitten like a baby in her sweater, but it kept squirming free. Henry was ducking down into the tent when someone called to him.

"Where've you been?" a woman's voice inquired and both children watched the opening, rooted in their hopefulness.

"Nowhere. Just here," he said walking not toward their mother, but Gladys. They stood a few feet off from the narrow lean-to he had fashioned as a three-sided outhouse, which was no more than a pole to squat against, a shovel, and bucket of lime. A tattered blanket served as door.

Almost as tall as his father, Gladys was a pretty strange-looking woman in her baggy dress and man's jacket and work boots. Thomas knew better than ever say as much though. Gladys and his father were like brother and sister almost, his mother used to say. His mother was always saying the trouble with poor Gladys was she had no self-respect, dressing the way she did and letting her father run her life. Gladys had gone away to nursing school, but when her mother died, her father ordered her home to take care of the place. Of him, really. His mother's pity for Gladys often seemed more like gloating in the way most observations were made in front of his father. And who could blame her? Until Irene had come along, everyone assumed marriage between the two friends would be just a matter of time.

Lately, Thomas had noticed the unnatural quiet that would descend over Gladys with any mention of his mother. It was almost as if she were holding her breath to force silence onto herself. Now that he thought of it, no one had said a bad word about his mother for leaving. All T. C. Whitby had really said was that she was a mill hand. It had been his sarcastic tone that had angered Thomas. His father had assured him Whitby was just mad he'd lost such a good bookkeeper. He said there wasn't a thing wrong with working in a mill. A lot of fine women did. In these times people were lucky to find work, men and women alike. A person did what he had to do.

Shirtfront still open, Henry Talcott came back into the tent to tell his children that Gladys was going to take him into town to see about spark plugs. His father never would have stood bare-chested in front of any lady but his mother, Thomas knew. Gladys stuck her head into the tent and asked Margaret if she'd named her kitten yet.

"Yes," Margaret said, lifting the cat from its nest of clothes in the trunk. "His name is Thomas."

"That's your brother's name," Gladys laughed. "You can't call him that!"

"Yes I can!" Margaret huffed.

"She does not!" Thomas scoffed.

"Yes I do!" Margaret said in the superior tone he hated so.

"I never heard you."

"Because you say, 'what?' " Shaking her head, she looked at Gladys. "He always thinks I'm calling him." Gladys and Henry were both laughing now. At him. But it was the first time his father had even smiled in days. "And I hate so to hurt his feelings," she drawled.

"Listen to you, you little imp," Gladys said, picking Margaret up and holding her out in front of her so that they were face-to-face. "You're so fresh you're just as fresh as paint!" she declared in her creaky voice before putting her down.

He was still trying to think of a clever retort when Gladys hugged his head to her bony chest. She announced that she was expecting them for dinner Monday night. And dress up pretty, she told Margaret. It was a very special occasion. A party! Margaret shrieked. "Yes," Gladys said, grinning. "August twenty-first! Your brother's twelfth birthday. And I have something special for him."

. . .

How strange that summer had become: not even knowing what day of the week it was, much less the date. He hadn't thought about his birthday at all. But now that it was upon him, it governed everything. He and Margaret had come to the same conclusion. Their mother had chosen his birthday for her return. Of course. For *she* was the special gift. The surprise. Yes, Margaret eagerly concurred. Something he had wanted for a very long time! (Had Gladys even said that?) But maybe Margaret had heard it and he had not. That's why his mother hadn't written him back. She was waiting for his birthday. And she knew he would know that.

3

OLD BIBEAU'S DREARY FARMHOUSE SHOULD HAVE SEEMED even bleaker that rainy evening. But how could it on so joyful an occasion? The sky was black with rain. The dull walls vibrated with each blast of thunder. Margaret's curls dripped from their giggly run inside. She had smuggled in the still unnamed kitten.

"I'm going to let Mommy pick it," she had whispered to Thomas when they had been searching through the big black trunk for their best clothes. Their mother was very particular about how they looked when they went out—especially with her. The fancy lady and her ragamuffin kids, Aunt Lena would tease her sister when by the end of a visit brother and sister were bedraggled and grimy. For this wonderful evening Thomas wore his good white shirt, yellowed and short in the sleeves as it was. Margaret's pink and white dress had started out a clutch of wrinkles. By the time they arrived the rain had smoothed out all but the most compressed creases. As soon as their father had put on his best shirt they had known for sure she would be there. He had even tipped his head into the water bucket to slick down his unruly black hair. Thomas was relieved when the curls sprang back up.

Their mother was usually critical of her husband's appearance. No matter how hard she tried to make him look like a gentleman, he always came back mussed. But she loved his hair. "That's what did it, these beautiful curls," she'd say, running her fingers through them until he'd push her hand away, embarrassed.

The dining table was covered with a white tablecloth. The yellow and blue flowers vining the hem had been embroidered by Gladys's mother, Gladys was telling Margaret. Boasting almost. No one had said much so far. Margaret kept looking toward the door. Thomas tried not to. The stewed meat and potatoes were delicious, but he was too happy and excited to eat much more. The hard times would be over soon, he was thinking, even as old Bibeau suddenly announced that the next hobo looking for a handout would be shot, point blank, no questions asked.

"I'm putting a sign on the gate. 'Posted Land. Bindle Stiffs Keep Off!' " he barked with a stab of his dripping fork. His chin stubble glistened with grease.

"The one yesterday was so young," Gladys said. "He couldn't have been much older than you, Tom. Maybe he was fourteen. Maybe. Him and his older brother, they were on their way down from Vergennes. Going out west, they said. California. 'You should stay in school,' I said, 'young boy like you.' 'Can't,' he said. 'Too many of us at home to feed, so we're on our own now.' "

"Not again, goddamn it!" The old man reached down his leg. He lifted the kitten by its scruff. "Scratching me in my own home!" He shook the curled-up little cat over the table.

"Please don't hurt him!" Margaret cried, reaching. "He was just playing! He does that to feet."

Their father had been eating steadily and in silence, but now fork in one hand, knife in the other he paused to look at old Bibeau. Thomas held his breath. The skin on the kitten's head was tight back from its scruff, pulling its eyes to slits. Once he'd seen the old man kick his dog in the ribs, just to make him move.

"Put the cat down, Dad," Gladys said, staring at him.

The old man grinned. "C'mere," he said to Margaret. She scrambled from her seat and hurried to the head of the table. "Now, don't you know better'n bring a cat to someone's house?"

"Yes, sir. But he's just a little kitten."

"I don't like cats. They're sneaky. Like women, always coming up on you when you least expect it." He stared at her. Thomas's stomach churned with nerves and joy. This was the old man's twisted way of announcing their mother's appearance.

His father's knife and fork clattered onto the plate. He stood up and held out his hand for the kitten. "I'll put him out in the truck," he told Margaret. She called after him to be sure and close the windows. Henry Talcott returned a moment later. Alone. Thomas's gaze lingered on the door, but it stayed closed.

Old Bibeau had fallen into silence. Gladys and Margaret were clearing the table. Henry told his son to help, but Gladys wouldn't hear of the guest of honor doing a bit of work. When she picked up her father's plate, he growled at her to get her hands off; couldn't she see he wasn't done? But everyone else was, and she wanted to bring out the birthday cake, she said. They'll just have to wait, the old man said. All he had left were a few carrots, which he didn't even touch.

Or want, Thomas thought bitterly. The old man had to be in charge at all times.

Thomas always knew when his father was getting mad. He'd lick his lips a lot and take long deep breaths the way he was now. Old Bibeau seemed happier now that he had Henry Talcott to himself. He was telling him how someone from the bank had come out last week to see if he needed any kind of a loan. As if he was some kind of fool. As if he didn't know what the thieves were up to.

His father only nodded. "Crazy times," he murmured when the old man paused for comment. Even Thomas knew how foolish old Bibeau sounded. It was his constant obsession, that his land, his rock-heaved, spent pastures were coveted by everyone. It was all the old man had left, this falling-down house, twenty-three acres, and a thirty-five-year-old daughter no one wanted either.

"Happy birthday to you! Happy birthday to you!" Gladys and Margaret sang in surprisingly sweet harmony, carrying through the doorway a chocolate cake blazing with candles. "Happy birthday, dear Thomas. Happy—"

"I'm not done yet!" the old man growled and hit the table with his fist.

". . . birthday to you!" Gladys set the cake in front of Thomas. He closed his eyes and wished his mother would never leave again. Then, he blew out every candle.

"I know what you wished for." Margaret looked around, eyes glowing.

It was suddenly very still. Outside, the rain had stopped.

"I said I wasn't done, didn't I!" The old man shoved his plate away.

"Oh, Dad, please. It's his birthday," Gladys said quietly.

The old man was boiling with bitterness. He had lost Henry's respectful attention, and all his daughter worried about were these two brats, whose own mother didn't care about them. He watched sourly as Gladys gave Thomas her gift, wrapped in white butcher paper on which she had drawn brown-eyed daisies. It was a blue and white striped shirt. Thank you, he said, holding the huge shirt to his chin. It was a little big; to last the year, she explained. More like ten years, he thought, wanting her to sit down so he could see the door when it opened. The next gift was from Margaret. Wrapped in a scrap of cloth, it was a smooth, thick birch stick. He thanked her happily even though she had just grabbed it on the way in to have something to give. And here it was, Gladys announced, his very special twelfth birthday surprise. Something he really, really wanted. She handed the small package also wrapped in butcher paper to his father to give to him.

"Here, Thomas. This is for you."

Already disappointed, he was still opening it. No matter what was inside it was not what he wanted.

"A two-blade, nickel-plated Palomino jackknife!" Gladys grinned.

"Brand-new," his father said, the grave nod alerting him that the crime had not been forgotten and the lesson was far from over.

"You can use it on the stick I gave you." Margaret's jaw trembled.

There would be no more surprises. Gladys was cutting the cake. Thomas got the first and biggest piece. She told him that this was father's favorite cake too, chocolate with chocolate frosting. Once, she was telling both children now, on her tenth birthday instead of the white cake Gladys liked best, her mother forgot and made chocolate. "I burst into tears, so then next time when it was your father's birthday, he had his mother make a white cake with chocolate frosting.'

"I did?" Henry Talcott seemed surprised and embarrassed.

"Yes, you most certainly did." Gladys grinned.

"Where's my piece?" old Bibeau finally asked. He'd been simmering. Gladys said she'd been waiting for him to tell her when he was ready.

Whatever he muttered was lost in the sudden volley of thunder. Margaret stared at the door. "I think someone's out there."

Just more rain, her father said as she went to the door and looked out. She turned back slowly.

"That reminds me," Gladys said placing a big slice of cake in front of her father. "What was Farley doing here this afternoon? I saw his truck. He was leaving when I came up the road."

Old Bibeau cut a chunk of cake with his fork and put it into his mouth.

"What did he want?" she asked, beginning to eat herself.

"None of your goddamn business!" old Bibeau snapped with a hateful stare.

"No, but I . . ." she stammered, turning from the children. Her face was red. "I just thought maybe he wanted to ask about the—"

"Shut up!" old Bibeau spat, pointing with his fork. "Just shut the hell up."

Her eyes closed for a moment and she seemed to sag over the table. She was ashamed. She rose quickly and went into the kitchen. With that, Henry put his napkin on the table and stood up. He told his children they'd better be going now.

"Oh, come on!" old Bibeau bellowed. He waved both arms. "Stay! You stay. She's always doing that, and she knows damn well it's none of her business." He looked toward the kitchen. "But the problem is she's got no business of her own!" he shouted.

Thomas's father licked his lips. He took a deep purposeful breath as he stood over the old man. He leaned so close, his voice so low and hard, Thomas thought sure his father would hit him. "You shouldn't be treating her like that. Especially in front of people. It hurts her pride." He spoke quietly so she wouldn't hear.

"Her pride?" Red-nosed, the old man exploded. "If she had any pride she'd be married instead of turning into a . . . a dried-up old stick nobody wants." He seized Thomas's whittling stick from the table. "And that includes me!" he shouted, flinging it at the kitchen door.

. . .

Her letter arrived days later. His father tore open the envelope and began to read. "August twenty-one," he sighed, then shook his head as if in disbelief. "She wrote this on your birthday."

"She did? What'd she say?" Thomas couldn't stop grinning.

His father took a deep breath. "Let's see . . . she says, 'I am thinking of you today. Twelve years old. Imagine that! My little boy is growing up so fast.' " There was silence as he read the rest to himself. The children stood in front of him, neither one moving. Henry hunched on the edge of the cot, the letter close to his face. He must be reading it again, Thomas thought. It was short, just one page. Seeing the loops of his mother's delicate handwriting raised an ache in the boy's heart. Her fingers had touched that paper. His father folded the letter.

"Read the whole thing!" Margaret cried. "Please, Daddy!" She tugged at his sleeve.

"I did."

"No, you didn't. You only read about Tom. What about my part? What'd Mommy write for me?"

Thomas watched his father's chin sag as if he'd just had the wind knocked out of him. His father looked away, down at the floor. Even as he spoke, Thomas knew it was a lie. All of it. Probably even the "thinking about you" part.

"She said she misses you very much and that she wants you to be a good girl," he was telling her.

Thomas sat on his cot, studying his father's struggle, alert to every pause, every clearing of his throat. He was amazed his father could lie so easily.

"A very good girl. She wants you to be sure and help Tom and me."

"Help you do what?" she asked and Thomas bristled watching her, Margaret the receiver of all helping, giver of none.

"Help us . . . help us . . ." He looked down, stricken by her expectant gaze, by her trust.

"When's she coming home?" Thomas asked with a coldness born of his sudden conviction that things had changed forever. Until now his brain had been like a clock, referencing each disappointment, fear, or deprivation as just another tick, moving him a second, minute, hour, day closer to the comfort of his mother's arms.

. . .

The next day his father didn't go out looking for slaughtering jobs. He spent most of the morning working on the truck. Thomas sat on the front fender whittling a short knobby stick, not watching so much as biding his time.

"This here's the camshaft," his father murmured, reaching into his back pocket for a smaller wrench. "Gotta get some of this here gunk off." He glanced back over his shoulder. "Pay attention now, Tom. You gotta know how to do things. You can't be expecting others to do for you. You gotta be self-sufficient . . ."

Thomas had stopped listening. He was remembering how his mother used to busy herself scrubbing woodwork or shaking out throw rugs when his father got in one of these moods. Anything to be out of his way. He was just too hard on her, Aunt Lena would say. He should have married Gladys Bibeau if all he wanted was a farmhand. His sharp temper had driven her away. Thomas was sure of it. Having been the object of much of his father's displeasure these last few months made him forget the long stretches of his mother's silences in which she barely spoke, even to her children. Dr. Creel said Jamie's death had done her in. But Thomas remembered Aunt Lena saying it was Jamie's birth that made her feel horribly trapped. She said his dying only confirmed it for her. On days like this Thomas yearned for those few months they'd lived in town, where they'd moved after Jamie died and they'd lost the house. He could overlook the tension at home because when they would go out shopping or just walking, his mother was a different woman. Animated and cheerful with everyone along the way. That she could be two such different women was a mystery. But then he would be too caught up in her happiness to puzzle over it for long. Everywhere they went people loved his mother. He loved his mother. Until that day she just up and left.

Last night in the dark, he had watched his father take the letter from his pocket and slip it into his tobacco pouch. He had been counting on reading it as soon as his father left for work this morning, but then the truck kept stalling when he tried to start it. Thomas jumped off the fender. He said he was going to see what Margaret was doing. His father said she was cutting pictures out of the ladies' magazine Gladys had given her the other night. Thomas said he'd just take a look anyway, see if she wanted a drink or anything. There were still some of those apples left, his father reminded him. They're sour, Thomas said, and his father's head drew back from under the hood.

"I paid good money for those apples," he said, scowling in the hot sun.

"I just said they were sour. I didn't say I wasn't going to eat one!" he called back.

His father hadn't paid a penny for the apples, but had traded work for them. That's how they got most of their food, from the different farms he butchered for.

"Don't you be talking to me like that!" his father barked, pointing the wrench and squinting with one eye as he came toward him. Grease smudged his cheek. "You be grateful for every thing you've got even if it's a no-good, sour apple, you hear me? You hear what I'm saying?" His fingers clenched Thomas's upper arm, squeezing into the bone.

"Yessir."

His father glared down at him. "And don't be writing your mother any more letters."

Thomas stared back. That was wrong. Nobody could tell him such a thing, not even his own father.

"What'd I just say? Don't just stand there looking at me, say it!" His father squeezed harder, pulling Thomas until his cheek pressed against his father's sweaty chest. "Say it!"

"Why? Why can't I write to her?"

"Because!" his father snarled, holding him so close Thomas could smell the rage seething in his unwashed sweat. "Because I said so." His father's rank heart beat against his ear. He didn't dare pull away. The seizure had become an embrace, more desperate in its grief now than the anger.

Nothing made sense. And for the rest of that day and most of the next, his father stayed nearby. Thomas had no opportunity to look for his mother's letter. It was late afternoon when the sputtering truck finally drove off. His father was afraid he needed a new battery. He had just remembered Mrs. Cobb, the old woman in Pawlet whose husband had fallen through the ice and drowned last winter. If his truck was still around she might be willing to trade some of its parts to have her hog butchered. Or for whatever else needed doing on her farm.

"How far's Pawlet?" Margaret asked their father.

"Sixteen miles."

"But that's far. What if the truck breaks down. How'll you get back?"

Don't worry, he told her. He'd be fine as long as he kept the motor running. And if he did get held up, her big brother knew what to do. There were still some eggs and pole beans left. And salt pork, he called down from the truck, to give them a good flavor. "And get more wood. We're running low," he hollered in a squeal of shifting gears.

He and Margaret headed toward the tent, dragging along, both thinking the same thing. The truck sounded real bad. His father never left for work so late in the day as this, Margaret said grumpily. He has to. Times are bad, Thomas said, searching for the tobacco pouch. It was exactly where his father had hung it the day before, on a nail behind the wooden crate they stored the canned goods in. Margaret asked if they could go out in the boat. Maybe in a while, he said, slipping the letter out. He told her he'd be right back. He had to go to the bathroom. It was the only place he could get away from her. Her kitten trailing behind, she followed him to the lean-to. When was a while, she called in at the blanket. When he was done, he called back, struggling to see the handwriting through the deep shade. If he stepped outside or even lifted the blanket she'd know what he was reading.

"I don't hear anything," she said with a giggle. "So you must be sitting down then, huh?"

"The sooner you leave, the sooner I'll be done!" he yelled, sounding again like his father. He peered from the side of the blanket and saw her move off only a few feet. "Go wait in the boat," he shouted. And if she didn't there wouldn't be any boat ride. Margaret ran down to the pond and he stepped outside.

August 21

Dear Henry,

How dare you use the children in your twisted efforts to make me come back to you. If it is pity or guilt you hoped to instill in me by having Thomas write, please know that you have failed miserably. I am, of course, concerned for the children's welfare, but I am absolutely unable to have them here on my paltry earnings. And you know this! This room is small even for me, and my landlady would throw me out into the street if I were to bring children here. I tried and failed at being a good wife. I can do no more and you know this. Please inform the children of our unfortunate situation. If you do it in a reasonable and kind way, then they can accept the truth. I long ago accepted your disregard of my feelings, Henry, but a letter like Thomas's makes me see just how cruel you really are. I have tried to be completely honest. And now you must do the same.

Sincerely,
Irene

Please tell the children that I am thinking of them.

So now he knew. It was all a lie. She wasn't coming back and she didn't want them there either. She wasn't working hard to save enough for them all to be together again. This was it, that tent, that trampled grass leading down to the muddy pond edge, he kept thinking as he rowed out to the middle of the still, dark water. The silvery sky was a hot mist of light trying to burst through a bubble. It was an ache, and it hurt so much he couldn't even look at Margaret for fear he would cry. She just kept talking, chattering on about nothing all the while their life was ending. He longed to reach over and pinch her until she cried. He resented her happy ignorance. She should also be hurting in the knowledge that only bleakness lay ahead: a life of tents and bucking, smoking trucks; instead of their mother's kiss goodnight their father's blunt orders to wash out their underpants, to throw more lime into the latrine, to eat sour apples and shut up about it. Instead now, she called for him to look, giggling with delight to see her kitten so perfectly poised on the stern. He seized the oars and began to row again. Hard, fast as he could, poling the oar blade deep into the dark water to change course.

"Thomas! Thomas! Stop!" she screamed with the sharp turn. She leaned out as far as she could, straining to reach into the water. He kept rowing. She scrambled toward him over the seat. He had to go back. The kitty had fallen over the side. "Please, Thomas! Quick before he drowns!"

How frightened she was. Horrified. Devastated that something she loved and needed so much was gone. "Please, Tommy!" she bawled with snot bubbling from her nose, her eyes swelling red. "Please get kitty before he drowns."

Of course he would. Would dive into the dead emptiness, deep down where an entire wagon and team of horses had vanished into bottomless muck.

"Back there!" she sobbed as his head burst through the surface. The boat was already drifting. He swam, thrashing in the direction she pointed to. But there was nothing there. No kitten. He swam back and, holding on to the side, told her to look under the seat. Behind the tackle box. Maybe it was hiding. But no, she had seen him fall in. She had seen him bobbing in the water. "He was trying to keep his head up!" she wailed.

"Cats can swim, can't they? Can't they?" he screamed back, for of course he had thought they could, had assumed it would just paddle behind them. Give her a little scare. Teach her a lesson. But what? That the cruelest people were the ones she loved and trusted most. Please don't cry, he begged, but he was crying too.

. . .

The letter in his pocket was wet, the smeared ink running into the creases when he opened it. Later, when it was dry, he folded it and slid it back into the tobacco pouch on the nail behind the box of cans.

His father came home as the night sky lowered. The old woman had given him the truck battery, but not for the expected exchange. She had sold her pig just last week, but her well had gone dry. She needed a new one dug and couldn't afford to pay anyone. The battery was his, if he would dig the new well. By his estimation the job would take three straight days of digging. Four at most. His father said he was sorry about the kitten's drowning. He held Margaret on his lap for a long time and told her he was glad nothing had happened to her because he loved her so much. She told him how brave Thomas had been jumping in to save it. His father looked over and didn't say anything.

The next morning his father was up before the sun had risen. The first light filtered through the trees along with the clear trill of a bird. Cans rattled. From under the crook of his elbow Thomas watched his father lift the pouch from the nail, then with a sigh sit down at the table. He rolled six cigarettes for the day, licked the end papers, then put them into his shirt pocket. He took out the letter. With the crinkle of the unfolding paper Thomas closed his eyes. His father got up and stood by his cot. Those few seconds were the longest agony the boy had ever endured. He tried to breathe slowly as if he were sleeping. Even through his closed lids his father's shadow was consuming him, the way the pond's blackness had overcome the kitten. His father knew that he had killed his sister's cat, just as he knew he had read the letter. Now he would pay. He waited, almost straining toward the blow. The air stirred as his father walked out of the tent.

4

THOMAS WAS BACK IN HIS OLD SCHOOL IN BELTON. ALL THE students were taught by Miss Hall. Each grade sat in its own row. Last year for those few months they had lived in town, the school he and Margaret had attended had different rooms for each class. It had been less confusing than this babble of so many lessons going on at once, first grade reciting the alphabet, eighth graders naming presidents, but it had been boring.

He didn't know how old Miss Hall was. It was hard to tell with fat ladies. Fifty probably, judging from her thin gray hair. She lived in town with her shy, unmarried brother whose only job was driving her to the little schoolhouse every day, earlier on cold mornings so she could get the coal stove fired up before her students arrived. Everyone knew Miss Hall preferred girls to boys, but for some reason Thomas was the boy she liked least of all. So far this year her favorite girl was Margaret. The first day of school Miss Hall had gasped when Margaret walked in the door. "Your hair! What happened to those long ringlets?" Like so much else from their old life, Thomas had almost forgotten the bedtime ritual of his mother wrapping the long strands of his sister's hair in rags.

Most days now Margaret's hair was snarled and frizzy. Her arms and legs were scabbed with bug bites and the mysterious scratches they invariably emerged from the woods with. Now that he thought of it, watching his sister from the end of the row, she was starting to look like poor Carol Pfeiffer, whose large family lived in a tar-paper shack. Carol sat in front of him. Every day the split seam on her dress tore a little more at the shoulder. Her brown, fuzzy hair was short as a boy's. Bugs, most likely. Tracks of grime ran up the back of her neck and she reeked of kerosene. Her long fingernails were caked with dirt. Instead of shoes she wore floppy black rubber galoshes, the buckles long ago broken off. Her mother wasn't right, crazy as a loon people said. Carol didn't act too right herself. She swore and hit kids and was always stealing things. Miss Hall didn't like Carol at all, though she tried to be kind, bringing her pears or apples and sandwiches to eat at school when many of the other children went home for lunch.

The stove in the little schoolhouse was glowing. The week's rain and cold nights had turned life in the tent raw and miserable. For the last few weeks his father kept saying he was going to look for a place to rent. They couldn't live there during the winter, which already seemed hard on their heels. This morning had been so cold that Margaret wouldn't get out of bed. Their father had left earlier, so it was up to Thomas. He had tried everything—bribery, threats, false promises. He couldn't leave her alone and if they both missed school Miss Hall would tell their father.

Finally, he had no choice but tip her off the cot. Margaret cried as she dressed in her damp clothes. Still wet from yesterday's washing, her socks sagged over her ankles. She ate her stale biscuits then whimpered through the drizzle all along the puddled road. Actually, this was the best place for them, Thomas knew the minute they stepped inside the warm schoolhouse.

The Battle of Gettysburg started on July 1, 1863. He had forgotten there was going to be a test on important Civil War dates. Studying in the tent was difficult with so little light. Now that the nights were so cold, they got into bed soon after they ate supper. Sleep seemed the only thing his father looked forward to anymore. If his mother had written again, the letter hadn't gone into the tobacco pouch. The water-streaked letter had disappeared and his father had never said a word about it.

Carol Pfeiffer spun around and demanded that he stop kicking her chair. He told her he wasn't. Actually he'd only been tapping his foot, nervous that he'd be called on. Yes, he was, she said, and if he did it again she would tell Miss Hall. Abraham Lincoln was the sixteenth president and he was assassinated on April 14, 1865. Miss Hall rose quickly from her desk and went to Margaret, who was crying again. At the touch of her shoulder Margaret sobbed loudly. All recitation stopped. Every eye was on his sister.

"What is it, dear?" Miss Hall bent close. "Tell me. You can tell me."

Thomas froze. This morning he'd gotten so angry at her bawling under the covers that he'd told her it was all her fault their mother had gone away. He told her about the letter and how in it she said she was never coming back again because Margaret was such a spoiled crybaby. Why had he done it? To hurt her. To make her feel as sad as he was inside. But he could see what a horrible mistake he'd made. Miss Hall would tell his father, who would punish him not just for his cruelty, but, finally, for having read the letter.

"I'm cold," Margaret cried through chattering teeth. "My socks are wet and I don't feel good."

Miss Hall put Margaret's shoes under the stove and hung her dingy socks to dry on the mitten rack for everyone to see. Thomas was ashamed. Miss Hall took a crocheted afghan from the closet, and bundled Margaret in it. Thomas tapped his foot uneasily. Margaret seemed to be settling down. From now on he would take better care of her. She had always been loyal in the big things and yet he had hurt her in the worst possible way.

"Stop it!" Carol Pfeiffer turned and shouted.

"Carol," Miss Hall warned, hurrying toward them. There was a pitch Carol reached, a line few dared cross.

"He keeps kicking my chair!"

"I was only tapping my foot."

"Thomas was only tapping his foot, Carol. Now you just turn around and mind your work."

"Who does he think he is kicking my chair? He's so poor he has to live in a tent."

"Carol!"

"Him and his sister both. And they don't even have a mother—"

. . .

Apparently that was how Miss Hall learned of their living conditions. He and Margaret had to stay after school and answer a thousand questions while Miss Hall's brother waited in his car to drive her home. Did they have enough food to eat? How long was their father gone when he went off to work? Finally, Miss Hall gave Thomas a note for his father and sent them on their shameful way.

The next day Henry Talcott was at the schoolhouse door when the bell rang at three. It was a temporary arrangement, he explained, just until he got enough saved for a new place. He was doing his best, but with so many having such hard times it was the low man on the totem pole that got least. What could Miss Hall say to that? Especially since she was one of the few people in Belton with a salary, fifty-two steady dollars a month no matter how poor her neighbors were.

Gladys was at the tent when they got home. Arms folded, she had been waiting for them to come.

"What happened?" Henry called, jumping down from the truck. He hurried to her.

"She looks sad," Margaret said as they watched Gladys shake her head with a sweep of her arm.

"Maybe old Bibeau died," Thomas said. The old man had been so sick the last time they'd gone to supper there that Henry had to help him up to his bed. The next day Henry returned to move the old man's bed downstairs. He set it up in the parlor from where the old man harassed Gladys throughout the day. At night she would be startled awake by her father's clanging cowbell.

The children climbed down from the truck, then lingered outside pretending to play. Alert as always for news of their mother, they were desperate to hear what was being said.

"There's nothing you can do," Henry said.

Gladys paced back and forth, her scratchy voice too low now to hear. ". . . Some sense into him" was all Thomas could make out.

"Of course not," Henry said. "It's his land. I have no say in it."

"But he's not thinking straight," Gladys suddenly cried. "You know he's not."

"But it's still his land. And if he wants to sell to Farley then there's nothing anyone can do."

"He knows my father's confused. That's why he's in such a rush for this, the bastard!"

"Get inside!" Henry ordered his children.

The details were slow in coming, but the boy learned enough to understand if not why, at least how all the rest of it came about. Fred Farley had offered to buy old Bibeau's land, leaving him the house and one surrounding acre. For years the old man had held him off, but Farley had finally convinced him things were going from bad to worse, and that soon the land would be worthless. This might be his last chance to sell and not die a pauper. At least he'd have something for his old age.

. . .

The transaction took place a week later in the office of Fred Farley's lawyer. Henry drove Gladys and her father, then helped the old man up the steep stairs. Gladys wanted Henry to come in with them, but he said it wasn't his place. He sat in the waiting room until they came out. Thinking himself a wealthy man with Farley's check in his breast pocket, the old man clung to his benefactor's arm and let Farley lead him down the stairs and back into Henry's truck. Farley shook the old man's hand, then stepped aside as Henry helped Gladys into the truck. Never one to hide her feelings, she had barely spoken to Farley and was saying less to her father.

"Henry," Farley said after Henry shut her door. "Where do you think you'll be going now?

"I'm bringing Gladys and her father home."

Farley drew back his pointed chin in the pinch-mouthed scowl all the men in his family had. "I meant where will you be moving to now?"

"Don't know yet." Henry climbed into the truck.

Farley came to the window and spoke past Gladys and her father. "Have you got a place?"

"Nope."

"Well, Phyllis wants you to know the children are welcome to come stay with us."

"Tell Phyllis we'll be staying in our own place."

"You said you don't have a place."

"Not yet, but I'm looking."

"I can give you a couple, two, three weeks, Henry, but after that you're going to have to be off my property."

"Don't worry, I will." He started the truck.

"Tell you the truth, Henry, I am worried. Worried you're going to put me in a position I don't care to be in."

. . .

In the next week and a half four new slaughtering jobs came Henry's way. He began to think his run of bad luck was finally over. He had just finished the last job when Jim Tomkins drove up and asked if he'd come by and do one of his two cows. He couldn't afford feed for both through the winter. Of course Henry would. In fact he'd stop by that very afternoon on his way home.

He had found a small house for rent not too far from Gladys's. Empty for the last year, it was dilapidated and swarming with hornets the day he'd seen it. There was a lot of dry rot in the outhouse, but it wouldn't seem half bad after their summer using the lean-to. The well was in good working order. Henry could have it, the widow who owned it promised, but she wanted a month's rent the day he moved in and he'd have to fix the broken windows.

Two more dollars and he'd have the thirteen they'd settled on from her wanting fifteen and his offer of ten. This last job of the day would put him enough over the top for the rent and to buy a couple panes of new window glass. The work went well. Tomkins apologized for paying in change; he'd had to break into his little one's piggy bank, that's how far gone he was. He and Henry commiserated a while. Henry wasn't a Democrat by a long stretch, but if Roosevelt thought he could do something, people ought to at least give him a chance. Tomkins said it was a rich man's world, always had been, always would be, and that Roosevelt was just one more rich man looking to get richer.

"You ever hear him talk, that fancy-boy accent of his?" Tomkins said, following him to his truck.

"Be seeing you, Jim," he said, climbing up into the truck anxious to be on his way. Even small talk was wearying lately. It was past suppertime and he couldn't remember if this was the night Gladys was bringing supper by. Days like this fogged his brain. He was afraid he might fall asleep at the wheel. Tomkins lingered by the window complaining about the banks now. They were like cannibals, feeding off their own. Once again Tomkins bragged what a genius his oldest was. Up at the state college there in Burlington, the boy was studying to be a doctor. Tomkins didn't know how much longer he could keep coming up with tuition. If he didn't get a break soon, the boy would have to come home. That'd be a shame, Henry said, looking over the wheel at the handsome black-trimmed barn. It was as hard to believe they were all in the same boat as it was to feel much sympathy for a man like Tomkins, who'd been born in that big, brick farmhouse. Even the wife was having to work now, Tomkins admitted. Piano lessons; maybe Henry's children might want to take from her. She had studied in Boston when she was a young woman. At some conservatory or something, Tomkins wasn't exactly sure which. Henry said he didn't think so. Well, if both children took together, Tomkins proposed, he'd only have to pay for the one.

"They don't have a piano," he said. Or even a room to put one in, he thought, pulling out the choke, then turning the key, but nothing happened. Nothing. Not even a sputter. Must be the battery, Tomkins said, already raising the hood. Couldn't be, Henry told him. It was new.

"New?" Tomkins hooted.

"Well, new for me." Three and a half days of digging it had cost from Mrs. Cobb's dead husband's truck.

"Well, it's deader'n Cobb," Tomkins declared and, from the looks of it, as old.

. . .

So, that was the first setback. A brand-new battery, the biggest chunk out of the rent money. The next, Thomas was witness to. Margaret's shoes hurt worse than ever. She had grown a lot over the summer, but nowhere was it more apparent and painful than her longer feet crammed each morning into tight shoes that rubbed her heels and big toes raw. All summer long she'd gone barefoot, but now with the cold and the walk to school she had to wear the only shoes she had. Margaret begged for new ones. Be patient, her father said. Next month after he had enough saved to move them into the house he'd bring her into town for the best pair a girl ever had. What about me? Thomas wanted to ask. His own were lined with paper and cloth, cardboard, anything he could salvage to keep from walking on bare ground. Because the bottoms of his socks had worn out, he had cut them off, but still put on the tops every morning so he'd at least look like he had socks on.

No one wanted a house to live in more than Thomas. He was convinced that as soon as they were settled his mother would return. It had been the tent that had kept her from coming back as soon as she read his letter. Now, with enough time having passed, he was certain that he had misunderstood her letter. He wished he'd never read it. Like so much that grown-ups said there were different meanings and shades of truth a kid could never untangle.

How Mrs. Farley found out about Margaret's "miserable shoes" Thomas didn't know, but "miserable" was Margaret's word every time she jammed her feet into them. Probably from Miss Hall, he decided. He had seen the two women talking at recess one day, all the while glancing over at Margaret. He had seen Mrs. Farley there a few times before with items she'd brought for the Pfeiffer children. Last year, when the back half of the Flanagans' house burned after a lightning strike, Mrs. Farley hauled boxes of clothes and dishes into the schoolhouse for Miss Hall to give to the family. When he wondered why she hadn't delivered it directly to the Flanagans, his mother had answered that it was to keep people from knowing of her largesse. It wouldn't be until high school that he would discover the real meaning of that word. Yet for all the rest of his life whenever he came across the word "largesse," it was the threat of Mrs. Farley's pillowy roundness that would come to mind first.

"Hello-hoe! Hello-hoe!" The cheery greeting sounded long before they saw Mrs. Farley emerge from the leafless trees. At first Thomas was confused. The large canvas bag she carried looked like a suitcase. Was she here to pack them up? One of Mr. Farley's workers had come by last week with a notarized letter from Farley demanding they vacate the property by October 26. Thomas's father had seemed amused that Farley had gone to so much trouble. He told the worker he expected to be in his own place in another few days.

"Look what I've got for you, Margaret!" Mrs. Farley sat on the trunk with Margaret between her pudgy stockinged knees while from the bag she drew a blue and white dress which she'd smocked herself. She held it under Margaret's chin. Next came the shoes, shiny black with silver buckles. Margaret couldn't stop grinning. Even Thomas could tell they were special shoes. The only other girl with such a pair was Dora Tomkins, who always had the best of everything. There was also a doll, which Mrs. Farley said (and Thomas had to agree) greatly resembled Margaret with her clear blue eyes and light, curly hair. Both excited and torn between envy and the certainty of his father's displeasure, Thomas watched from his cot. Just having a visitor was pleasant.

Mrs. Farley's perfume filled the tent and made him ache for his mother. With old Bibeau sick these last couple of weeks Gladys hadn't come by much. His father was working long hours trying to get them into the house. You shouldn't've let her in, his father would bark the minute he saw the gifts. And as always it would be Thomas who would bear the brunt of his anger, Thomas who hadn't been responsible or strong enough. But how could he tell a grown-up lady to leave and take her things with her? The only way would be to say his father didn't let them accept gifts from strangers. Well, people then, he'd say, because obviously she wasn't a stranger. Now she was unwrapping a plate of butternut cookies.

"Mrs. Farley—"

"But what about Thomas?" Margaret interrupted, still holding the shoes. "Doesn't he get any presents?"

"Yes, of course! Look what I brought you, Thomas." She offered what appeared in the shadows to be a brown stick. "A flute! Just like Jesse-boy's. Now you two can play together."

But he didn't know how to play the flute, he told her. Well then, Jesse-boy would teach him, she said, the two red dots glowing on her cheeks. Why didn't they go there right now? Jesse-boy was hoping they'd come back with her. He hadn't seen them in so long. In fact the flute had been his idea. Thomas said they couldn't; his father wanted them to stay in the tent. Oh, he won't mind a bit, Mrs. Farley said; and it'll just be a quick visit. Jesse-boy was waiting.

Suddenly they were in her car and on their way. She told them how Jesse-boy wanted to hear all about their summer in the tent. He thought it was the most magical life anyone could have. Her chatter swamped Thomas's weak protestations. Margaret was so excited sitting up front that she was no help at all. Mrs. Farley urged her to put on the new shoes so Jesse-boy could see them.

As they were led into Jesse-boy's bedroom, Margaret wilted into her brother's side and squeezed his hand. The room smelled of talcum power and stale urine. Pictures of cowboys and Indians hung on the red striped walls. Jesse-boy's face had a gray wet sheen against the propped pillows. His childishness was belied by the wispy fuzz on his upper lip. His frail body seemed even thinner under the bedsheets, his soft voice weaker. He asked Margaret why she wasn't wearing her new dress. When she didn't answer right away he looked in exasperation to his mother. Mrs. Farley drew Margaret closer and told her to show Jesse-boy her new shoes. Margaret lifted one foot. Jesse-boy strained to see, but couldn't.

"Up you go!" Mrs. Farley swung her onto the bed. "See, Jesse-boy!" She lifted Margaret's foot and her son smiled happily.

Margaret sat stiffly beside him. He asked Thomas if he liked his present. Thomas nodded.

"Let's play together then," Jesse-boy said, slipping an identical flute out from under the sheet. Thomas said he didn't know how, but that didn't bother Jesse-boy. He played two or three weak notes, paused for breath, gasped three more notes, paused wheezing, played again. This went on for what seemed to Thomas (and surely for Margaret, frozen at his side) the longest time. Finally, he did not set down the flute so much as let it drift lightly, wearily from his wet, tremulous grin.

"Oh! Oh!" Mrs. Farley cried, clapping, then covered her mouth against her tearful joy. "Oh, Jesse-boy, that was so beautiful." She threw her arms around Margaret. "He's never been able to play that all the way through before!"

Margaret stared out at her brother over Mrs. Farley's embrace.

Standing against the wall, Thomas felt as if he were being pressed back by a great force that would consume his sister just as it had his mother.

"Mummy! I need to!" Jesse-boy said, pressing his hand over his crotch.

"Yes, yes!" Suddenly Mrs. Farley was snatching Margaret from the bed and opening the door.

Just then, there began a great commotion downstairs. Banging, thudding, then raised voices. Men, shouting.

"Henry, you wait outside! Don't you go up there now or I'll—"

"You've got my children. I don't care what the hell you do, I'm getting them!"

"Daddy!" Margaret cried, running down the stairs, the strangeness of it all erupting with the sight of their father, who scurried them outside.

Mrs. Farley ran out to the truck and tried to pass the new flute up to Thomas. His father grabbed it and threw it onto the ground. She had no right to come and take children out of their home. No! Mr. Farley thundered back—off of his property, that's what it was. She was sorry; she was so sorry, Mrs. Farley kept saying and Thomas wasn't sure who she was sorry to because both men seemed mad at her. All she wanted was for Jesse-boy to have company; he'd been so lonely lately. Well, that's not how you do it, her husband shouted. If only the children could live here a while. Even just during the week, poor things, she tried telling Henry as the truck inched ahead. She held on to his window well, pleading as she skittered alongside. They'd have so many advantages, a fine home, a good education—

"Look, Phyllis," Henry Talcott said, stopping the truck dead. "Just because your kid's not right doesn't give you any claim on my two."

Her head drew back as if slapped. Her eyes seemed to lock on Thomas's. He felt both shame and pity for her. His father didn't have to say it like that, as if Jesse-boy were some freak. After all, she'd only been trying to give them what they didn't have, which was more than most people did.

"You get the hell off my property, Talcott, tonight! You hear what I'm saying?" Mr. Farley shouted and threw a rock against the roof, running after the truck in such a rage Thomas was sure he'd chase it all the way back.

When they got to the tent, Henry Talcott balled up the new shoes and the doll in the dress, tying the bow strings and sleeves into a tight bundle while Margaret wept. They were never again to take handouts from anyone, did they understand? Because there was always a price. Always. But Daddy how could she go to school? Margaret bawled. She didn't have any shoes at all now. Her old ones were in Mrs. Farley's car. Then she'd wear Thomas's to school and he'd have to wear his father's dress shoes. But they'll be too big and flop, they protested.

"Then they'll flop!" Henry Talcott roared into the night so angrily they huddled on their cots. "They'll goddamn flop! And you'll just keep on walking! And if they fall off your goddamn feet you'll put them back on, you hear me? You hear what I'm saying? Do you? Do you?" he raged through the darkness.

His father's despair was terrifying. His father was the strongest man he knew. If he couldn't cope with the forces against them, then who could? What would become of them? Thomas lay very still, arms over his head. No wonder his mother had left. He would too if he could. If he had someplace to go. And if Margaret would come with him.

. . .

All that was left when they got home from school were their clothes in a heap. The tent and everything in it had been torn down and hauled away. It had been a raw, gray day, damp under the threat of low dark clouds, snow probably if it got any colder. Thomas's breath spouted to vapor in the air as he told Margaret to shut up and stop crying. At least he had his jackknife.

"Daddy! Daddy!" she screamed, tearing through the pile as if her father might be at the bottom.

Thomas assured her their father must have taken it all down to move them into the new house early.

"No, he didn't! He left! He's gone too!" she wailed, then ran back the way they'd just come through the woods.

"Margaret!" he grabbed her arm, but she punched his chest, pushing him away. He lunged and this time caught her wrist. Writhing, she shrieked to be let go, but now he clenched both wrists. Her face twisted into pure hatred and she kicked his shin bone. His painful bewilderment, that she would hurt him when he was only trying to help and comfort her, soured to outrage and he slapped her. Right across the face. Hard, hard as he could because she deserved it. Because, somehow, this was all her fault. For being too pretty and weak and always wanting more than they had. Because he was as helpless as she was. And now her tears streamed into the blood pouring from her nose. She let herself be led back. He grabbed a ragged shirt from the pile and pressed it to her nose. It was all right, he kept telling her. Everything was going to be all right. They'd just wait here and she'd see, pretty soon Daddy would be back to take them to the new house. But he doesn't have enough money for the rent, she cried. Yes, he does, he said. But the windows are all still broken. No, he probably fixed them, but didn't say anything to surprise us. But what about the hornets? She blew her nose and the bleeding started all over again. Press harder, he told her. Daddy must have killed most of them. They would finish off the rest, the ones he couldn't. Are you sure? she asked with a last deep shudder that finally seemed to calm her, though her thin shoulders continued to tremble. Yes, and they'd probably be finding dead ones all winter long, he said.

"I know! Let's keep them in a jar. See how many we end up with. Thousands probably," she sniffed.

Probably. Past her, he watched the sky deepening into cold, dull lead.

It was almost dark when the children arrived at Gladys's. That goddamn Farley, she swore when Thomas told her what had happened. Hearing this, Margaret burst into tears and could not be consoled. Gladys picked her up in her long, strong arms and sat with her, in the warm kitchen, assuring her as Thomas had earlier that everything would be all right; she'd feel better as soon as her daddy got here.

"I want my mommy," Margaret cried, sobbing again. Thomas was getting annoyed with his sister's breakdowns. But he was afraid to say anything for fear she would tell that he'd hit her. "I want my mommy!" she gasped again.

"Yes, I know you do." Gladys clasped Margaret's wet face against her own coarse cheek. "How could she have done this. Such a terrible wrong to you poor children. Such a terrible wrong!"

Thomas glared up at her. He was angry that she had said the very thing he'd been thinking. But who was she to criticize his mother, his beautiful mother? He remembered a conversation on their way home from T. C. Whitby's Christmas party in town. Gladys had been at the party and his mother teased his father how Gladys's lazy eye turned straight in, she got so excited whenever she saw him.

"That's not nice, especially in front of the children," his father had scolded in a low voice.

"No, but it's true. Gladys Bibeau thinks she's just biding her time!" she had giggled, flushed with punch and the attention she always got at parties. "I'll bet she goes to sleep every night dreaming of you, Henry."

"One more word like that and I'm stopping the truck!" he had growled.

"And then what? What're you going to do, make me get out and walk like last time?"

"I didn't make you. You said to."

"Well, that's what you meant by stopping."

"I just do what I'm told, that's all."

"You do? Is that what you think? Then how come I've only got two—"

"Irene. Don't. Please, don't."

Thomas had fallen asleep then. Sometimes he thought grown-ups argued just to hurt the other person, not because what they said was true or even mattered to them. At least that's the way it always seemed with his mother. In some ways she could act as much like a little girl as Margaret. Sometimes even Margaret had more sense about people's feelings than her own mother did.

That argument was as much a mystery to the boy now as then. He couldn't ask and all he knew was that it had to do with his father's temper and Hemmings, the tipsy cloth salesman from Massachusetts, who had been teasing his mother at the party. The same man in the pin-striped suit had been at their house months earlier when their father wasn't there. They had come home from school to find him sitting at the kitchen table, his tie loose and collar unbuttoned. T. C. Whitby had given him her address and he had just dropped in on her. His mother wanted him to leave. He ignored her and began telling the children about the stack of picture cards on the table. He mounted one in the stereoscope for Margaret to see. Thomas hadn't liked him at all. His mother was nervous and the man was too pushy.

After a while though Thomas had forgotten about it until one day when they were driving home from supper at Aunt Lena's. Out of the blue Margaret asked what happened to that man in the kitchen who had shown her the pretty bird pictures. Thomas tried to hear, but couldn't make out the words up front. Then the truck stopped and his mother got out and started walking. She got home a while after they did.

Gladys set Margaret down and moved around the kitchen taking pots and pans from the wide metal shelf over the stove and covered dishes from the icebox. "Ham steak and home fries," she said, slicing a baked potato lengthwise, then into cubes. She chopped a red pepper and then an onion. The knife's racket on the metal drain board drew them closer to watch.

"See what you did!" Gladys laughed, wiping her sniffly nose on the back of her wrist. "You made me cry, Margaret Talcott!"

"No, I didn't. It's the onion!" Margaret squealed and all three of them jumped, startled by the cowbell clanging from the parlor.

"Shut up!" old Bibeau yelled. "Shut the hell up in there."

5

THE NEXT DAY THOMAS RODE ALONGSIDE HIS FATHER TO Farley's. He could tell his father expected trouble, was working up to it, nodding grimly, lips moving in silent fury, readying himself for the fight to come. Thomas was more excited than scared. He knew his father's reputation as someone not to mess with, though he'd never seen him actually hit a person. Once in his younger days, three men had been waiting for him by the side of the road. The one who said he had a gun demanded the money Henry had just been paid after a long day's butchering and dressing hogs. The other two had clubs. They ordered Henry down from the truck, but he said they'd have to come get it if they wanted his money. When it was over one man sobbed like a baby with a broken arm dangling at his side while the others ran away.

Old Bibeau loved to tell that story, gumming his tobacco and grinning. Sometimes there were only two men, often as not, five or six. Thomas had asked once if it was true. His father laughed and said it didn't matter now that people thought it was true. Even T. C. Whitby had alluded to it the last time he'd been with his mother when she picked up the store's books to work on. He said he'd warned Hemmings that Henry Talcott was one man not to get mad. Oh, Mr. Whitby, what're you talking about? Clyde just wants to be everyone's friend, you know that. Friends like him you don't need, Whitby had snapped and, as always, his mother, his out-of-the-house, in-town mother, only laughed.

And then what? How much time had lapsed between the man with the bird picture on the stereoscope, sitting at the kitchen table and his mother's leaving, to now? He couldn't be sure. Time had never been of much consequence. One day he was rowing through summer heat and here he was now bouncing along through snow flurries on his way to a showdown.

The truck rumbled off the road onto the long gravel driveway in to Farley's Dairy Farm. As they drove past the house Thomas wondered what Jesse-boy would do if there was a fight. Probably cry and wet his pants. His father parked in front of the first red barn. Of the three it was the smallest. Dairy Office, said the sign over the dented metal door.

"Wait!" Thomas yelled as his father jumped down.

"You wait!" His father slammed the truck door.

Fred Farley stepped out from the office followed by a scowling man in knee-high barn boots. His father towered over Mr. Farley. Thomas rolled down the window, but it was hard to hear with the wind blowing. His father did most of the talking at first, with Fred Farley's high, nasal twang cutting in to say he was sorry. But Henry'd been given fair and legal warning. Of course he was sorry the children had to find such a scene, but hadn't Henry put his own children in that desperate situation by not providing them with a proper home. This angered his father more. He said something, pointed at Mr. Farley. The worker stepped forward and Mr. Farley spoke up loudly. He said Henry's belongings were right out back in the shed behind the barn. This man, Arnold, would help Henry load them onto the truck.

"No need," Henry Talcott said on his way back to the truck. "I brought my boy." He drove behind the barn. Farley made a great show of trying different keys before finally unlocking the padlocked door. The heavy smell of cow dung rolled out from the shed. Thomas followed his father inside. Surprisingly, everything was carefully stacked. Even the kerosene lanterns had been wrapped in newspaper before being put into the fruit crate. The tent was neatly folded. Thomas and his father moved quickly between shed and truck. His father ignored the men watching him and his son hustle their sad belongings like migrant workers. Farley'd gotten him good, Thomas thought. Was that what was happening? Was this the way life would be, lower even than the Pfeiffers, hauling their fire-blackened pots and pans from site to site, the boy wondered, head down like his father.

"One of the poles cracked some," Arnold, the worker, said on the last trip in.

This, Henry ignored. He looked around. Just one more cot and another chair. "Something's missing," he told Farley.

"It's all here. Nothing's missing," Farley said.

"My spare tire and my boning saw."

"I don't remember seeing any spare tire or boning saw. Do you?" Farley asked Arnold.

"No!" Smirking, Arnold drew in his double chin.

"Well, they were there. And now they're gone," his father said.

"You accusing me of stealing them, Henry?" Farley looked amused. "An old tire and a saw?"

"Somebody did."

"Well it sure as hell wasn't me and you know that. You're just looking for trouble now, aren't you? Or maybe you're trying to make a little money off me now, is that it?"

"Yeah, that's exactly what he's trying to do," Arnold said with that insulting grin. "There weren't no tire or saw or I'da seen 'em."

Thomas couldn't understand why his father didn't just smack the grin off his face. One quick left and a right. Pow-pow! Instead, he was handing Thomas the chair and picking up the cot. Meekly. Like the whipped man he was, worn down and grim, averting his gaze as he slunk past Farley and this idiot barn man who reeked of the stalls he'd just been mucking.

"No! Because I saw them! They were there all right!" Thomas declared. "The tire was out back of the tent, and the boning saw, that was . . . that was there too! You're lying, the both of you. You're nothing but liars. Damn liars!"

He couldn't remember where anything had been. Adult possessions in a boy's life were vague objects that existed, but in some other realm of consciousness.

"Thomas!" His father's hand clamped over the back of his neck. "Get in the truck!"

"But they are! They're—"

With that whimpery outburst his father shoved him along, then one big shoe snagged the other and he staggered into a heap by the side of the truck.

"Don't you ever do that again, ever, you hear me?" his father called over the engine.

"But they were, they were lying!" he cried as the truck pulled onto the road. "And you let them. You didn't do anything!"

Thomas's head snapped back as his father wrenched the truck sharply onto the soft shoulder.

"What? What can I do?" he bellowed, eyes wild for an answer. "Go ahead, tell me! Tell me! Don't you see? There's nothing I can do! Nothing! Nothing, goddamn it. Nothing! Nothing! Nothing," he groaned into his arms over the steering wheel.

. . .

Time resumed its vapory flow with one day lasting the length of a week and four gone in the wink of an eye. Their stay at Gladys's was wonderful. Except for old Bibeau, of course, but even his foul moods were endurable with good food and clean clothes always available, not to mention real mattresses to sleep on. In the evenings after Gladys finally got her father settled for sleep in his parlor bedroom, she and Thomas would play bridge at the kitchen table. Margaret busied herself cutting pictures out of the old Montgomery Ward's catalog Gladys had given her. Each night Margaret would arrange her dozens of beautiful ladies, handsome men, and pretty children into various families. Their names were forever changing, but she would never admit as much. She would insist that this blonde lady in the polka dot dress had always been Norma. He and Gladys would tease her and say they distinctly remembered that last night she had called her Annabelle. No I didn't! she would insist and, if in one of her mopes, might come close to crying.

Thomas was learning he had to be the one to change the subject. More than kindhearted, Gladys almost seemed to care for them in a way their mother never had. But there was a ferocity in her attention that could be as overwhelming as it was comforting. She was a strong woman who met life head-on. She said what she meant. And meant what she said. Sometimes her forthrightness left a child like Margaret flattened in her path. Sensitive as he was to Margaret's pain, there were times, however, when he had to admit he enjoyed her misery. She'd always been spoiled. But no more.

The scouring efficiency of Gladys's ways was rough enough on Margaret, but old Bibeau was deliberately cruel. Gladys only meant well, but her father seemed to delight in upsetting the little girl. Little Miss Priss, he called her. Out of the way! he'd warn, then let go a gob of tobacco juice into the tin can by his bed. One day he missed and it hit the tatted antimacassar on the chair arm. Gladys had gone into town for his medicine, leaving the children and the old man to mind each other. Everything he needed was bedside, well within arm's reach: water, his plug of chaw, the thunder jug. With his sight too weak for reading, his only entertainment was watching out the window for the occasional car or truck, or, even rarer, a neighbor to pass by. Gladys had put the radio by his bed, but its staticky transmission with his poor hearing made it a difficult companion. To hear anything, he'd have to turn it up so loud that no one in the house could think. Most of his contemporaries had died and the few left had never liked the sour old man anyway, certainly not enough to come fill his idle hours. According to Gladys, the chickens had come home to roost. He was getting back just what he'd given, not a kind word or deed for anyone. The one man he'd ever liked was young Henry Talcott, who had always treated him with respect. On the frequent occasions of old Bibeau's bilious eruptions, Henry had taken it in stride, both as a boy coming to play with Gladys and now as a man, down on his luck and needing shelter.

The old man had never forgiven Henry for betraying his "plug-ugly, but decent daughter" for a woman like Irene Jalley. "Nothing but a painted face and a wiggle when she walks," he had come right out with it at the time, telling Henry if he married Gladys instead of Irene, the farm—every acre, down to the last inch of dirt—would be his. "You don't even have to have those kinds of feelings for Gladys and I'd be surprised to hell if you did," he confided. For *that* there was always a quick trip to Albany. Henry said he was sorry, but he couldn't do that. No, no! the old man had grabbed him and thundered. Let her do what women do when that happened. The most important thing here was loyalty; rejecting Gladys was the same as rejecting him. Not only had he trusted Henry like a son, taking him in after his father left, but through all those years of Gladys's spinsterhood had assumed Henry would marry her. Why else did Henry think he'd been allowed "full access" to her. As if she were one of his cows in heat, Henry must have thought, for he was as angry as he was insulted for Gladys. Henry told the old man he should be ashamed of saying such things about his own daughter. The old man hauled off and backhanded him across the mouth. "You'll pay for that, you jackass, you stupid jackass!" he bellowed as Henry stormed off.

Most of the acrimony between old Bibeau and his father Thomas wouldn't understand until he was grown. One thing seemed clear to the boy now. All of the old man's bitter hope for revenge had appeared in the form of these two children. Margaret heard it first from the kitchen where she was mixing flour and water for paste. Thomas sat on the porch steps whittling with his knife. It was okay to let the shavings fall where they might when they were living in the tent, but Gladys had ordered all whittling to be done outside. The bell clang-clang-clanged, but Thomas ignored it. Whatever it was, the old man could wait a minute. Suddenly the door banged open and Margaret burst outside screaming. A shiny brown splatter ran down her dress.

"Look what he did!" she cried in disbelief, plucking the wet bodice out from her chest. "He spit on me! He did!"

He had rung the cowbell and ordered Margaret to clean the chair arm doily before Gladys saw it. If Thomas wasn't so mad, he might have been amused at the old man's imperious assumption that finicky Margaret would ever go near his mess, much less touch it. "That's disgusting!" she had told him, cringing from the soiled doily. And with that the next stream hit her right across the chest. He had done it on purpose, though he would deny it later to Gladys, claiming instead that the girl had barged in on him right when he was spitting. With Margaret gagging in the kitchen while she pulled off the stained dress, Thomas marched into the parlor. Old Bibeau's open pajama top revealed the waxy yellow skin on his sunken, bony chest. His head trembled as he tried to fix Thomas in his filmy gaze. He demanded that the boy earn his keep and clean up the chair. Thomas knew better than talk back, especially when the insult to his sister had been far greater. Behind him Margaret was insisting they leave. Thomas said he'd clean the antimacassar, but first the old man should tell Margaret he was sorry.

Sorry, the old man repeated, almost eagerly. Thomas practically had to pull his sister into the room. Wheezing, the old man strained up one elbow. Instead of being pitiable, his feebleness was repulsive, creepy the way it emphasized the great effort it took to wage such cruelty. Instead of apologizing he asked why the hell they weren't with their mother.

They would be soon, Thomas said, secure in the lie as long as his father did not acknowledge his brief possession of the water-stained letter. Soon as she could, he added. Of all the ways a child keeps safe, easiest is the lie no one dares refute. You mean she's coming back? the old man said quickly. Thomas nodded. So then the old man told the story of taking Henry Talcott in and raising him along with his daughter, certain that one day Henry would reward him and do the right thing by marrying her. To that end old Bibeau had taught him a trade and sold Henry the land he'd built his house on. "And you know how he paid me back? By knocking Irene Jalley up, that's how. So the way I look at it is I've given all I'm gonna give. So don't be telling me to say sorry. I'm the one should be said sorry to. And now I want you out of here! Now!" he yelled, pointing as they backed out of the room. "And keep on going! Get outta here! Get outta my goddamn house, go on, you little bastards, the both of you—"

They were moved out by morning. The argument between Gladys and her father was bitter and quick. She stormed from the room and slammed the door. The cowbell clanged and clanged. The old man hollered her name on through the night until hoarseness paled his outrage to a rasp.

Even in the driveway she begged Henry to stay. He knew how unpredictable the old man was; he'd probably already forgotten what he'd said and why. Henry said he was sorry, but he couldn't do that to the children. Or to her, he added. "You've got a tough enough job as it is, Glad. No need of me making it worse." He patted her hand.

In a way Thomas was sad they were leaving. He really hated old Bibeau now, and though he didn't know for sure what it all meant, saw through the fire in his father's eyes that it was vile. But now they had nowhere to go. It was too cold with a snowy skim of frozen ground to go back to living in the tent. His father still didn't have enough for rent.

"Here." Gladys tried to give him three dollars, but he wouldn't take it. "For God's sake, Henry, it's just a loan."

"Well, hold on to it then. If I need it I'll ask you for it."

"Just so you'll know, Henry, I ran into Phyllis Farley yesterday. She was asking all kind of questions about the kids and didn't I think they'd be better off with a family that could take proper care of them."

"I hope you damn well told her I do take proper care of my children!"

"Of course I did! But then she said what a hot-tempered, coarse man you are." Upset as Gladys was she couldn't hide her amusement. Thomas squirmed, envious of their easy banter. His father talked to Gladys in a way he never had to Thomas's mother. His father and Gladys always found humor in the same things, while his father had usually been closemouthed at home, and his mother usually resentful. Was this why she had gone away? Had it been Gladys?

"And what'd you say to that?"

Gladys burst out laughing. "I said, 'So? He still gives them proper care.' "

"Thanks for the hinds-end compliment," Henry called with a wave as he drove off.

When they came into Atkinson they passed a For Rent sign on a porch, and Thomas groaned.

"What's that for?" his father snapped.

"Nothing." He didn't want to go back to the big town school where everyone thought they were better than the country kids.

Margaret was happy. "Look!" she called, pointing out the window. "The church, that's where Mommy took us, remember? And the park, remember we had a picnic and we listened to the band play up there in the bandstand!"

It was all he could do to keep from pinching her. How could she be so happy to be back in the very town where their mother had abandoned them? Because she was stupid, that was why. That, and the fact she didn't know the half of what was really going on here.

"Wait here. I'll be right out," his father said grimly as he pulled in front of Aunt Lena's battered gray bungalow with the purple shutters, half of them missing slats.

"Oh no!" Margaret watched their father trudge up the weedy path, then pause on the top step to rub the back of his neck. "Don't!" she gasped, willing him back to the truck. "Please, don't."

"Yeah, and it's all your fault!" Thomas poked her leg hard and she yelped, then cried, wanting her mother back. Why did Mommy do this? Why did she go away and leave them like this, she wept into her hands.

"Because of you!" he spat. "Because you're a mean, bad

girl and she couldn't stand being near you anymore. Nobody can," he continued as the door opened and Aunt Lena appeared, clutching the front of her bathrobe closed, squinting blearily out at the truck. "You always ruin everything for everybody."

6

"AW, THEY'RE OKAY. THEY'RE NICE KIDS, MAX. AND THAT little Margaret, now you gotta admit, she's hot as a pistol, hon. A lot like her Aunt Leenie, don't you think? Cute as a button. I was just like her. Here, look . . . look . . . ," tumbled Aunt Lena's blowsy voice up the stairs through the dark. She'd been drinking since they got home from school. Maybe all day. So unsteady was she that Thomas had had to help her cook supper. Something fell with a thud.

"Jesus Christ. Can I just read the paper?" Uncle Max grumbled.

"Just look. Look a minute. Look at this picture. See? That's me in front. Wasn't I pretty? Wasn't I? Wasn't I, Max?"

"Yeah."

"Irene and me, you know what they called us?"

Paper rustled with a turning page.

There was a pause, brief as a slap. "The It girls!" she cried, hard on the course of her dogged nostalgia. "We had so many boyfriends, we couldn't keep 'em all straight, who belonged to who, we—"

"Shut up, Lena, will ya?"

"Well it's true. We—"

"Go to bed, will you just go to bed?"

"No! I feel like talkin', and you're—"

"All right then, I'm leaving. Is that what you want?"

"No! No, don't leave! Come on, Maxie! Please! Please don't go!"

Just like the night before, the door closed and Uncle Max was gone. Everything had seemed all right their first few days here. Uncle Max made little effort to make them feel welcome. He wasn't mean like old Bibeau, just uninterested. If they had to be there, fine. Just keep out of his way.

Uncle Max was a preoccupied man. His marriage to Aunt Lena was held together by her ownership of the house they lived in and his reliance on her increasingly sporadic income. Once considered the best beauty parlor in town, LENA'S operated out of her winterized sunporch with two chairs and the latest perm and coloring techniques. But life had gone sour for Lena. Max hadn't turned out to be the adoring husband such a sultry woman deserved. Worse than not finding her in the least bit amusing, he had little interest in her physically. But then again when they finally did get married Lena had been deep into her thirties and thickening around the ankles and waist.

Everyone knew the marriage was an empty one, a sham really. All it ever took was a few sips for Lena's tumbler of troubles to spill over. Max's latest stake in the future was a wealthy older lady whose long ailing husband just couldn't seem to die. Even Max had expressed concern, "as a friend of the family," to Dr. Creel about the mounting cost of the old gent's round-the-clock nursing care. The scandal, like so much else, existed on the periphery of Thomas's awareness. Gladys had been one of the old man's nurses before her own father took sick. Certain people deserved her professional discretion, but as Gladys had told Thomas's father, Max Lessing was a snake.

The more Max stayed away, the more Lena let herself go. Then, she would struggle up from her boozy depths to a four-, maybe six-week run of perfect sobriety. Her "ladies" would return. The money would cover enough of Max's gambling debts to make life good. But little by little she'd start getting the blues again, hearing all the talk of other women's children and the cute, nutty things their husbands were always saying. "Excuse me," she'd say slipping into the bathroom, where the brown glass flask lay in the bottom of the hamper. In the past year the last of her ladies had stopped coming. Lena blamed the times; things were bad all over.

. . .

"Beauty is a terrible curse," she was telling Margaret now as she brushed snarls from her hair. "It's like a magic spell, but then it starts to wear off and you look in the mirror one day . . ." Her voice trailed off, as it often did.

Thomas was beginning to recognize when it was time for her trip into the bathroom. Sure enough. The hamper lid banged against the wall, then closed with an even more heedless bang. Even Margaret could tell now. At first she had enjoyed her aunt's silliness, but last night long after midnight she had crawled into Thomas's bed. The terrible sobbing from Aunt Lena's bedroom frightened her. She's just drunk, that's all, he said, pushing his sister nearer the edge, away from him.

This morning Aunt Lena had been sleeping when they left for school. Actually Thomas had been grateful. She was usually so jittery first thing in the morning that everything she cooked she ruined. Yesterday it had been burned oatmeal. Ever since they'd been home from school today she'd been struggling to make it up to them. First, she tried to sew a button on Thomas's cuff, but got so many needle pricks in her fingers that she'd gotten blood all over his best shirt, the one Gladys had given him. He put aside his homework and finished the job himself. Now she wanted to set ringlets in Margaret's hair. Margaret waited in the chair while the curling iron heated. Aunt Lena came out of the bathroom smiling. She stood over Margaret a moment looking confused, as if not sure what to do next.

"Was my mother beautiful when she was little?" Margaret asked. She looked tiny under the soiled yellow cape over her shoulders.

"Oh yes! She was such a pretty little girl. I used to dress her up. I'd tie ribbons in her hair and bring her everywhere. She was my little, little dolly girl, my pretty little . . ."

Margaret's eyes raised, waiting. Aunt Lena had paused midsentence, the brush still in Margaret's hair.

"Does she write you letters?" Margaret asked.

Aunt Lena blinked. "Who?"

"My mother."

"Oh. Yeah. A couple. Two or three maybe." She picked up the curling iron and twirled it around a strand of Margaret's hair.

"Will you read them to me?" Margaret asked, looking up sideways. Her aunt squinted as if trying to remember something.

Thomas's pencil had fallen, unnoticed. He couldn't believe it. Not one letter from his mother, but Aunt Lena had gotten two or three. He didn't understand. Couldn't figure it out. Did she love her sister more than her own kids?

Margaret asked again. Would Aunt Lena read her the letters?

"No, I can't, dolly, I . . . I threw them out. Wasn't much in 'em. Nothing you'd care anything about." Aunt Lena undid the curled strand and rolled up another. "Lady talk, you know."

"Did she tell when she's coming home?"

"Uh . . . no, hon, she didn't. Not that I remember anyhow."

"How come she left? Did she say?"

"There was all kindsa reasons. I think . . . well, gee. I don't know, she wasn't happy . . . and sometimes . . . well, things just weren't going too good here and she figured maybe she'd have a better chance some other place. That's what happens. You know what I mean?"

Her face pinched and fearful, Margaret shook her head no. Thomas glared up at his aunt for dragging this out, for not having sense enough to change the subject and spare his little sister this pain.

"Well, having kids wasn't really what she . . . what I mean is, she—"

"Margaret, you know why," he interrupted. "Daddy told us. To save enough—"

"No!" Margaret cried out. "Because of me. Because I'm mean and bad, that's what you said!"

"You said that?" Aunt Lena staggered over to him. "You vicious thing, you!" She grabbed his shoulder and yanked him up from the chair. "How could you say that? Don't you know how bad things like that hurt?" Her hot liquory breath spewed out as she shook him. She was crying, still berating him, but with a dull cast to her eyes, as if already forgetting why. "You have no right to do that. No right! Do you hear me?" she panted, slapping the side of his head. "Do you hear me? I don't deserve this! It's not fair! It's just not fair!"

Hard as he struggled, he couldn't pull free. From her rage had emerged the strength of a man.

"Aunt Lena! Aunt Lena!" Margaret screamed as she burst from the chair. At first Thomas thought his aunt was backing away because Margaret had pushed herself between them. But it was her head. The curling iron was burning her scalp.

All this did was cause Aunt Lena to bawl even more. She watched helplessly while Thomas untangled the hot metal from Margaret's singed hair. He had smelled this same smell before, at a farm where some of the cows had taken sick. After his father put them down, a tractor dragged the carcasses far from the rest of the herd and pushed them into a pit, where they were doused with gasoline. Just as it had with those cows, the sharp smell of Margaret's burned hair would be with him for days, deep inside as if he had breathed the damaged hair, and pain, into himself.

. . .

Two hard weeks had passed. Their father was shaved and smelling of Bay Rum when he picked them up on a Sunday. He took them for a ride a few miles out of town, then back. He didn't dare go too far without a spare because two of his tires were real bad, patched so many times he'd lost count. There hadn't been any deep snow yet, but he'd put the chains on just to get normal traction, the treads were so worn. He had brought them each a piece of hard candy and a couple of old books Gladys had found in her attic and sent along for Thomas. And for Margaret a sock doll with brown yarn hair Gladys had bought at the Grange Ladies Fair. Margaret took one look at the drably pitiful thing and laid it on the seat. Thomas hoped she didn't say anything. No doubt she was remembering the blue-eyed doll from Mrs. Farley that her father had so callously bundled and returned.

He looked better than the last time they'd seen him. He and Aunt Lena had never gotten along anyway, but her connivance in her sister's leaving him was more than he could overlook. He hadn't been to her house since the day he'd brought his children there in desperation. He almost seemed happier. Probably was, Thomas thought, without two kids to worry about feeding and dressing every day. He had been staying with some cousin of his and the cousin's wife. They had a spare room he could have until somebody or other's mother moved back in after her trip somewhere.

Thomas had stopped listening. First his mother; and now his father had found another life apart from them. Like two birds they had flown off in different directions, leaving him and Margaret to fend for themselves. He was angry, resentful that his father still had a whole other family they'd never even heard of to be happy with, while he and Margaret were stuck with Aunt Lena. Uncle Max was back and Aunt Lena was trying not to drink as much. Uncle Max had yelled at Thomas this morning for spreading too much jelly on his toast. Ever since his return he'd been irritable as a wounded bull. Try and stay out of his way, Aunt Lena had confided. Apparently his older lady friend had sent him packing. He was just a lot more interested in her bank accounts than in her. Or at least that's what someone had told Lena.

Thomas was attempting to list all the bad things that had happened since they'd been with Aunt Lena. He felt panicky. They were nearing the house and nothing he'd said seemed to matter to his father. "And last week she even burned Margaret's hair!"

"And it's still sore." Margaret touched the back of her head.

"How'd she do that?" The noisy truck turned the corner.

"With the curling iron!" Thomas shouted over the racket. "She had too much to drink, then she started hitting me and she forgot all about the curling iron in Margaret's hair."

The truck pulled up to the curb. Sighing, his father shook his head. "Just be patient, please? I've almost got enough for a place. It's just that everything's so slow right now. But it's gotta get better. Sure can't get much worse anyway."

They both stared at him. It felt as if he had turned into someone else. The same way their mother had.

Nothing had panned out anywhere around here, so starting tomorrow he was heading farther north. Try new places. Farms he'd never been to before. Somewhere, there was work out there. He just had to find it, that was all.

But how could he go that far on such bad tires? Thomas asked. Maybe his father was lying to them. Lately it seemed most grown-ups did.

"Cuz I don't have any other choice, do I?" he said so bitterly that Thomas looked down and Margaret rubbed her chin on her shoulder. "I just want us back together, that's all."

"All of us?" Margaret grinned as if at some secret he couldn't yet share.

"You go inside now. I'll be by in a couple days. Soon's I get back. Go ahead. Go on now," he said with a stiff smile.

. . .

The chain rasped back and forth on the front porch floor. Thomas was pushing Margaret on the lopsided swing when the car passed by again, this time slowing near the curb. It kept going. Margaret asked who it was. He wasn't sure. Maybe Mrs. Farley. Maybe she had some more things for them, Margaret said. She told Thomas to let her get off. He pushed harder. With one of the front chains broken, the trick was to hang on to the swing back to keep from falling off. They'd been sent out to play while Uncle Max read the newspaper. Aunt Lena didn't want him "riled." There was a hiss as the cold rain turned to sleet on the front steps. Margaret begged him to stop; she had to go to the bathroom. He kept pushing. She screamed. He grabbed the dangling chain and jerked the swing to a sudden stop. She fell, landing on her knees. She ran to the door, but it was locked. Crouched and wiggling, she rang the bell.

How long would it be before she remembered it didn't work. If she had to go so badly why didn't she just bang on the door? And how could he enjoy her misery this much and still hate his aunt and uncle for not letting her in. Was he just as mean as everyone else? Poor little kid. It wasn't her fault for taking the kitten, or even his for telling his mother he hated her the morning she left. No, it was James's fault. James for dying. James for having been born. Poor sick little baby James, he thought, hitting the door frame with both fists as Margaret groaned. The pee made vapor as it streamed down her legs, turning her baggy sock cuffs bright yellow.

Uncle Max opened the door, then swore when he saw the puddle at Margaret's feet. "You're not coming in like that. Lena!" he bellowed, turning from the doorway. "Lena!"

Aunt Lena came quickly. Her eyes darted in frantic confusion between Max and the children on the other side of the threshold. Margaret cowered in shame against the warped shakes. Thomas had never seen her look like this before. She wasn't the same. She was different now. She was turning into what other people thought, what they expected. Like Carol Pfeiffer, sly but scared. Made dumb by her desperation.

"Why'd you do that?" Aunt Lena demanded when she returned with one of her dye-stained towels. "Don't I have enough problems? It's not fair. I don't need this too," she whined and patted dry Margaret's shivering legs. "If I'da wanted—"

"It's not her fault!" Thomas exploded. "She couldn't help it. She was trying to get in, but the door was locked!"

"Yeah!" Margaret chimed in. "And he wouldn't let me off. I said I had to go, but he kept pushing, so finally I jumped off, but then it was too late!"

If Aunt Lena was going to reply she had already forgotten her rebuke. Her head trembled, her eyes heavy with self-pity. Down on the street a car door slammed and high heels clicked up the walk.

"Lena!" Mrs. Farley cried, covetous eyes on Margaret as she hurried on to the porch.

"Phyllis? Oh. Phyllis. Phyllis!" Aunt Lena wielded the name like a broom against her troubles.

"Margaret! And Thomas. How nice to see you both. How've you been? Are you still with the Bibeaus? What're you doing here, visiting your nice Auntie Lena? I was just going by and I thought"—now she looked at Lena—"my heavens, now when's the last time Lena Jalley did my hair? Too long, right? From the looks of it you're probably thinking." She patted the side of her head. Try as she might she couldn't hold her gaze on Aunt Lena. She kept smiling down at Margaret, who grinned back at her.

"You could use a cut maybe." Aunt Lena sidestepped around her in blurry appraisal. "Definitely a set."

"When could you take me?"

"I'll have to check," Aunt Lena said with some vestige of professional dignity. She hurried into the house. The only hair she'd done all week had been Margaret's and the old lady's next door. According to Max, who'd been berating Aunt Lena this morning when she asked him for money to buy milk, the half-blind old woman could barely walk and had no choice but her "boozy neighbor" for a hairdresser.

In Aunt Lena's brief absence Mrs. Farley had managed to find out everything from Margaret. Thomas couldn't even feel angry. If anything Mrs. Farley seemed a great relief. It was almost a pleasure talking to such a kind, normal person again. The quick conversation had roused Mrs. Farley too. Her cheeks burned with giddy excitement when Aunt Lena returned to say she had a nine o'clock appointment open tomorrow.

"Oh! That's wonderful! I'll be there! And I won't be late, I promise!"

Mrs. Farley's hair appointment sent Aunt Lena into bursts of frenzied busyness in her little shop. She combed hair out of the musty brush, washed towels and capes, then with snow falling outside had to hang them inside on chair backs, banisters, and radiators. She swept pelts of dust and cut gray hair from the floor and had Thomas throw it into the backyard for birds to use in their nests. The storm had intensified. It would be months before birds would be building nests, but in such frivolous ways his aunt reminded him of his mother. Even Uncle Max was helping. The prospect of Lena's support had become a great energizer. He hadn't complained about the children once all day. He lay on his back, head under the big sink trying to stop the pipe not just from leaking, but from squirting water out onto the floor.

At the end of the day Aunt Lena sat in the big black hairdressing chair watching him. Thomas knew she was waiting for Uncle Max to leave her alone in there so she could have a swig, just a quick one, the way she'd been trying to do since he'd been back, just enough to keep her going. Aunt Leenie's tonic, she'd confided once. Her medicine.

. . .

The next morning they could hear Uncle Max trying to wake her up. He kept calling her name. Over and over, he reminded her that Phyllis Farley was coming. Her appointment was in an hour. This was her chance. To get her business back again. If she did a good job, Phyllis Farley would tell all her friends, and they'd come too.

"Leave me alone," she moaned each time he went into her room.

Downstairs, Margaret and Thomas had already eaten breakfast—toast and an apple they'd split. Aunt Lena's kitchen never had much in it. She and her sister had not been trained in the domestic arts, she liked to boast. Their mother had wanted them to be professional ladies and make their own way in the world. But, poor Irene, with three children and a husband to feed she'd had no choice but to cook, uninspired as the meals might be.

"Yeah, go ahead then!" Uncle Max roared overhead. "You do that! You just rot in that bed. But not me! This time I'm gone for good!" A door slammed. Uncle Max stalked into the kitchen straightening his tie knot. Margaret backed into the pantry. He told the children he was sorry, but he couldn't keep doing this. From now on she was on her own. Grabbing one of the damp towels he put his foot up on a chair and buffed one shoe then the other. They should do themselves a favor and get the hell out while the getting was good. She was useless. "Just plain useless!" he shouted, threw the towel onto the floor, then was gone.

Margaret scurried out from the pantry. She hung the towel back on the chair to dry. She paused and thought a moment. "Didn't Mommy say he was the useless one?"

Just then Aunt Lena appeared in the kitchen, her wrinkled dress unbuttoned and spattered with dye. Her bright red lipstick was smeared, her hair still uncombed. Where was Mrs. Farley? Had she been waiting long? Aunt Lena sank into the chair and leaned over the table, head in her arms.

"Do you need some medicine?" Margaret asked, not even waiting for an answer. She hurried back with the square brown bottle.

Aunt Lena unscrewed the cap then turned her back a little while she took a long drink. "There," she said quietly with her eyes closed then sat holding the bottle.

"Want me to put it back?" Margaret asked.

Aunt Lena shook her head no. Thomas watched in disgust. Uncle Max was right. They had to get out of here. He'd walk to Gladys's and find out where his father was staying.

Margaret touched her aunt's shoulder. "Mrs. Farley's coming. Don't you want to fix her hair?"

Aunt Lena nodded. She let Margaret take the bottle and then followed her into the beauty shop.

Mrs. Farley arrived five minutes early. Thomas and Margaret let her in. Just as Margaret had predicted, she had presents for them. A picture puzzle of the Statue of Liberty for Thomas and a white fur muff and matching hat for Margaret. Fluffy pom-poms hung from each tie string. Margaret insisted on wearing the hat the whole time. Mrs. Farley couldn't get over how beautiful she looked with "fur framing that sweet face." Thomas sat on the beauty shop floor working on the base of the Statue of Liberty. He was trying to be polite for his aunt's sake. Actually, he hated puzzles.

Seeing Aunt Lena's shaky hands, Mrs. Farley changed her mind about the cut. "Just a set," she said. "Fred always likes it a little bit long," she tried to explain. "And Jesse-boy too."

Aunt Lena combed the thick, pink setting lotion through Mrs. Farley's hair. She began to twist the wet ends into tight pin curls all over Mrs. Farley's head. She worked with the rhythm of an old skill. Mrs. Farley leaned slightly forward to tell Thomas he was doing a wonderful job. Jesse-boy loved puzzles. In fact he could do that one in just a few minutes, with his eyes closed almost; he could tell by the shapes. Jesse-boy's teacher couldn't get over how smart he was. And how creative. He could draw just about anything. Mr. Wentworth said he might even be a famous artist someday.

"Lena!" Mrs. Farley seized Aunt Lena's wrist. She leaned back and looked up at her. "If the children ever get too much I'd love to give you a hand."

"A hand?" Aunt Lena blinked, reverie broken.

"Well, like now when you're . . . when you're not feeling quite yourself . . . I can take them. They can stay with me. With us." She smiled at Margaret, who now wore the muff around one ankle. "In fact, I can even take them now. Give you a little rest. Some time to yourself. It must be hard when you're not used to all the commotion children bring." Mrs. Farley was out of the chair and tying a silk scarf over her bobby-pinned hair. "I'll take good care of them, you know I will." She opened her purse and handed Aunt Lena a twenty-dollar bill.

Aunt Lena held it, confused. "I don't have enough change, Phyllis. I'm sorry."

"No, that's for you." Mrs. Farley patted her arm. "You need some rest, Lena. So why don't I take them with me, then maybe when you're feeling better I'll bring them back."

"No, I can't."

"Why? Why not?"

"Well. Well, first I have to ask Henry. He'll be mad. I mean, if he comes and they're not here."

"But Lena, you're the one in charge. You're the one taking care of them. The only one now."

Aunt Lena didn't seem to understand. Mrs. Farley asked Thomas and Margaret if they would please go into the other room. She needed to speak with their aunt for a moment. Privately. Waiting in the kitchen, they tried to hear, but couldn't.

When the women came out Aunt Lena looked even more dazed. Dollar bills stuck out of her pocket. Mrs. Farley was abustle with gay energy. Here they were, coats and hats; can't risk getting sick. Good food and warm things. Mrs. Farley pinched Margaret's chin. The slightest cold and Jesse-boy'd catch it. Their clothes, Lena called, heading up the stairs. Mrs. Farley opened her mouth as if to say not to bother, then changed her mind.

"Where are we going?" Thomas asked on their way to the car. Eager as he was to get out of here, he knew his father wouldn't be pleased.

"Don't you worry now, young man," Mrs. Farley said with such fierce conviction he knew there was good reason to worry. "From now on everything's going to be all right. I promise!"

Even Margaret could tell that something had just happened. Something very bad.

7

THOMAS AWAKENED EASILY TO THE SHIMMERING LIGHT through the gauzy curtains. He had never slept in such a warm room or in so soft a bed. The sheets lay like silk against his arms and legs and the blankets smelled of cedar, without a single hole in them. Even getting out of bed was pleasant, his bare feet sinking into a thick rag rug. Across the hall in Margaret's bedroom was a dollhouse, three stories high, almost as tall as she was. There was beautiful furniture in every room on small oriental carpets. There were miniature brass lamps that lit up and gilt-framed paintings on the papered walls. The cherry dining room table was set with blue and white china and tiny silver flatware. The dollhouse had been Mrs. Farley's as a child. Now that Jesse-boy was too old for it Margaret could consider it hers. As long as they were there, Mrs. Farley had added.

That had been for three days now. Not only was Thomas never cold, but he was never hungry. If anything he felt too full most of the time. Mrs. Farley loved to bake and not just for special occasions, but every single day. Jesse-boy was a finicky eater. Cakes were his favorite food and the only way Mrs. Farley could keep any weight on him, she said.

Even now for breakfast Jesse-boy was having a thick slice of chocolate cake with buttercream frosting and milk with Ovaltine. After only a few spoonfuls of oatmeal Margaret pushed the bowl away and asked for cake. Thomas kicked her foot under the table, but she would not look at him.

"Here you go, dear," Mrs. Farley said, bearing it to her. She scraped the oatmeal into the covered pail under the sink. When the pail was full it would be carried outside and dumped into the slop bucket for the pigs. The pail always filled quickly, usually with Jesse-boy's spurned food. It almost seemed that Mrs. Farley cooked mostly for the pigs. Even Mr. Farley didn't clean off his plate, not the way Thomas's father always did. As much as Thomas would have preferred cake he finished the gluey cereal, his spoon noisily scraping the empty bowl. Margaret was falling into the trap. He'd warned her again last night how careful they had to be. Mrs. Farley wouldn't tell him when they were going back to Aunt Lena's. When he asked if his father knew they were here, she told him not to be "such a worrywart." He stared at Margaret. Ignoring him, she asked for more Ovaltine.

He kicked her foot, harder this time.

"Ow!" She rubbed her ankle.

Turning from the icebox, Mrs. Farley asked what was the matter.

"Nothing." Margaret glared at him.

"Thomas kicked Margaret," Jesse-boy said, licking frosting from his fingers.

"Now, Thomas," Mrs. Farley said coming quickly to the table. "Why did you do that?"

"Because he's mean," Jesse-boy spoke up. "He's always picking on Margaret."

"Why, Thomas? She's such a sweet little girl." She stood behind Margaret, twirling a lock of her hair around her finger.

Margaret's eyes closed. Since his mother had gone away no one ever touched him. Not in tenderness anyway.

"I think that's why," Jesse-boy said in his soft, scratchy voice. Maybe it was from being together so much, but he and his mother were lapsing into one of their singsong, whiny choruses. One spoke and the other's lips moved. "Thomas is jealous. He thinks Margaret gets all the attention."

"Oh, dear. Is that why? Is that what you think? Well, it's because Margaret's a girl. And girls just need special care, now don't they?" She smiled at her son.

"No, he wants cake, that's why," Jesse-boy said irritably.

"Well, he can have cake. Of course he can. My heavens, here!"

"No, thank you. I'll have mine tonight. For *dessert*."

Margaret still wouldn't look at him.

"You don't have to be such a Spartan, you know, Thomas. Cake is actually very nutritious, all the eggs and butter and cream." Mrs. Farley sounded hurt.

The massive grandfather clock chimed in the front hall. Eight o'clock. Hurry! Mrs. Farley said. Mr. Wentworth would be here any minute now. He was very excited to have two more students in his little class, she was telling them, almost giggling, as she pulled Jesse-boy's enormous wheelchair back from the table. "Come along now, Thomas," she called on her way out of the kitchen. Margaret helped push the wheelchair. For reasons he couldn't fathom Margaret found that exciting.

"Why aren't we going to our own school?" Thomas asked again. Last night Mrs. Farley had changed the subject when asked. He liked the idea of not having to go back to that big, confusing school in town, but he didn't understand why they couldn't go to their little schoolhouse with Miss Hall now that they were back in Belton.

"This will be much better, and you'll like Mr. Wentworth." Mrs. Farley slid the pocket door open into the front parlor, which was now a classroom. Two chairs stood behind a narrow table facing a large oak desk. The bay of floor-to-ceiling windows flooded the room with so much light that Thomas didn't notice the older man in the corner until he spoke.

"Good morning, Jesse-boy. And a very special welcome to our two new students, Margaret and Thomas," he said, clapping enthusiastically with Mrs. Farley and Jesse-boy. For such a thin, stoop-shouldered man, Mr. Wentworth had a booming voice.

The hours dragged on. Jesse-boy was a most uninterested student. He only wanted to draw pictures. He leaned over the pad closely, his chin grazing the paper. He could barely read and long division so easily frustrated him that he threw his tablet onto the floor. Mr. Wentworth spent half the morning on spelling, while Jesse-boy doodled on his drawing pad. Mrs. Farley visited from time to time with "treats," hot molasses cookies, warm fudge. Though Mr. Wentworth's frustration with Jesse-boy was obvious, he never reprimanded him. Instead, he drilled his new pupils with a relentless fervor that drained them. If they were here to spark Jesse-boy's desire to learn, it wasn't working. Mr. Wentworth recited "The

Raven" by Edgar Allan Poe. He paced in front of them, waving his arms as he thundered, "Nevermore, spoke the raven. Nevermore."

Jesse-boy slept with his head on his arm. Drool seeped onto his paper. Mr. Wentworth tiptoed to his desk and sat down. He pulled a newspaper from his valise and whispered that they should read quietly while the boy rested. Like the other rooms in the house this one was hot. The radiators hissed as shafts of dusty light streamed from the windows. Minutes later Margaret's head sank into her arms. She was asleep. Thomas poked her and she grunted irritably. "Margaret!" He poked her again.

"Leave her be, Thomas," Mr. Wentworth whispered. "And you may rest too if you'd like."

Thomas read for a while, then doodled in his composition book, something Miss Hall would have never allowed. At noon Jesse-boy finally woke up and looked around, his cheeks red with the heat. He declared himself tired of school, so that was it. School was over for the day. Mr. Wentworth ate lunch, then left quickly. Margaret ran upstairs to play with the dollhouse. Thomas sat on the porch petting Mr. Farley's collie. Two more dairy trucks pulled in and drove down the road to the larger barn. Two men came out and unloaded the empty milk cans. One was the barn hand Arnold, his head still bandaged. Seeing Thomas, he looked away. Thomas had gotten some revenge the other day when he told Mrs. Farley that Arnold had said a bad word in front of him and Margaret. Goddamn! Arnold had yelled when the barn door swung back and split the back of his head open. Mrs. Farley wanted him fired. Mr. Farley tried placating his wife. That wasn't such a bad curse, particularly under the circumstances, but Mrs. Farley demanded that Arnold be read the riot act. Him and every man on the farm. One bad word in front of these dear children and they'd be fired on the spot.

The trucks had left early this morning. Soon after, Mr. Farley had come in to say he had to get to the courthouse. He didn't know how long he'd have to be there so Mrs. Farley shouldn't expect him for lunch. No backing down now, Mrs. Farley had warned in a low voice. I know, Mr. Farley had answered.

His father still hadn't come to see them. Thomas watched another shiny Farley's Dairy truck turn onto the gravel road. His father's truck had probably broken down again. If it had, he couldn't work. But if he wasn't working, then they could at least be together. Why were they here? In a million years his father wouldn't want them with the Farleys. It didn't make sense. Unless—fear rose in his bones—unless his father had gone away and left them too. Or maybe—maybe he'd gone down there to Massachusetts to be with her. Maybe he was bringing her back. Or maybe he'd stay there with her.

He hurried into the house. Mrs. Farley wasn't anywhere downstairs. Through the kitchen window he saw her outside taking clothes off the line. She put each clothespin into her bulging apron pocket. She smiled as he ran around the corner of the house. She dropped a towel into the basket by her feet. "Look at you." She wet her finger and tried to flatten his cowlick. "You're all mussed. I just realized." She held his chin and turned his head from side to side. "You need a proper haircut, Thomas!"

He jerked his chin away. "I want to see my father. Where is he?"

Her mouth opened and closed the way it did whenever Jesse-boy spoke or when she was nervous. "Don't you speak to me in that tone, young man. Don't you just dare!" She perched the basket on her hip and marched toward the house. He wanted to run and grab her by the arm and make her answer him. "But Mrs. Farley!" he called, but she went inside. He yanked a towel off the line and threw it to the ground, then another, then sheets, shirts. Underpants. He stood there looking down at the big wide white pair of Mrs. Farley's in his fist. He dropped them, then ran down the road.

. . .

It took a while, but Gladys finally told him. His father didn't want them to know, but better Thomas hear it from her than anyone else. It had happened when he and Margaret had still been with Aunt Lena. His father's tire had blown out and there weren't enough slaughtering jobs to keep him going, so he'd tried to find any other work he could. No one needed help, but then someone in town told him he'd just heard that Farley's Dairy was looking for a man. So he swallowed his pride and went, hat in hand, to ask Fred Farley for a job. Farley made him stand outside in the freezing rain for almost an hour, then sent one of his hands out to say he'd just hired someone else. That night Henry went back. He slipped through a window inside the truck barn and searched until he found his saw and the spare tire Farley's men had taken when they demolished his tent site. Soon after that, the sheriff arrested him coming out of the woods where he'd hidden the tire and saw, intending to pick them up the next day.

Gladys said the sheriff tried to talk Farley out of pressing charges. He couldn't see putting a decent man in jail for an almost treadless tire and an ancient saw hardly worth owning, much less stealing. Even the sheriff thought they probably did belong to Henry, but Farley wouldn't budge. Talcott had broken into his place of business and stolen from him. The sheriff said Mrs. Farley was even more adamant. Henry Talcott thought he could make up his own rules in this world and it was about time someone taught him a lesson. His father had been in jail ever since.

Mrs. Farley barely spoke to Thomas when he returned. He was sent to his room, where he would wait until Mr. Farley came home. The only reason Thomas had come back was Margaret. He couldn't leave her alone here. And, he had nowhere else to go. Even Gladys thought Farley's was better than staying at Aunt Lena's again. She'd take the two of them in a minute if it wasn't for her father, who was sick with pneumonia. While Thomas was there the old man called out that he was dying. Gladys said he wasn't even close to dying. Hearing Thomas in the house made the old man frantic for her attention. He was afraid she would leave him alone as she'd threatened when he'd caused Henry to move out with the children.

Thomas sat on his bed. He could smell supper cooking. Voices rose from the kitchen, yet no one called him down to eat. He opened his door, then tiptoed to the end of the hallway. Margaret and Jesse-boy were laughing. Mrs. Farley said something and now Mr. Farley laughed. The yellow-warm smell of chicken and gravy was thick in the air. He crept back to his room and waited.

An hour later Mr. Farley knocked on his door. Thomas didn't answer, but Mr. Farley came in anyway. He said he understood from Gladys Bibeau that Thomas had found out about his father. He was sorry, but some violations couldn't be overlooked. No matter the circumstances. Thomas sat on the edge of the bed staring up at the wiry little man. The muscles in his jaw and temples clenched. His nasally voice was hard, the words tightly strung, pauseless. In this driven, humorless way, he reminded the boy of his father, except that his father would have gotten to the point long before this. Farley said that, his father being unable to, Aunt Lena was in charge of their care. And she wanted them with the Farleys. Thomas and Margaret had a home here, a very good home, as long as they acted properly. What Thomas had done today was completely unacceptable. Not only had he hurt Mrs. Farley's feelings, but he had frightened her terribly. She didn't know if she could trust him. Margaret was no problem; she would certainly stay. But they weren't so sure about him. "So from now on, you should consider yourself here on a trial basis only," Mr. Farley said before opening the door.

"I don't care. I don't even want to be here." He spoke just loudly enough to be heard or not heard as would be Mr. Farley's choice. His heart pounded.

Mr. Farley stepped back into the room. He closed the door quietly, as if this had to be just between them. "It would be difficult to have to separate you from your lovely sister, Thomas, but maybe that's the way it's got to be. For the good of everyone."

Thomas glared at him.

Mr. Farley seemed to be smiling. "Is that what you want? Is it? Well? Is it?"

Thomas forced his stare downward. He shook his head.

"Then don't upset Mrs. Farley." Mr. Farley leaned close, the grind of his voice like unoiled, rusted gears. "God knows, she has problems enough without the likes of you scurrying around."

Bastard. Son of a bitch. His father was in jail for trying to get back what had been stolen from him. But this time Thomas kept his mouth shut.

. . .

Sometimes the lessons lasted as long as an hour and a half. Today, though, Jesse-boy had fallen asleep after only a few minutes. Mr. Wentworth was annoyed. His private school was not turning out well. Thomas made little effort now and all Margaret wanted was to play. Every day, when she ran upstairs, there would be on her bed a beautiful new dress for her doll, and matching cape. The thump of Mrs. Farley's sewing machine treadle would go on through the night. Jesse-boy loved dressing the dolls with Margaret.

Hearing voices late last night, Thomas had gotten out of bed. He stood in Jesse-boy's doorway, disgusted by the sight. Jesse-boy was making his doll kiss Margaret's. "I love you," Jesse-boy was saying in a tremulous falsetto. "And now I want to marry you." He jerked the doll up and down as he spoke. "Will you marry me?" His gray flannel pajama top was unbuttoned, revealing the bony hollow that was his chest.

"Oh, I don't know," Margaret answered. Thomas had never minded her high, make-believe voice when she played with him, but now it made his skin crawl. She moved her doll's head from side to side. "How do I know you're not the evil king?"

"Because." Sweat trickled down Jesse-boy's ashen face.

"The evil king has no heart. Listen." He pulled her head against his chest. "Do you hear it? That's the heartbeat. That's how you know." Closing his eyes, he lowered his face into her hair. He rubbed her back.

More frightened than repulsed, Thomas backed into the shadows. She was just a little girl, and Jesse-boy . . . he didn't know what he was, man or boy, with that whiskery smudge above his lip.

Margaret pulled away. "Marybelle's tired," she said, but her pretend voice was thin and forced. She held the doll out at arm's length as if it were a shield. "She needs to go to bed now. So good-night. Good-night," she called, running to her room.

. . .

Mr. Wentworth read his newspaper for ten minutes then got up and gently shook Jesse-boy's arm. "Wake up. Would you please wake up."

Thomas could tell he only pretended to be asleep.

"Leave me alone," Jesse-boy groaned.

"No. We accomplished very little yesterday, so today we must be diligent." Mr. Wentworth stood over him, waiting. "I said, wake up. Please."

"No, I can't. I don't feel good. I'm sick," Jesse-boy whined.

Mrs. Farley was summoned. Mr. Wentworth usually deferred to Jesse-boy's brattiness with feigned concern, but now even Thomas could sense the old teacher's shame. A day off with pay was nothing to sneeze at in such demeaning times, but how could he squander his professional authority in front of these normal children, his more promising pupils.

Jesse-boy was sick, Mrs. Farley concurred after pressing her cheek to his brow. He made a face behind his mother's back, and Margaret giggled. Then school would continue without Jesse-boy, Mr. Wentworth declared. Thomas and Margaret's studies needn't be interrupted by another pupil's illness. Like a dash of vinegar into buttermilk, the sweetness in Mrs. Farley's face curdled. Jesse-boy was *the* paying pupil here, and Mr. Wentworth would do well to remember that. And be not only willing, but eager to meet whatever special circumstances her son's condition called for. *She* would decide if there was to be school or not. Red-faced and weak with dread, Mr. Wentworth tried to explain. He had only thought to continue lessons with "the other two" not in exclusion of Jesse-boy, but as an enticement. To get the boy feeling better and back to class sooner.

"I'm surprised, Mr. Wentworth, being a teacher that you know so little about children. Not being able to participate is very painful for a sick child and only prolongs their convalescence. School will start up again as soon as Jesse-boy feels better."

So there it was. Mr. Wentworth had been banished. Thomas and Margaret were cut loose, free to do anything they wanted. Or nothing at all, which was the case for Thomas.

Margaret had a new kitten, orange, white, and black. It was always sleeping on her lap, head on its double-toed paws. With nothing else to keep him occupied, Thomas spent most of his time outside, whittling or roaming through the barns. Yesterday, Otis, one of the workers, rolled an extra cigarette and offered it to him. At first he'd said no, fearing the trouble he'd be in if he did. But of course he wouldn't be. No one would know. And if they did, no one around here cared. Without school or parents, he could do as he pleased. He inhaled so deeply that he choked. He couldn't stop coughing. Tears ran down his cheeks.

"You should've said it was your first smoke," Otis chided, then coached him the rest of the way through. "Take in just a little at first, hold it, then breathe out slow and easy does it. Yessir, now you got it. Here. Here's for later." Thomas liked the feel of the cigarette and matches in his shirt pocket. The tobacco smell reminded him of his father. But he had no desire to smoke. Ever.

Every morning Jesse-boy woke up, panting for breath and groaning with awful, stabbing pains in his chest. By ten o'clock the symptoms usually eased enough for him to be able to "play." Dolls had been banned from his room. Mr. Farley had come upstairs unexpectedly yesterday and been startled by his son's shrieky falsetto demanding to be taken "to the queen's ball." Tonight no one spoke at supper. Mrs. Farley's hands shook and her pale lips quivered. She barely ate. Sulking, Jesse-boy picked at his food. Coaxed by his mother to at least eat his favorite, the mashed potatoes, he tried, then gagged. A windy darkness pressed at the windows like bad dreams peering in. Margaret's eyes darted between Jesse-boy and her brother.

"There, there," Mrs. Farley said, rubbing the back of her son's neck. He should just spit it out and then he'd feel better. She was sorry she'd made him try the potatoes. Would he like applesauce cake? Or custard? There was still some custard left. Jesse-boy wanted to go to his room. His father lifted him from the wheelchair and carried him up to bed. His mother hurried after them.

"I want to go home. Please, Thomas," Margaret whispered. Now that she had become so housebound her face was sickly pale. She was beginning to resemble Jesse-boy in pallor and nerves.

"I know, but we can't," he whispered. She didn't know their father was in jail. Gladys had made him promise not to tell her. Upstairs, a great commotion had begun. Jesse-boy shrieked in outrage. Mrs. Farley sobbed. And Mr. Farley shouted, "You'll damn well do as I say! And that's that!" Brother's and sister's eyes widened on each other; life just got stranger and stranger, the look said.

With his napkin dangling from his collar, Mr. Farley strode back into the kitchen. He sat down and ate slowly, determinedly. Staring, he blinked with each hard swallow. He was in charge here, and there was supper to be eaten. Finally, he pushed his plate away. His anger was fading to sadness, as if he knew how hopeless it all was. No matter what he said or did, just plain hopeless. He glanced at their empty plates. "You finished?"

"Yes," Margaret whispered, and Thomas nodded. Yes, finished his and Margaret's too. These last few weeks he couldn't get enough to eat. He was always hungry.

Mr. Farley looked at Thomas. "Go up and . . . play with him," he added sourly.

Eager to escape Farley's gloom, Margaret jumped up too. Mr. Farley said she could go to her room. He wanted Thomas to do it, he said with a stiff nod that sent Margaret scurrying up the stairs.

"Play boy games. Please," Mr. Farley called so desolately that Thomas felt something hard and sharp give way in his chest.

He turned back. "That tire was my father's. The one he took. And the saw, that was his."

"He broke into my property," Mr. Farley said grimly.

"To get his own things back." Thomas could barely swallow.

"Do you really think I'm going to sit here at my own table and listen to your fresh mouth?"

"No, sir! It's just I don't see how they could arrest my father for—"

"What you don't see is your father's a thief."

"No! He's—"

"Shut up! And if you don't, if you can't, there's the door. Go!" He pointed. His face twisted with pain as if trying not to cry.

Upstairs, Jesse-boy lay curled with his back to Thomas. He was still sobbing. He hated his father, his mother, Mr. Wentworth, Thomas, Dr. Creel, the whole pissing, goddamn world. Thomas continued lining up the checkers. Like smoke, Jesse-boy's sorrow filled the house. Everyone was hiding from it.

"You want to be red or black?"

"What I want is for you to get out of here!" Jesse-boy's narrow body arched with his scream. "That's what I want!"

"It's not my fault. I don't want to be here neither." Thomas's eyes moved from the wretched boy to the cowboy pictures. The windows not only had curtains, but on them a design of crossed Indian peace pipes. He wondered if Jesse-boy had ever even noticed them. He sighed. "But we gotta play a game or do something. Your father said."

"I hate my father! I hate him so much!"

"Yeah, well you can still play checkers or something." Expecting it to go flying, he gripped the edge of the board. Mr. Farley's words had numbed him. No one ever spoke badly of Henry Talcott. He was a good man, respected and admired.

"If I play will you do me a favor?" Jesse-boy grunted, pulling himself up against the pillows.

"Okay." Thomas slid the board between them.

"Black!" Jesse-boy moved his checker though they hadn't chosen turns. "Will you do something if I ask you?"

"I don't know, what?"

"You know the gun cabinet? Can you get me a rifle?"

Thomas moved his checker. "Why?"

"Why do you think?"

"I don't know, play cowboys?" He nodded toward the *Saturday Evening Post* pictures Mrs. Farley had framed. In some, text on the back page showed through.

"No!" Jesse-boy scoffed. He moved.

Thomas shrugged and made two quick jumps. "How'd you miss that?" He couldn't hide his smile. "Your move."

"I'm gonna kill somebody, that's why," Jesse-boy whispered, finger on the checker.

"Who? Who you gonna kill?" Thomas asked distractedly, eyes darting over the board.

"Somebody." Jesse-boy made another losing move.

"Who?" Thomas jumped, seized the black checker.

"My father." He had Thomas's full attention. Squinting, he

raised one trembling arm, the other stiff, aiming his imaginary rifle. "I'm just gonna sit here and wait and the minute that door opens 'psew-psew-psew,' " he whistled, jerking back with each shot.

"What if it's your mother?"

"I know his boots, how they bang on the stairs."

"Why do you want to do that, shoot your father?"

"Cuz he's such a mean bastard, that's why." Jesse-boy pushed a checker, threatening Thomas's. "And I don't have any other choice."

"But you'd go to jail. And they'd hang you, that's what they do. Same as Red Tully."

"Who's Red Tully?"

"He killed his brother and sister once and that's what they did. He was only a kid and they hung him. They did!"

"How old was he?"

Thomas's eyes flashed in appraisal. "Fifteen. Yeah, that's what he was, all right. Fifteen. Just turned too."

"Red Tully; how come I never heard of him?"

"My father told me about him. He said he never did anything wrong, well, not real bad as that anyway. Then this one day he just got mad at his little brother. His sister was there, so he shot 'em both, quick as that. Didn't mean to neither, which was the sad part, cuz then it was too late."

"Too late for what?"

"To change his mind. To bring 'em back."

"But maybe he was glad. To finally be rid of them."

"No, because then he was real alone," Thomas said, sliding his checker forward a square, then another, unnoticed by Jesse-boy. "No family. Nothing. My father said he was so happy to die he thanked everybody that was going to hang him." Thomas moved again, but Jesse-boy wasn't even looking.

"What'd they call him Red for?"

"His red hair, I guess. Your turn. Or maybe his temper. That's why my father always says, 'When you start seeing red, think of Red Tully.' "

Jesse-boy leaned closer. "Want to see something? Something really secret?"

"Sure."

Jesse-boy told him to get his box from under the bed. Thomas knelt down and dragged out the locked wooden box. Checkers scattered as Jesse-boy lifted one hip and took a key from his pocket. "Pretty good, huh?" He passed Thomas the drawings, one by one. They were pictures of naked ladies, faces crudely sketched, the features dashed with little interest or aptitude for the details of humanness. The breasts were like round balloons, with bright red nipples crayoned in.

"What's that?" He pointed, knowing the minute he did what the scribbled snarl was between the legs.

"That's where girls get laid," Jesse-boy explained.

Thomas didn't let on, but he was confused. He'd seen dogs and cows going at it, but didn't remember anything that looked like this.

"You never seen a naked girl, have you?" Jesse-boy's red-rimmed eyes gleamed with rawness.

"One time I did. It was a picture. In a magazine I found." The woman had had fancy underwear on.

"Was it your father's?" Jesse-boy leaned closer. "It was, wasn't it?"

"No! It was old Bibeau's. Out in his barn. I found it."

"You ever see Margaret naked?"

"No!" Though of course he had.

Jesse-boy smiled in gleeful disbelief. "Yes, you have! You just don't want to say." He opened his pajama top. "She got any"—he touched his own nipple—"things here yet?"

"No!" Thomas still held the picture.

"How 'bout hair there? She got any—"

"Shut up!"

Just then a light tap, tap, tap came at the door. "Jesse-boy, it's me, dear," Mrs. Farley called apprehensively.

"Wait! Don't come in yet! We're not done playing!" Jesse-boy tossed the papers into the box, then locked it. "Put it back!" he hissed.

As Thomas leaned over and slid the box under the bed the cigarette fell from his pocket. He picked it up and Jesse-boy snatched it from him.

"You smoke?" he asked with awe as he slipped it inside the pillowcase.

"Yeah. Sometimes."

"Give me a match."

Thomas lied and said he didn't have any. Jesse-boy said there were some in the tin can over the kitchen stove. Mrs. Farley tapped on the door and asked if they were through yet. They were, Jesse-boy called back.

"Oh, checkers," she said, beaming as she backed in with her tray. There were two tall glasses of chocolate milk and two plates of applesauce cake with hard sauce. "Who won?" she asked, delighted that her son finally had a playmate.

"Thomas. But he cheated," Jesse-boy said. He broke off a forkful of cake.

"Thomas wouldn't cheat, Jess. He probably just doesn't know the rules the way you do." She glanced Thomas's way, then fixed her loving gaze on her son. "Jesse-boy and I've been playing since he was just a little tiny boy."

"I don't feel too hungry," Thomas said, making his way to the door. As much as he wanted that cake and milk, he wanted more to get out of here, away from the stifling heat of this invisibly webbed room, away from this peculiar mother, whose lips moved now in perfect cadence with her son's.

"Don't forget, you're gonna get that for me, right?" they both seemed to be saying in Jesse-boy's voice.

Thomas nodded, opened the door.

"Oh! Get what?" Mrs. Farley asked with shivery delight. Their voices trailed him down the hall.

"A book I want."

"What book?"

"I don't have to tell you everything, do I?"

"Well, no dear, I just wondered. I—"

"See! That's what I mean. I can't have secrets. I can't have friends, I can't have anything of my own! Ever!"

"No! That's not true, dear, you—"

"You spy on me! Can't you leave me alone? Why did you have to come up here and ruin our game? You ruin everything! You always do!"

"Jesse-boy! I'm sorry. I'm so sorry!"

Mrs. Farley burst into Thomas's room and ordered him to go back and play with Jesse-boy. Had he gotten the match, Jesse-boy asked the minute his door closed. Yes, here; Thomas gave him the match and then started to leave. No!

Jesse-boy hollered. First he had to show him how to smoke. Thomas lied and said Margaret was waiting for him to say good-night. It was easy, all he had to do was light it.

"Please," Jesse-boy begged. "You have to. What if I drop the match and I can't get it, and then the whole house burns down?"

Thomas hurried back to show him. "The first thing you gotta do's tamp it. Here. Like this." He tapped one end on the night table the way Otis had on the step.

"Why?" Jesse-boy giggled with excitement.

Thomas said he didn't know; you were just supposed to, that's all. But what was the reason, Jesse-boy persisted. To make it taste better? There wasn't any reason, you just do it, Thomas said with a worldly shrug. Jesse-boy put the cigarette in his mouth. Thomas struck the match on the floor grate and then held the flame to the cigarette. "Do this," he instructed, curling his lips and sucking in air.

Jesse-boy tried, but opened his mouth too wide. The cigarette fell, smudging the sheet with ash from the burned-out paper.

"Like this." Thomas demonstrated with the unlit cigarette. "Like sipping in air."

Jesse-boy snatched it and put it in his own mouth. Thomas struck another match and tried, but the cigarette wouldn't light. It was getting limp. Jesse-boy thrust the cigarette at Thomas and told him to light it for him.

"Your spit's on it!" Thomas cried with the wet end in his mouth. He struck another match. The cigarette flared red and lit with Thomas coughing out the smoke. His eyes watered and his nose ran. "Here. I took too much in. Just take a little." He passed it to Jesse-boy.

Jesse-boy puffed in then stared back with swollen cheeks.

"Blow it out!" Thomas said, and Jesse-boy did. "That was good. You didn't even cough." Thomas sat on the edge of the bed.

Jesse-boy smiled. He took another puff, again blew the smoke out easily. Pleased with himself he immediately took another, this time inhaling deeply. He began to choke, deep chest-wrenching gasps. With the cigarette still in his hand he bent over gasping for air. "I can't breathe!" he finally wheezed.

The door opened and the blue haze swayed overhead.

"What's going—Jesse-boy!" Mrs. Farley screamed, running to him. She began to pound his back. "Breathe! Breathe!" she cried, but he had gone limp. "Fred! Fred! Fred!" she screamed, arms around her gasping son.

It was then that Thomas noticed the smoldering black circle widening on the bed. He grabbed the glass of chocolate milk and poured it onto the burning blanket. Mr. Farley ran into the room, half ready for bed. He was bare-chested in his undershorts with just one sock on. He swooped up Jesse-boy and swayed him in his arms like a baby, all the while shouting his son's name. Jesse-boy's legs swung like useless puppet sticks in the thick green wool socks Mrs. Farley had knit for him. "There, there," Mr. Farley soothed while his wife tore about the room begging God to spare her son and take her. Because if He didn't, she threatened, she'd kill herself. That's what she'd do. She'd have to! Without Jesse-boy she had nothing to live for. Her life was over.

Thomas watched warily for a clear path to the door. His eye caught Margaret's. Roused by the commotion, she peered in from the hallway, small and even whiter-faced in the white ribboned nightgown sewn from one of Mrs. Farley's many patterns.

"He's all right," Mr. Farley cried. "He's all right!"

Jesse-boy tried to lift his head. He looked around then moaned and closed his eyes.

"He's all right! He's fine!" Mr. Farley declared, and with that as her signal, Mrs. Farley sprung at Thomas, pinning him against the wall. She shook him so hard his head banged the wall. "Why'd you do that? Why'd you do that to him? You bad thing! You horrible, horrible boy!" Spray from her mouth hit his face. Out in the hallway Margaret sobbed, shrieking for her to leave him alone! Leave her brother alone!

"I told you it wouldn't work," Mr. Farley said as he settled Jesse-boy into his wheelchair. "They're from a whole other place, kids like them."

. . .

School started up again the following Monday. Jesse-boy's breathing was back to normal, wheezing only when he got excited. Mr. Wentworth was extremely considerate of Jesse-boy. When Mrs. Farley peeked in to wave hello, he insisted she come in and hear Jesse-boy recite from the Declaration of Independence. The smoking incident had terrified Margaret. She begged Thomas to be good so he wouldn't be sent away. Sent away? Sent away where? She didn't know, but she'd heard them through the floor grate. The boy was no good. Just like the father and mother. One more incident, Mr. Farley told his wife, and he'd have to go. Boys do those things, she tried to placate her husband. Jesse-boy was just learning how to be a boy, that's all. He's almost sixteen! Mr. Farley said. It's time he learned how to be a man.

. . .

It was a blustery day when Gladys came to visit. She was all dressed up; well, dressed up for Gladys in a faded navy blue dress, the seams worn lighter, shiny like the seat of her skirt. Her run-down black loafers were like a man's, they were so wide on her big feet. She had business in town to see to, she told Mrs. Farley through the door screen, but first she'd like to say hello to the children. They were at the kitchen table eating lunch with Mr. Wentworth, leftover pork chops and milk gravy. It was the old teacher's main meal of the day, so when Mrs. Farley told Gladys the children had to get right back to their lessons, he was quick to allow them fifteen extra minutes. He slid the last chop onto his plate and held his tie back in his reach for more gravy. "Take your time," he called after them.

They stood in the musty-smelling dining room. "I thought you might like these." Gladys handed Margaret a wrinkled cloth bag. In it were her paper dolls and a red haircomb with missing teeth that Gladys had found once at the movies. "Sat on it the whole time." She laughed. Even though Margaret tried, her gratitude sounded thin. By now she was used to finer gifts. For Thomas Gladys had brought a tattered book of snakes. Its cover was torn. He thanked her and quickly turned pages, looking closely to make up for his sister's spoiled ways.

"It's good to know the names. And the ones that're poisonous," Gladys said, adding a little self-consciously that the book had been hers as a girl.

"You liked snakes?" Thomas asked, surprised. His mother was terrified of them.

"Not liked them, so much as liked to know about them," she said.

Just then Mrs. Farley bustled into the room. Time for school; Jesse-boy's energy, the little he had, would be running low soon. She steered Margaret toward the door.

"Wait." Margaret turned back to Gladys. "Is my father back yet?"

"Back?" Gladys said.

"From that slaughter job, the one way up north," Margaret said.

"No," Gladys said with a look at Mrs. Farley. "Not yet. Soon's he is, though, he'll be here. And that's for sure."

"But when? It's been so long!" Margaret said.

"Look at this girl." Mrs. Farley pulled Margaret close. "She's just blossomed, hasn't she? And Jesse-boy too, he's so happy having her here. Just like brother and sister, they're so close. And of course, Thomas, he's very . . . very nice."

"And honest too. Like his father. He'd never take what wasn't his," Gladys said. "And you know that, don't you, Phyllis? You and Fred both."

"Gladys! I'm surprised at you. Really! In front of the children. Come now, time to get back," Mrs. Farley said, blotchy-cheeked and herding them down the hall.

Gladys must have waited, because even with the door closed on the stifling parlor classroom the women could be heard, not words, but sharp, angry voices. Beaks, Thomas thought, pecking at one another.

8

THOMAS HAD BEEN SICK FOR A WEEK. EVERY DAY HE GREW sicker. Tonight his fever was so high he could barely open his eyes. With little distinction between dreams and wakefulness he drifted in and out of sleep. The dark slipped into day, then dark again. The wordless, watery voices came and went, whether in and out of the shadowy room or surfacing through delirium he could no longer tell. He had no need of food. When she tried to force broth between his parched lips it dribbled down his cheek and stained the pillow. Hearing his mother moan he hit the spoon away and struggled to see. It was his own voice. He couldn't lift his head.

"See? He's waking up." Mrs. Farley wrung out a wet towel over the basin on the night stand then laid it across his burning forehead.

A rough hand grazed his cheek. "Even hotter than before," Mr. Farley said. "He's burning up."

"It's got to run its course, that's all."

"He's just getting worse."

"Go down and chip some more ice. He's taking that at least."

"We should call the doctor. You know we should."

"Will you stop saying that? Please, Fred. Please?"

Barefoot in his red plaid pajamas, Mr. Farley hurried downstairs to the icebox. Margaret tiptoed along the hallway close to the wall. She had already been sent back twice. Hugging herself, she watched from the shadows. Mrs. Farley dipped the towel into the basin again, then wrung it tightly.

With so much traffic past his door Jesse-boy called in a high, panicky voice. "What's wrong? Will somebody tell me what's going on?" There was a pause. "Mommy! Mommy!" he shrieked and banged on the wall.

Mrs. Farley rushed into the hallway. "Get back to bed, Margaret!" she snapped on her way to comfort her son.

Margaret ran to Thomas's bedside. When she said his name, he struggled to open his eyes. They rolled to whites, then closed again. With his agitation his chest rose and fell rapidly against the piled blankets. His teeth chattered.

"Get away from him!" Mrs. Farley cried, coming back into the room. "You'll catch it!" She tried nudging Margaret to the door, but the little girl backed into a corner. She would not be moved. Mr. Farley returned. He gave his wife the bowl of ice chunks. She told him to get Margaret back to bed. Margaret said she wanted to stay. He looked at his wife.

"You gonna call Dr. Creel?" Margaret asked. She stared at her shivering brother.

"He's going to be fine, Margaret." Mrs. Farley wedged a chip of ice between Thomas's teeth as if to make her point.

"You better. He's awful sick. I never saw him so sick before," Margaret gasped. "Look! He's shaking! Same as

James. And then he died. He died real fast. Mommy waited too long. She should've got the doctor!"

"Get her into her room! Please?" Mrs. Farley hissed at her husband.

"She's right. What's the point of waiting?" Mr. Farley asked.

"It's chilblains, that's all. Open the closet and get me the blanket up there." Mrs. Farley shoved more ice into Thomas's mouth. Mr. Farley pulled a heavy woolen blanket from the shelf. "Cover him up!" Mrs. Farley ordered. Her voice was tight with intensity, but her face was not.

"No." Mr. Farley clutched the blanket to his chest. "Not with such a fever, Phyllis. He'll get even hotter."

Her head snapped up. "You don't know what you're talking about! Look at him! If the chilblains get any worse he'll go straight into a fit. I know he will. I've seen it happen." She fixed a hard, wordless warning on her husband. Margaret crept closer. Mr. Farley continued to hug the blanket. As with discipline and education, in matters of health he always deferred to her. And so it was that he was usually stymied in any decisions regarding Jesse-boy. Thomas moaned. His cheeks burned.

"Please call Dr. Creel," Margaret begged.

"Yes. He's getting too sick." Looking closely, Mr. Farley bent over the boy, the blanket at his chest. "His breathing, it's too . . . too forced. I'll go call."

"Don't! Don't you do that! Don't you dare!" Mrs. Farley hissed.

"But—"

"No! Not with *her* working for him. I don't want *her* here."

"But Phyllis. The boy's sick. He's got to be seen. Dr. Creel will come alone if I say to."

"No!"

"I'll tell him, I'll say, don't bring Gladys Bibeau," he pleaded.

"I'm more than capable and I will take care of this in my own way. And alone, Fred."

"For God's sake, Phyllis, this isn't right. Send the boy away if you want, but don't do this," he pleaded in a low, frantic voice as Margaret slipped out of the room.

Downstairs, she kept dialing the operator, but no one answered. Finally Mrs. Pierce's sleepy voice came on the line. Margaret told her to get Dr. Creel up here right away to the Farleys'. Her brother was awful sick.

"Who? Phyllis? Phyllis has a brother?" Mrs. Pierce said. "Not any I know of."

"No! My brother! Thomas!" Margaret shouted. "He's upstairs and he's gonna die. He's gonna die just like little baby James did."

"Hang up then! Hang up and clear the line!" Mrs. Pierce commanded, jolted now to duty.

Dr. Creel did come alone, though it took a while. His night vision was almost gone. As it turned out, old Bibeau had blood in his urine and the doctor hadn't wanted to call Gladys away from her father's care. He directed Mrs. Farley to fill the tub with cold water. He and Mr. Farley carried Thomas downstairs and gradually immersed him. Mr. Farley held his shoulders to keep him from sliding down while Dr. Creel patted his forehead and neck with a washcloth he kept dipping in rubbing alcohol.

All the lights were on in the big farmhouse. Up in his

room Jesse-boy raised such a ruckus demanding to know what was going on that Mrs. Farley insisted Margaret go keep him company.

"But I want to stay with Thomas."

"He's in good hands," Mrs. Farley said as she scrubbed Margaret's face and hands with Borax over the kitchen sink. She dabbed more camphor onto the flannel pinned to Margaret's undershirt. With influenza in the house, they'd all been wearing the strips for days.

"I want to see him."

She clutched the girl's shoulders. "No. You will do exactly as you're told." She glanced back at the stairs. Her son was calling, shouting her name. "This is all too much for him. He mustn't be agitated. Do you understand? Do you? Well, do you? Do you?" she demanded until Margaret finally gave a teary nod. "All right then." She marched Margaret up to his door, shut for days against turmoil and contagion. She put her hand on the knob then turned instead to Margaret. She knelt down and held the girl's face between her hands. "I'm sorry, Margaret. I'm sorry for speaking to you like that. It's just that Jesse-boy . . . he . . . well, he loves you so much. And he needs you, honey. He needs you very much. In the whole world the only thing that makes him happy is you." Her smile quivered.

"No," Margaret gasped as Mrs. Farley scooped her up and carried her to Jesse-boy's soft bed. "Make room, dear. Margaret's afraid. She doesn't want to be alone, and you're upset too so this will work out just fine," she whispered as she drew the covers to their chins. "Sleep tight," she whispered through the closing door.

"Here, hold my hand." Jesse-boy groped between them.

Margaret hit his hand away.

"Don't be scared."

"I'm not."

"What are you then?" He curled on his side facing her.

"Nothing."

"Nothing!" he giggled. "You have to be something. You know what I am?" When she didn't answer he moved closer. "I'm happy." He touched her cheek. "I'm so happy. I love you," he said in so small a voice it sounded like a question.

"Shut up!" She moved as far as she could to the edge of the bed without falling off.

"Your hair's so soft," he whispered, then suddenly pulled her close.

Her eyes opened wide as his hand clamped over her mouth. With her back to him it was hard to fight him. She couldn't understand his thick voice, but she was scared. And mad. Mad as hell, she would say later. Her elbow rammed into his belly. He groaned and she bit his finger then jumped down. She ran into her room. Even with the door shut she could hear his bawling.

. . .

When Thomas was strong enough he came downstairs for meals. Classes had started without him, but he was expected to complete the lessons Mr. Wentworth prepared daily. Margaret delivered them every afternoon. She had grown very quiet. And paler. There was a sadness about her he could neither penetrate nor tease her out of. She seemed almost angry now. She sat on the side of his bed and said she knew he was pretending to be sick just to get out of school.

"No, I'm not!"

"Yes, you are. Just like Jesse-boy, you're a whiny-boy weakling."

"Shut up!" he said, then quickly laughed for fear she'd cry.

"You are. You're a sissy. You just want to be up here all the time."

"That's not true. Mrs. Farley says I'm not strong enough yet."

"I hate it here. I hate it here so much." Her face twisted in her struggle not to cry.

"You do? How come? You keep getting new dresses and things for your dolls. That's pretty good, huh? And your very own kitty cat, right? That's not so bad."

She stared at him, jaw set with stubbornness.

"And it's just for now," he continued. "You know it is. Soon as Daddy gets our own place we'll be outta here and back in our old school. And then Mommy'll come back too, she'll be so glad we're all settled down. Happy and everything." His voice trailed off.

"Daddy's in jail. Jesse-boy said we gotta stay 'til he gets out. Ten years, he said."

"Well don't believe him," Thomas said, sitting straight up. "He's a liar. A goddamn liar, that's all he is."

"But Daddy *is* in jail. Aunt Lena came by yesterday and I heard them talking. She was all blubbery crying and bumping into things, the way she gets, and she said she'd go tell the judge what a bad father Daddy is. Mrs. Farley said she appreciated that and how she'd let her know when. Aunt Lena got crying again how broke she was and alone now with Maxie out on the road again. So then Mrs. Farley gave her five dollars. And Aunt Lena says how she can't take charity. Mrs. Farley says it's not charity. 'Consider it a debt paid,' she says, now that she's got us, 'the dear children,' that's what she calls us. And Aunt Lena got her scissors out. 'No. I gotta work for my keep. I always do,' she says and she's stumbling around the divan, tryna get at Mrs. Farley's hair. But Mrs. Farley, she didn't want her hair cut. She went out in the barn for Otis to come give Aunt Lena a ride back into town."

"So how'd you hear all that?" He was poking the satin point on the blanket binding inside and out.

"I was in the pull-out closet."

"What were you doing in there?" He laughed uneasily. The cedar pull-out closet under the stairs, that was where the good woolen coats were kept.

"Hiding. On Jesse-boy." Her clear blue eyes showed the dread. "And her too."

"Why?"

She shrugged. "She makes me sit with him and ride. In the chair."

"Oh yeah? Seems kinda dumb to do, huh?" He reached for the tumbling man on the wooden sticks. Mrs. Farley had brought it up the other day. To keep his mind off being so sickly and weak, she'd said.

"She thinks it's funny," Margaret said, watching the little man spin up and down between the sticks.

"Must look funny, huh? You getting a ride and him working the wheels."

"That ain't it! That ain't why!"

"Don't say ain't! Mommy says that's ignorant farmer talk. And you don't want people thinking you're ignorant, do you?" All the while he was squeezing the sticks so fast the wooden man was a blur of tumbles.

She grabbed the toy and flung it across the room.

"You better not've broke it, damn you!" He scrambled over the side of the bed. The toy had hit the round mirror and landed on top of the dresser. He examined it carefully for cracks. There weren't any, but he wanted her to squirm.

"He made me look at pictures."

Thomas turned dizzily, teetering to be so newly on his feet again. "Who?"

"Jesse-boy."

"What kind of pictures?"

"Bad ones." She looked down. "And he says bad things."

"What? What bad things?"

She shook her lowered head. "I don't wanna stay here any more. I just wanna go."

"We can't. We got no place to go to."

"What about Mommy? We could go there, and then when we tell her, she'll let us stay. You know she will. She will, Tom! I know she will!"

He considered this a moment. "But how'll we get there? Massachusetts, that's far off."

"Down the depot. The bus."

"But we'd have to buy tickets. You need money for bus tickets."

"I know where her pocketbook is. In the pull-out closet."

"No! We can't do that. That'd be stealing."

"I don't care. I'm gonna go live with Mommy. You can stay here if you want, but I'm leaving." She ran out of the room. He started to climb back into bed.

"Margaret! Margaret!" Jesse-boy called from somewhere. "Come down here. Mommy wants you to meet somebody. Reverend Tillotson. He and Mrs. Tillotson want to say hello."

First Mr. Farley came, looking. He opened Thomas's door and asked where Margaret was. Thomas said he didn't know. Then Mrs. Farley came. She opened doors along the hallway, calling softly for Margaret. She burst into Thomas's room, demanding to know where Margaret was. He didn't know. She opened the closet and pushed back the few clothes in there. Grunting, she bent down, hand on her knee, and looked under the bed.

"This is so embarrassing," she said, plump hands on her flushed cheeks. "They're here to see Margaret."

"How come to see her? We're Catholics. Well, kinda, anyway."

"Tomorrow morning she's supposed to start Sunday school. And they've come to say hello first."

"But we don't go to church."

She opened her mouth as if to say something, but instead hurried out of the room. Across the way the wide door to the linen closet creaked open. "Margaret!" Mrs. Farley cried.

He peered out. Margaret's ringlets were mussed and wild-looking. Goose feathers were stuck to the back of her dark green dress. Mrs. Farley led Margaret toward the stairs. He dressed quickly and came downstairs.

"Well, Thomas! Good to see you finally out of bed," Mr. Farley said.

Mrs. Farley blinked when he came into the parlor. She introduced him to the Tillotsons as if she'd been expecting him all along, but annoyance crimped her mouth. Her eyes narrowed every time she looked his way. Jesse-boy was all dressed up in a shirt and tie. The unscuffed shoes on his dangling feet gleamed with polish. He giggled happily. The grown-ups were drinking tea. Jesse-boy and Margaret had mulled cider in little clear glass cups with handles. There was a plate of cookies, fudge, and penuche on the side table. Thomas took a piece of fudge and Mrs. Farley's eyes darted his way.

Mrs. Tillotson was a tall, strong-faced woman. Even in the chair she towered over her husband. He was slight with thinning hair and full red lips and a preacher's strong voice. So far he'd had little to say. Every few minutes there would be another lull in the conversation. Now, everyone began to speak at once, Mrs. Farley about the Christmas pageant, Mrs. Tillotson about the ham and bean supper, Reverend Tillotson about Alice Pfeiffer. She had been sent to the sanitarium up in Burlington. Tuberculosis. It was pretty bad. Yes, Mrs. Farley said with a vague look. She thought she'd heard something or other like that.

"Now Roddy's alone with the six young ones," Reverend Tillotson said, pursing his lips for a sip of tea. Mrs. Tillotson fidgeted with the button on her faded needlepoint purse. Mr. and Mrs. Farley stared straight ahead at nothing at all. Mr. Farley's face was puffed and red as if he'd just swallowed the wrong way. "He's having a real rough time of it," Reverend Tillotson said, pausing as if to let this sink in. "Even with relief there's never enough food, all those many mouths to feed."

"He might try working!" Mr. Farley said testily. "That'd sure help, don't you think?"

"If there were any jobs around, especially for someone like poor Roddy, being so slow and with the six little ones to look after."

Now, no one spoke. There was only the squeal of Jesse-boy's chair as he wheeled closer to the table. He took two cookies. He offered one to Margaret.

Her face soured. "I don't want it," she said.

"How about some fudge, dear?" Mrs. Farley reached for the plate. "Margaret has quite the sweet tooth," she told Mrs. Tillotson.

"No thanks," Margaret said sullenly. She plucked a feather from her sleeve.

"Oh, dear. You're not sick, I hope." Mrs. Farley got up and felt her brow. "See, Thomas, that's why you shouldn't be down here. We can't risk everyone catching what you have. He's been sick almost two weeks now," she informed Mrs. Tillotson with raised eyebrows, then sat back down with a sigh.

"What's he got?"

"Influenza," Mrs. Farley said and Mrs. Tillotson shrank back in her chair.

"But I'm all better now," Thomas said, and Margaret looked at him. "I feel good."

"You've done a fine thing taking in these children," the Reverend said.

"How could we not?" Mrs. Farley smiled at Margaret. "Especially Margaret. Such a dear little thing. And not the least bit shy. She'll talk to anyone, just march right up and tell you right off what she thinks."

The Reverend glanced at Margaret, uneasily, as if she might be getting ready to tell him a thing or two. She certainly had that kind of nasty look, Thomas thought. Talk returned to the Sunday school's pageant. One of the wise men had shot up over the summer, almost a foot taller, Mrs. Tillotson fretted. Last year's robe would be up to his knees. Mrs. Farley said she'd be glad to make a new one for him.

"I was hoping you'd say that," Mrs. Tillotson said, relieved. "It's hard now, asking for extras when there's so little around."

"My pleasure. More than glad to do it." Beaming, Mrs. Farley poured another round of tea from her blue and white Spode teapot.

"You're such a good seamstress." Mrs. Tillotsin glanced at her husband. "Phyllis sews all her own clothes. Every year at the fair she wins the blue ribbon for tailoring."

"Well, not every year." Mrs. Farley blushed.

"Just about though," Mr. Farley added, beaming.

Bored, Jesse-boy rolled his chair back and forth, bumping the side of Margaret's chair. She glared at him. Her legs were crossed and her foot swung up and down. He hit her chair again. This time she shoved his wheelchair and he rolled back against the piano.

"Margaret!" Mrs. Farley scolded with a shocked look.

Thomas laughed. Jesse-boy gave a menacing giggle. He was embarrassed and angry. Margaret's stare dared him to do it again.

"I think we're boring the children with all our talk," Mrs. Tillotson told her husband.

"Oh no," Mrs. Farley protested. "It's good discipline for children to sit through an adult conversation."

"We shouldn't overdo it though." With a look at her husband Mrs. Tillotson put her hands on the arms of her chair.

"Just one more thing then, Fred," Reverend Tillotson said. "If there was some work, just some kind of chores here Roddy could do. That's really what I came to say. Part time. Just a couple hours here and there, it'd sure help."

Fred Farley's eyes had gone dead.

"Cleaning out stalls even. Roddy's got that kinda mind, you know. Don't matter what, just tell him where and he'll go right to it, not look up once 'til he's done."

"Sorry, Reverend, but I'm not hiring just now. And especially not Roddy Pfeiffer."

"But if you could just make an exception. Some men're even stealing they're so desperate. If you could just see it in your heart—"

"My heart!" Mr. Farley interrupted. "And these two here, what do you think they are?"

"Now, Fred," Mrs. Farley warned.

"Yes, of course," Reverend Tillotson said uneasily.

"I didn't cause any man his troubles. That one, he went looking for them. If you know what I'm saying."

Thomas looked between the two men. The women stared at their knees.

"I know what you're saying," Reverend Tillotson allowed with bowed head, almost ashamedly.

"I don't think you do," Mr. Farley said. "Because I work hard, always have and I never once asked anything from anybody, much less trespassed another man's property and stole from him, besides. I don't expect handouts, no sir, never did. So don't be expecting them from me." With that Mr. Farley got up and left the parlor.

"Oh dear," Mrs. Tillotson said. "I'm sorry we came, that we upset him like that."

"He's a little sensitive on the subject," Mrs. Farley said. Her eyebrows raised in the Talcott children's direction. "All the criticism he's been getting. As if he was the one broke into his own barn."

"I never would've brought that up," the Reverend said. "Tell Fred that. Tell him it's Roddy I meant."

"Well, anyway, we're managing," Mrs. Farley continued sweetly. She absently stroked the back of Jesse-boy's hair. "Aren't we, dear?"

"Yes, Mummy. We are," he said as sweetly while making a goofy face at Margaret. He bobbed his head as if to bump her again.

"It does seem a little harsh though." Reverend Tillotson looked at Mrs. Farley as if the intensity of his stare might override the children's presence. "Considering."

9

THOMAS SAT ON A STUMP, WATCHING THE BIG MAN SPLIT firewood, then stack it behind the house. Otis had already been yelled at once when Mr. Farley caught him talking with Thomas while he stopped to smoke. Otis worked double time now. He rumbled up in the tractor pulling another load of logs in the cart. He climbed down and emptied the logs onto the ground.

"I never saw so much wood! How many trees's that now?" Thomas asked.

"This? This is just part. Last spring we cut thirty-eight all told. Cut more tomorrow." He looked up at the heavy, lowering sky. "If it don't snow, that is."

"Where's it from?"

"Down Post Road. Straight in by the pond." He kicked a stray log, rolling it back to the pile. "Mostly all maple. Some ash and birch though."

"That's where I used to live. You must've seen my house. Up the hill some, it's white. There's a green door and it's got a tin roof. And a barn. Not big as these," he said, gesturing around. He was talking about their old house, before the tent, before the move to town, their old life, before their mother just disappeared into thin air. He walked back and forth alongside Otis, who dragged the logs into a neater pile. "But still, we had two cows. Two pigs and a goat. And the chicken coop, it was down back of the house. We used to play in the back part, Margaret and me, in the little room back of the chicken coop. It was our playhouse." Thomas laughed and held his nose. "Pee-you, but we put all kindsa junk in there."

"Junk?" Otis grunted pulling a knobby log straight.

"Secret things. Like our spears, ones we made. Snake skins and lime for potions. And rope. We were always looking for rope."

"How come rope?"

"Case we ever needed to tie a prisoner up or something."

"You ever do that, tie someone up?"

"No. Well, Margaret. But just for practice. And that was easy. She's strong, but she's not very big."

"You make your own fish poles?"

"Yeah, we did."

"With bent hat pins for hooks?"

"Yeah! But they were my mother's so we had to hide them. How'd you know?"

"Found 'em."

"You did? Where?"

"The little room back of the coop." The big man's face clouded and he closed the back of the cart. He dropped the long metal peg through the latch and Thomas felt its clunk in his chest. "That's where I live. Me and my wife. In your old house. Farley takes it outta my pay."

"Oh."

"Don't wanna make you feel bad." Otis lit a cigarette. "Want one?"

"No thanks." He followed Otis to the side of the tractor.

"For later then."

"No, Jesse-boy took the other one. He got so sick he took a spell, then all hell broke loose."

"You didn't tell them I give it to you, did you?" Otis looked sick.

"No! I said I found it. Out by the road."

"That's good." He climbed onto the tractor. "Wanna go for a ride?"

"Sure!" He climbed up and perched on the edge of the seat next to Otis. Otis drove down the wide, rutted cow path to the shortcut to the back road. He stopped suddenly; maybe Thomas better go ask Mrs. Farley first.

"She doesn't care," Thomas shouted over the engine.

"You sure?"

"Yeah. And besides she's sewing. And when she's sewing she doesn't want anyone bothering her." They passed the Farley burying ground, a cluster of thin, blackened headstones encircled by a wrought-iron fence. Thomas let his jaw hang loose, laughing as his teeth rattled with the rumbling tractor. Now came a grove of birch, the silvery limbs flashing by. Ahead was a farmhouse. The shutters had been nailed shut over the windows. In the front yard a wheelless wagon sagged into bittersweet that twined over it.

"That's Creedons'. Billy, he was in my school! Yeah! We were both the same! Fifth grade. I didn't know they lived so close. To Farley's, I mean. Maybe I could walk there and see him sometime."

"Creedons're gone!" Otis shouted. "They went on up to Burlington, live with his family or hers, I don't know. But it's the bank's now. Like everything else. Probably Farley's someday if he wants it."

They drove the rest of the way in silence. At the edge of a clearing where raw stumps posted the frozen ground, the cut wood lay piled in four-foot lengths. This side of the pond had always been thickly wooded. Thomas glanced up the hill. A thin drift of smoke rose from the wide center chimney.

Otis turned off the engine. "Up there's your house." He jumped down and so did Thomas. Otis tossed a log into the cart.

"Yours now." Thomas got the end of a smaller log and tried to heave it into the cart. It hit the edge and bounced back, banging into Otis's ankle.

"Jesus H. Christ!" the big man hollered, jumping on one foot.

"I'm sorry!"

Otis closed his eyes and took a deep breath. "That's okay," he groaned, then limped toward the pile. "I guess I had it coming, huh, for living in your house." He tossed two logs into the cart.

"I didn't do that on purpose! You think I did? I didn't! Swear to God I didn't! It wasn't your fault, us losing the house. It wasn't, right?" His voice rose dangerously high and cracking. He wiped his nose with the back of his hand.

"No. 'Course not." Otis worked for a few more minutes, then paused. "Maybe someday things'll get better and your father maybe can buy it back."

"He's in jail, you know," Thomas said, and Otis nodded. "For stealing. From Mr. Farley."

Otis paused with an armload of short lengths. "I'm gonna tell you something. But you gotta keep it to yourself. Promise?"

"I promise."

"I'm just telling you so you won't feel so bad. About your father, I mean." There was a clatter as he dumped in the logs. He brushed dirt and bits of sawdust and leaves off his sleeves while he spoke. "But I ain't never gonna say it again—even in a courta law. I can't, you understand?" He waited until Thomas nodded. "That time, your tent got pulled down, and all the rest? Well, that was your father's spare that got taken. And his butchering saw too."

"I know."

"What you don't know is, it wasn't no mistake. Farley, he knew what he was doing. A man like Henry Talcott. Any man, 'course he'd come back for what was his. For what he needed to keep his family going. So then Farley, he was just waiting for him to come. Every night, I had to sit out there. 'You see anything, you shoot first, ask questions later,' he says. But acourse, I wouldn't. I never would. 'Specially not him."

"Will you tell the sheriff?"

"No! I said. I told you I'm just telling you, so you won't think bad of your father."

"But the sheriff, he'd—"

"He knows. 'Course he knows, everybody does."

"But—"

"But the thing's the breaking and entering. That, he did do. It's the reason that ain't fair."

Thomas picked up a log and ran at the front of the tractor. With the bang Otis lunged at him. "What the hell're you doing?" he shouted and grabbed the log. Thomas ran back and picked up another. This time he drew the log back higher, bringing it down, crashing into the engine casing with all his strength and outrage and pain. And tears. Otis grabbed that log and threw it down. "That's enough! That's enough!" he shouted as Thomas scrambled to get it again. "Ain't gonna do no good." He held out his arm to keep Thomas from the log. "Just gonna get me fired, that's all."

Thomas ran into the woods a few feet, gave a deep shuddering moan of a sob, then blew his nose in his shirt-tail. He was peeing into a leafless, viny thicket when Otis came up from behind.

"Thought that's what you were doing," Otis said as he unbuttoned his pants and began to pee alongside the boy. The yellow stream gave off faint musky steam, a hiss onto the frozen ground. "I was in school with your mother. 'Til seventh grade anyhow. That's when I left. You see her, tell her Otie Johnson says hello. Prettiest girl in school. In the whole town, I always said so. Where's she at now?" he asked on their way back to the dented tractor.

"Massachusetts. Working someplace, a factory."

"Well, good for her! So there! She'll get you all together settled, and you'll forget all this mess. 'Course she will. Irene, she was a real lady. Not like her sister. That Lena! Woo-wee!"

Thomas laughed. "Sorry about the tractor! The dents," he called as they rumbled onto the road.

"Don't be. Damn tree fell the wrong way, that's all." Otis laughed.

10

OUTSIDE, A LIGHT SNOW HAD BEGUN TO FALL. THOMAS was in the parlor doing long division problems in his tablet before school started. Mr. Wentworth claimed that he had fallen behind during his illness. It seemed to Thomas that Mr. Wentworth gave him extra work probably at Mrs. Farley's request, just to keep him busy all the time. The door flew open and Margaret burst in.

"I been all over. I been looking for you!" As usual she was dressed as if she were going to church or a party, with a pink dress and ribbons in her hair.

"Here I am," he muttered, crossing out and carrying a one. It was the last problem.

"I hate Jesse-boy! I hate him so damn much!"

"Don't swear."

"Look! Look what he gave me!" She laid a sheet of paper on his tablet. "He said it's me. When I get big." She began to cry.

The drawing was of a woman's fat, hanging breasts and the same scrawl of hair between her legs.

"Good morning!" Mr. Wentworth called as the front door opened. "Something smells good today."

Thomas balled up the drawing and shoved it into his pocket.

"I said I was going to tell his mother if he didn't stop, and he said she'd send us to the home then."

"Send us home?"

"The home. The orphanage! Because no one else'll take us, he said."

Thomas jumped up. "He still upstairs?" he asked at the door.

"He's in the kitchen. Having cake," she said with disgust, though she too had eaten cake this morning.

The long hallway amplified Mrs. Farley's screechy laughter. Whatever she said next made Mr. Wentworth roar laughing. Thomas told his sister to wait here; he'd be right back. Keeping close to the wall he tiptoed up the front stairs. They were right below him. The step creaked and Mrs. Farley's head shot up. "Thomas! Where are you going? What're you doing, sneaking up the stairs like that? I told you about that, about being so furtive all the time."

"I didn't want to make noise and bother you. I have to get my book. I'll be right down."

"Don't make Mr. Wentworth wait now."

"I won't." He bounded along the hallway, then down the back staircase, into the kitchen.

"Wentworth's here." Jesse-boy didn't look up. He was pouring milk into his glass.

Thomas pulled open the balled paper. "You're a creep. You're such a creep, giving this dirty thing to my sister. She's just a little girl!"

"What're you talking about?" Jesse-boy laughed and brushed the paper away. "She thinks it's funny. Like you did." He cut off a forkful of cake. "You thought it was funny, right?"

"No I didn't." In his pocket his hand closed over the jackknife.

"Yes you did. You laughed, remember? Just like Margaret does." He stuffed cake into his mouth until both sallow cheeks bulged.

"That's a lie! That's a dirty lie, and you know it, you no-good, dirty liar, you, talking about my sister like that!"

"Well, she does. She comes in my room late when everyone's sleeping and she climbs up on my bed and she whispers, 'Jesse-boy, draw me a titty picture, please, please, please. I'll kiss you if you do,' " he whispered, his eyes suddenly wide on the jackknife Thomas was holding. "Mummy! Mummy!" he screamed, covering his face with Thomas's lunge.

"She's a little girl!" Thomas panted as the butt of the unopened jackknife struck Jesse-boy's head. He pummeled his bleeding face now with both fists. "That's all she is, that's all she is, you—"

"Thomas! What're you doing?" Mrs. Farley demanded, then screamed for help. "He's hitting Jesse-boy! He's beating him!" She shoved Thomas against the stove. The jackknife fell as he caught himself on the glowing stove top. He ran to the sink and held his burned hand under the cold running water.

"He stabbed me! With a knife!" Jesse-boy screeched. Blood poured from his nose. His lip was split. "He's gonna kill me, Mummy! Make him go! Make him leave! I don't want him here anymore!"

Mrs. Farley stared down at the bloodied drawing on the

table and shuddered. "Get out of here! Go on!" she screamed, pushing Thomas out the door and through the back shed. "Go back and live in the woods! With the animals like the horrible, filthy boy you are!"

He stumbled down the steps then stood in the middle of the yard blowing onto his blistered palm.

"Fred!" Mrs. Farley screamed from the doorway. "Fred!"

His stomach roiled with the deep pain. He teetered a moment, closed his eyes against this next wave of throbbing. He staggered into the barn and collapsed in an empty stall. Directly below him, the last of the cows were being milked. Even their mooing made his hand ache.

"Fred! Fred! I need you! Get in here right now!" Mrs. Farley was still screaming when Mr. Farley came running toward the house from the office.

. . .

Trembling, he squatted in the stall. He'd been here for hours, it seemed. He couldn't stand the cold much longer, but he couldn't leave Margaret behind. If he could only get warm then he could think straight, decide what to do next. Maybe Otis would come soon. Otis would help, tell him what to do, where to go, maybe even let him and Margaret stay with him. At the far end of the barn, there was a small potbellied stove. He still had a match in his shirt pocket. He got up and looked from stall to stall. No wood, but lots of hay. He stuffed an armload into the stove then lit it. The hay ignited in a tinder-crackling blaze. He scooped up another pile and pushed it into the stove. Another pile. Another. It was a little smoky, but the heat felt good. Brow on his knees, he crouched near the stove.

"Thomas! Thomas!" Margaret called softly.

His head rose slowly over the stall board as he stood up. Alone, she hurried toward him, carrying his jacket. She wore her new navy blue wool coat and the red and white hat Mrs. Farley had just knit for her.

"It's smoky in here." She coughed. "Here." She held out the jacket. Shivering, he put it right on, but his sore fingers couldn't work the buttons. "I got the money," she said as she buttoned his jacket. "Eight dollars, that's all she had. You think we can get two tickets for eight dollars?"

"I don't know." His voice broke. He couldn't stop shaking. Before, he'd been too cold to cry. But right now he was about to. Smoke poured from the back of the stove where there should have been a stovepipe, but wasn't.

"They're all up with Jesse-boy. Come on, let's go." She was tugging him by the sleeve, out of the barn. "Come on, Thomas! Quick! We gotta go! We gotta run! Fast! C'mon!" She ran ahead, down the road.

He caught up to her. "It's five miles!"

"So what? We did that before. With the blackberries, we walked the whole way, remember?"

"Yeah, and you whining the whole time."

"I was little then."

He stopped and looked down at her. "You better go back. It's starting to snow, and it's not you they're mad at."

"No! I hate it there. And besides, Mrs. Farley's calling the sheriff. She wants you arrested. She said you tried to kill Jesse-boy."

"I did not!"

"Well how come she's got your jackknife then?"

"Because it fell on the floor."

They began to walk. Quickly now, as if on the trail of vapor their voices made in the air.

"You broke Jesse-boy's nose."

He stopped dead in his tracks. "I did?"

"And he's got a black eye," she called back over her shoulder. "The son of a bitch."

"Margaret!" He caught up, but before he could scold her the drone of an approaching engine sent them scrambling into the culvert. They lay on their bellies. An old truck loaded with baled hay, high over its cab, rattled by. Next, Thomas expected the sheriff's car. He said it would be safer to follow the brook into town, the way they had with their mother once. It had been a blistering July day the summer before last. The heat of the road had burned through the soles of their shoes. By going along the brook they'd kept mostly in the shade, and when they got too hot she'd let them carry their shoes and wade over the cool stones through the rippling water. It was shorter this way, and they wouldn't have to keep ducking off the road.

"How do you know his nose is broke?" he asked when they came to the brook. The snow had turned to sleet. Fallen leaves crunched underfoot. In here the sleet came louder, rasping down through the branches.

"Mr. Farley said so. He could move it back and forth."

"My hand's killing me." The knuckles were bruised and cut, the palm tender red.

"Here." She scooped up snow and pressed it into his hand.

"That feels good." He could almost make a fist. There weren't any sirens, just falling snow. Mrs. Farley wouldn't really call the sheriff because then he'd see Jesse-boy's dirty picture.

"You broke one of his teeth too."

Smiling, he scooped up more snow. "Damn tree fell the wrong way, that's all," he said under his breath.

"What tree?"

"Nothing, just something to say." He hurried on ahead. Every now and again she'd sigh or whimper some, but she kept going. It was a longer walk than he remembered. Here, the slowing brook was so wide in some places from bank to bank that boards had been laid to get across. Come spring the rockbed would be under racing water, but now was covered with snow.

"We should've stayed on the road," Margaret complained, adding how hungry she was. She had just sat down to breakfast when Jesse-boy showed her his drawing.

They were getting closer, Thomas kept assuring her. Pretty soon. Another mile or so. He curled his toes to warm them. At least he wore heavy leather shoes. Margaret's thin strap shoes were soaked. She whimpered as she limped, falling farther behind.

"I'm up here!" he called as he trudged on. "Can you hear me?" Each reply came fainter than the one before. "We're in town," he cried, running back to her. A little way ahead the brook tunneled under the road. There were two houses, one on each side. "See! It's Main Street!" he said, urging her on. She tried to run, but couldn't.

When they came out of the woods he suggested they stay off Main Street in case the Farleys drove by. Margaret said she could barely walk, much less go another way. "It might even be quicker," he said.

"And it might not!" she called back. "I'm going in there." She pointed ahead to a red house. She'd go ask them if they could come inside and warm up some. Maybe they'd feel bad and give them some food.

"No!" he said as she hobbled toward the brick walk. "We can't! We gotta get to the depot before they find us."

Again, he stoked her fear of the Farleys to keep her moving.

"I don't care. I gotta warm up. I can't even walk. I'm so cold, Thomas. You don't know how cold I am." She burst into tears. There she stood, halfway up some stranger's front walk, hugging herself, shaking all over and sobbing.

Clippety-clop. Clippety-clop. Clippety-clop came the sound of hooves, then the metal-rimmed clatter of the wooden wheels as the old wagon rolled closer. "It's Merton!" Thomas cried, pulling her by the hand to the edge of the road. "Hey! Hey!" he called, waving his arms and running alongside the stuporous old egg man, head turtled deep into his battered overcoat, his heavily lidded eyes locked on his blinkered horse. "It's me, Thomas Talcott! You used to buy eggs from us. Remember? Mrs. Talcott? Irenie! You used to call her that!"

"Whoa!" The wagon stopped. The horse shook his brown head with a wet snuffle that sent great puffs of breath into the air. "Hurry it up!" Merton the egg man said as Thomas helped Margaret climb into the wagon. He asked for a ride to the bus depot. He nudged Margaret and gestured for her to put her feet under the moth-eaten blanket covering the old man's legs. She shook her head no.

"Where you going?" The egg man shook the cracked harness and the horse started ahead.

"Noplace," Thomas said uneasily.

Merton thought this over. "How come you wanna go the depot then?" he said after a minute.

"I just said the depot. So you'd know. We're really going to the drugstore. To Leamings," Thomas said just in case anyone asked the egg man.

"Okay then. Leamings. You shoulda said so'n'a first place. Never been anywhere but here. All my life, ten times yours probably. I know every place. Every place there is." The horse slowed as they started downhill into the center of town. Leamings was a block from the bus depot. Thomas had to help Margaret down. He waved as the wagon continued on. The drugstore's gold-lettered windows were steamed with warmth. Margaret begged to go in for a hot chocolate and some pie at the counter, but he refused. For all they knew there might be only one bus going to Collerton, Massachusetts. What if it was right there in the depot now, taking on passengers while they dillydallied over hot chocolate. What if it left without them? Then what would they do? Where would they go? They'd have to spend the night somewhere until the next bus tomorrow. And she sure didn't want to go back to Aunt Lena's, did she? They wouldn't be there five minutes before she'd call the Farleys hoping to be rewarded with another twenty dollars. For their capture, he told his shivering sister. Yes, their capture! Because that's what they were now, outlaws. Hunted outlaws. "We're on the run," he said breathlessly as she plodded along, head hung in defeat and fatigue. "And when you're on the run, you can't take any chances. None!"

"You're the one on the run, not me," she said sullenly as he started to open the depot door.

He stepped back. "What's that mean?"

"Means I didn't beat up Jesse-boy. You did."

"All right then. So you want to go back?" They stepped aside as a man in a red hunting cap left the depot carrying a worn suitcase tied with rope. An old woman limped after him. "You want to go back to the Farleys'?" He grabbed his sister's arm and squeezed it, making his hand hurt again. "Is that what you want?"

She stared up at him. "I want something to eat, that's all I want."

. . .

They had to wait only a half hour before the bus arrived. There'd be a twenty-minute stop in White River Junction and then onto Collerton. Neither had been on a bus before. Margaret demanded the window seat, but it was wasted on her, so quickly had she fallen asleep. Thomas looked around for familiar faces, relieved that there weren't any. The bus was almost full. It started off with a roar, jouncing its passengers up and down in the rigid seats. Directly behind the children two ladies argued in low voices. The disagreement seemed to be whether or not their mother used to put ground cloves in her apple pie filling.

"Just because you do, doesn't mean she did."

"She's the one that taught me."

"For goodness sakes, I was there too. You act like you were her only child."

"You didn't care one fig about cooking. I was the one always in the kitchen." There was a pause. "Don't cry. Don't you dare cry or I'll move."

"Why do you do this? Why do you always make me feel this way?"

"Pauline," warned the lady who baked.

"I can't help it," Pauline wept. "You spoil everything. You always have. All my life." There was a wretched sob.

"Excuse me." The lady who baked reached over the seat and tapped Thomas's head. "Excuse me, young man, but we need to trade seats."

"Mary!" Pauline cried.

Ignoring her sister, the tall woman in the iron-gray coat stood in the aisle gripping a leather satchel while she waited for his seat. A little green hat perched low over her forehead. The hat's one long feather was frayed to a bare quill.

"That's my sister. She's sleeping." He looked up imploringly.

"Yes, well I'll be very quiet."

"Mary, please don't do this," Pauline pleaded.

"Her name's Margaret," he told the impatient woman. The bus lurched around a curve and she grabbed the seat with both hands. He rose, then leaned back in and shook Margaret's shoulder. Her eyes opened, wide and panicky as if unsure of where she was. He said he had to move, that he'd be in the seat right behind.

"Why?"

"Because. The lady said so."

When he sat down, Pauline wouldn't look at him. Right hand screening her face, she stared out the window. Margaret and Mary were having a lively conversation. The bus had grown noisy with voices vying to be heard over the loud motor. The sister next to him glared at the easy laughter in front.

"Well, here!" the tall lady said. From her satchel she

removed a crustless sandwich and gave it to Margaret. Margaret took a bite, then with a big smile handed the other half over the seat to her brother.

Pauline leaned forward. "That's my sandwich!" she declared before he could eat it.

"She's very hungry," the tall lady said.

"But the chicken sandwich, that's mine."

"The little girl doesn't like pork."

"Well I don't either. And you know I don't."

"I'm sorry. Here." Thomas held out the chicken and butter sandwich. "It's yours."

She looked at the sandwich, not at him, then snatched it away. She turned to the window, nibbling quietly. Paper rustled up front and then the tall lady handed him back half of her pork sandwich. He thanked her and tried to eat slowly. Dry and tough as the meat was, he devoured it before the lady beside him had finished hers.

With a little food in his belly he closed his eyes and fell asleep. He awoke to Margaret's voice. She was telling the tall lady that they were on their way to see their mother. To see her, the tall lady asked, surprised. Well, to live with her, Margaret explained. She told about leaving their father to live with their Aunt Lena and then with the Farleys. The tall lady knew the Farleys well. She and Phyllis used to be in the same bridge club. But that was before their son was born.

The little lady pressed her face to the space between the seat backs and asked for her apple. Her sister said to wait, they were almost in White River Junction. The little lady said she wanted her apple and she wanted it now. Ignoring her,

her sister said it was her opinion that Phyllis had turned that sickly child into a cripple with all her fretting and pampering. "Not that it's any of my business, of course."

"Which it isn't," the little lady said under her breath.

They pulled up to a small brick building. A few people huddled out front on benches, with suitcases at their feet. The sleet had turned to fast-falling snow. The bus driver said the toilet was in the shed behind the depot. Margaret and Thomas had to wait their turn. There were two men ahead of them and a pregnant woman who jiggled up and down, groaning anxiously. From here they could see the road. Margaret shivered in the gusting wind. A car's approaching headlights lit up the bus.

"Oh no," said one of the men in line as a black car with a gold star on the door pulled off the road with a squeal of brakes. "Not him again."

A square-bodied man in a tall sheriff's hat, high black boots, and big holstered gun hurried into the depot. A moment later he came out and climbed onto the bus.

"Looking for booze," the man said shaking his head. "And he'll keep every bottle he damn finds too!"

Thomas grabbed Margaret's hand with a nod toward the woods, but she pulled back. "He's looking for us," he hissed in her ear.

"No he's not."

"What if he is?"

The people in line were too interested in the sheriff's mission to notice the children disappear. They ran straight into the woods until they came to an oak tree so long ago fallen that a tall, spindly maple grew from its upended root system.

"Shh! Listen!" each warned the other through the stillness. The snow had suddenly stopped. They could hear the running water of a nearby stream. A clamor of squabbling crows broke out, then died. In the distance a car door slammed shut. They started toward the depot. Margaret complained that her feet were numb again. Thomas told her to whisper. Light shimmered through the coated trees. "And I'm not sitting with that lady again," she warned.

"You liked her well enough, telling her everything there was to know," he whispered.

"She asked me!" she cried sounding relieved, as if she'd been expecting that rebuke.

"Daddy's told you a hundred thousand times just cuz some people're nosy doesn't mean you have to tell them anything."

"I got us a sandwich, didn't I?"

"Wait! Wait!" Thomas burst through the tree line, waving at the departing bus.

. . .

His hand ached. They had been walking for a long time. Twenty miles anyway, Margaret insisted. Thomas knew better than argue. He was cold and too tired for any more of her temper. With the slightest disagreement she would cry. Their pace was even slower now, with them stopping every five or ten minutes so Margaret could warm her feet. His were just about frozen numb when a car pulled up behind them.

The driver was a skinny man with gaps between his teeth and a big hook nose. His bushy hair had been so badly cut that chunks were missing in back. The minute the door opened they could smell the liquor. He drove with a bottle between his thighs. He'd take a drink from time to time, wipe his mouth then start talking again. His only question had been to ask where they were going. Collerton, Massachusetts, well, that shouldn't be too hard to find, he'd said agreeably enough, then continued his soliloquy. He drove erratically, as if fueled by strange energies, veering suddenly onto narrow bumpy lanes, then finding his way back onto wider roads again. He'd been all over the world, first as a child with missionary parents, then as a soldier. Both his brothers were important men in Washington, D.C. But they were really small-minded men with no love in their hearts. This country was falling apart before their very eyes, men out of work, their families in rags, but what was the government doing? Nothing. Nothing, at all, he said. But he had a plan. He knew exactly how to end all this deprivation and suffering. His brothers wouldn't listen, so he'd gone straight to the White House. He had demanded an audience with President Roosevelt. It was his duty as an American citizen to tell him how to stop the misery. But for his trouble he'd been thrown in jail. Kept for thirty days and nights in a cell with common criminals, thieves, and murderers. "But now I'm safe," he declared. He reached under his seat and held up a long-bladed knife.

Thomas cringed back. His hand closed over the door handle. The winding mountain road was dark, lit from time to time by the onrushing headlights. Curled in a ball Margaret slept in back. Not to worry, they were in good hands, the man said. He pushed the knife back under his seat.

"My father's in jail," Thomas said in a bid for kinship, empathy, anything to spare their lives, but the man said nothing. Thomas's eyes burned for sleep, but he forced them wide as possible.

"Lord a'mighty, will you look at that. It's a sign!" the man said as he hit the brake. In the middle of the road the eyes of a twelve-point buck shone like two rubies. The man hunched over the wheel, whistling softly between his teeth. The stately creature did not move. "We could live off the meat for a winter. Make shirts and shoes out of the hide." He reached down for his knife. "What d'ya say?" he whispered, not moving, staring at the deer.

"No," Thomas said.

"Go on! Git!" The horn blared and in a leap the great buck disappeared into the black night.

"Thomas?" Margaret sat up suddenly. "What is it?"

"Nothing, little sister. Nothing at all," the man said. He began to drive again.

Margaret did not lie down. She asked if they were near Collerton yet. The man grunted something. The brief sleep had invigorated Margaret. She said they were going to live with their mother. She worked in a big factory. Margaret said she was very excited because she hadn't seen her mother since last winter.

Thomas's heavy eyes sank to the cadence of Margaret's voice through the dark as they sped round curves, lower down into the flattening valleys, the mountains shrinking in their wake.

"Thomas!" she whispered.

He awakened, confused, cold with hunger and fear. They were parked by the side of the road. The man was gone. "Where is he?"

"Going to the bathroom."

"Where?" He couldn't see out; branches pressed against his window.

"I don't know. He said not to look."

He squinted through the windshield. "It's so dark. I can't see."

"No, don't!" Her hand gripped his shoulder as she tried to pull him back. "It's him the sheriff's looking for. That's why he went on the bus!"

"How do you know?"

"I told about the sheriff and that's why we were walking. And he said, no, they're after him. They always are. Every place he goes."

"Why? What'd he do?"

"I don't know. I didn't ask. I was too scared."

"But you told him all about us, didn't you?"

"No! Not about Jesse-boy. Not that part. Thomas!" she gasped.

The door opened. The man scrambled in and drove onto the road. "Here you go." He handed back a stale soda cracker. He took another from his pocket and gave it to Thomas, then one for himself.

"Thank you," they both said quietly.

The eastern sky was brightening. A rim of pinkish light outlined the mountains behind them. Thomas kept looking over. Finally he said, "Your hand's bleeding."

The man sucked one knuckle, then the other. "Must've cut it on the window."

No one said anything for a few minutes.

"I got a sore hand too," Thomas said, cupping it to his chest, begging God to please, please help them.

"We almost there?" Margaret's voice was a small rasp.

"You could keep on going with me," the man said. "I got two brothers in Mexico. Very important men down there. They have horses. Wild mustangs. Hundreds. So many, you can each have two or three of your own if you want."

"Thanks, but we better not," Thomas said with a rueful shake of his head.

"Suit yourself," the man said. "But you won't get such a chance again. No sir, not in a blue moon you won't."

"Up there!" Margaret pointed over the seat. "The sign. See? It says Collerton."

"Probably just as well though," the man continued, heedless of the passing sign. "I'm not particularly welcome anymore. Last time I went they locked me up in the bunkhouse. Thirty days they kept me under the boiling hot sun with no food or water. In a dirt-floor, one-room cell with common criminals, thieves, and murderers. Banditos, all of us!" he cried with sudden pitched laughter.

"Turn here!" Thomas directed, and the man jerked the wheel. He turned onto a broad, treeless street with houses so near one another they almost touched. They hadn't driven too far when they came to an enormous brick factory. The tall iron gates in front were being opened by a man in a wool cap with earmuffs. There was a large whistle around his neck. Their driver eyed the man uneasily.

"Look for Common Street. Thirty-four Common Street," Thomas said, repeating the long-remembered address on his mother's letter.

"He's watching me," the man said, speeding off.

Men hurried along the sidewalk on their way to work. Some carried lunch pails, others, buckets with a cloth on top. A milk wagon came down the street, then stopped.

The milkman jumped down and filled his wire carrier with bottles of milk from ice-filled crates in the back of the wagon. He left the bottles on the doorsteps of the next two houses.

"Stop here!" Thomas said.

"I can't, they'll find me!" the man said, his voice breaking.

"Let us out quick then. We won't say anything!"

"Promise?"

"Yes! I promise! We both do! We promise, we do," Thomas kept shouting before the car finally pulled to the curb. Front and back doors opened at once and they leaped onto the sidewalk, running back toward the milk wagon as the crazy man sped off.

Common Street was only a few blocks away, the milkman said. He gave directions, then asked who they were looking for.

"Irene Talcott," Thomas said and couldn't help smiling to be so near with her name and his breath in the air. The milkman shook his head. He knew the address, but not the name. Thirty-four Common was a rooming house. People came and went; new faces all the time. Following the milkman's directions Thomas hurried around the corner.

"Wait!" Margaret squealed at his heels. "You're going too fast. Slow down!"

He couldn't, so he grabbed her hand and tugged her, running alongside.

11

THIRTY-FOUR COMMON STREET WAS A WEATHER-BEATEN, three-story house with different colored curtains in each window. As the children ran up the front steps a skinny black dog charged out from under the porch, barking at them from below. Margaret cringed against Thomas as he reached for the brass knocker. "You're not afraid of dogs," he said, noting the paper sign nailed to the door:

NO BEGGARS
NO HANDOUTS
NO WORK

"But that's at home. And I don't know him."

"He doesn't know you either." He had already banged the knocker three times. Just as he went to lift it again, the door swung open.

"Go on! Go! Get out of here, you stupid dog!" the woman shouted, then peered out through puffy eyes. "Do you know what time it is?"

"No, ma'am."

"It's six o'clock in the morning and some're still sleeping!"

"Oh. I'm sorry."

She gave a wave of disgust. "What is it? What do you want?" She had orangey hair and thin painted eyebrows of the same bright hue as her hair. Her black robe was covered with cat hair.

"Is Mrs. Talcott here?"

"*Mrs.* Talcott, is it? Her odd eyebrows arched. She seemed amused.

"Yes. Her first name's Irene."

"And who're you?"

"Thomas. I'm her son. And this here's Margaret. She's my sister. We're here to see our mother." He grinned.

Chuckling, the lady bit her lip and shook her head. "Well, what d'ya know. Can't say I'm surprised though." She leaned down and pinched Margaret's cheek. "But I know someone who will be," she teased delightedly.

Staring at the woman, Margaret rubbed her cheek.

The woman brought them inside. They followed her down a dank hallway past a parlor where two shawled women huddled in front of a coal stove with cats on their laps. Thomas and Margaret glanced toward every passing room, expecting to see their mother. The woman led them to the kitchen. A dark-skinned young woman with haphazardly bunned hair stirred a pot of cereal on the stove. She glanced back and asked if they were eating. The woman asked if they wanted some porridge.

"Sure," Thomas said. He and Margaret sat at the long wooden table and the sulky kitchen girl served them. The cereal was thin and flavorless but hot, and it felt good going down. The woman sat across from them. "These're Irene's children, Millie!" she called to the quickly turning kitchen girl. "She never told me she had such beautiful children. She ever tell you, Millie?"

"No!" The kitchen girl stifled a laugh.

They were almost finished when she asked where their father was.

"In—" Margaret started to say.

"Belton," Thomas said quickly. Belton, the woman repeated. Where was that? Vermont, he said. Why was their mother here and their father way up there, the woman asked, leaning close. She came down to work, Thomas said. In a big factory that makes cloth, he added. The woman smiled and tilted her head, as if she were trying to catch them in a lie. Did they know who owned that big factory? she asked.

"No," he said.

Margaret's spoon clinked as she scraped the last bit of cereal from her bowl.

"Louis Dexter. Mr. Louis Dexter," the woman said with a knowing glance at the kitchen girl, who had moved to the table. Arms folded, she stood over them, listening closely.

"He's the boss?" Thomas said.

"I'll say he's the boss, all right," the woman said. She and the kitchen girl smirked at each other.

"I have to go the bathroom," Margaret leaned close and whispered in Thomas's ear.

"Don't be telling secrets, you rude little thing," the woman scolded.

"She said she has to go to the bathroom." He stared at her. "That's all she said."

"Go show her, Millie," the woman said. Sullenness descended over the kitchen girl as she hurried Margaret from the kitchen. "So, what're ya here for, you two? You gonna be living with your mother now? Or just visiting, are ya?" Again came that calculating sideward gaze.

"Is my mother here?"

"No," the woman said. "What about your father, is he coming?"

"Well, is she at work then?"

She covered her mouth with a prim little giggle. "Depends on what you call work."

"What do you mean?"

A tall, skinny man shuffled sleepily into the kitchen. Suspenders hung down the sides of his baggy brown pants. "Mornin', Miss Noyes," he mumbled and sat down with his head in his hands.

"Serve yourself, Seamus. Can't you see? Millie's not here," she said irritably, then leaned into the boy. "Your mother left. She doesn't live here anymore."

. . .

Thomas and Margaret climbed halfway up the hill. He stopped to check the paper again. Twelve Kressey Court, the woman had written. Third right up the hill, then on the left was Kressey Court. There were six houses on the horseshoe-shaped street. Number twelve was the smallest.

"We're here," he said. There were no sidewalks and the road was cobbled with paving blocks. Breathless, they stood in the street looking up at the pale blue cottage. The door was gray as were the narrow shutters on the small diamond-paned windows. There was a black iron fence in front. Margaret rushed to open the gate, but couldn't. He ordered her to stand back so he could reach the latch. But it was locked. He swung himself over the fence, snagging his sore hand on the sharp tips of the wrought iron.

"What about me?" Margaret struggled to get a leg over, but wasn't tall enough.

"Stand on the lower bar there. Arms around my neck. Okay, climb up and get your foot between the points. Okay, now the other one." He stepped back with his arms out as she balanced, waiting. They had made it this far. Of course the last obstacle would be easy. She laughed and leaped into his arms.

Thomas rang the bell. They could hear its jarring buzz from here.

"Don't!" Margaret said before he could ring it again. "Mommy hates loud things. She'll be mad."

"I know that." He scowled at her. "I was just going to knock, that's all."

They both stared up at the door.

"Well, go ahead, knock on it then!" Margaret said impatiently.

"Don't tell me what to do. I'm waiting." He rocked back on his heels. "We have to wait."

"For what?"

"For Mommy! You're supposed to give people time to come, you know." Hands behind his back, he watched the door.

Margaret watched until she could stand it no longer. She rang the bell, holding her finger to the button.

"Louis, I was in—" came the soft, familiar voice with the opening door.

"Mommy!" Margaret screamed, springing at the tall, slender woman. She threw her arms around her mother, burying her face in the folds of her nightdress. It was so sheer that Thomas looked away in embarrassment.

For a moment all Irene Talcott could utter was their names. Margaret. Thomas. Repeating them in uneasy bewilderment. "How did you get here?" She quickly closed the door behind them, as if on others yet to come. The bus. And then a ride, Margaret said, clinging to her mother's hand. "With a crazy man," she added, making the awkward moment even more so. "He had a knife and he probably killed somebody to get us crackers."

"I don't understand." She looked at her son.

"Well we had to!" Margaret declared in a torrent of details too elusive for her mother, who kept blinking down at the unkempt dervish who had landed in her little parlor with the pink tub chairs. Margaret went on about life with the Farleys, the terrible heat of the rooms, so dry she could barely swallow some days, and not being able to go to a real school, and Jesse-boy, he—

"Margaret!" Thomas interrupted. "You're doing all the talking. I haven't said anything to Mommy yet." Irene looked at him. They both looked at him.

"So go ahead and say something," Margaret said in exasperation. "You're just standing there."

At that instant Irene seemed embarrassed, as if aware for the first time how revealing her nightdress was. Just a minute, she said then hurried into the next room. She returned, tying the belt of a white satin robe. She sat the children down, one in each chair, then asked how they had come. And why.

"To see you," Thomas said, bristling.

Margaret looked hurt. The attention she had desired for so long was on her brother now, its great beam eclipsing her. Thomas spoke hesitantly, though cautiously. He could sense his mother's discomfort. And yet, no matter their disappointment, no matter the surges of relief and fear each was feeling, they could not take their eyes off their mother.

In a loved one's beauty, there is solace, comfort in its presence, and the hope—no, the belief—the certainty that possession of so fine an ornament might be sustenance enough. Here it was, at last, the object of all yearning. They stared, relieved. She was more beautiful than ever before. Her dark, loose hair fell softly about her face. Her deep-set eyes were startlingly bright, bluer than the clearest sky, her cheekbones high, her long imperious nose perfect, her skin milky beneath the high color of her emotions, her wide mouth full and parting easily with the suggestion, promise, hope of a smile. And though it might as quickly quiver to nothing, it left its beholder hungry, needing more. They both felt it, though they weren't aware of holding their breath, of such grinning, of yearning forward in their chairs, abstracting from her hand-wringing, tongue-tied bewilderment the real proof of her love for them.

When Thomas finished talking, telling everything in much the same careening, out-of-sequence garble as Margaret, Irene finally spoke. "So your father sent you here?" Sighing, she closed her eyes.

"No," Thomas said. He went over it again, all their unhappiness in the different places they'd been. And so because their father was in jail they had nowhere else to go, but here. To their mother.

"He did this." From the delicate loveseat she spoke quietly, her voice dulled by sadness. They had heard and seen her like this before. The death of baby James had cut the heart and the life right out of her. Day after day she had sat this way, for weeks, contained and staring, numb with loss, not seeming to see or hear them, the living children, the only ones she had left.

"But it'll be all right, Mommy." Margaret hurried to take her mother's hand, to comfort her again as she had after baby James. "Because now we're here. We can stay with you."

Irene's head lifted. She did not look at her daughter, but past her, across the room at the wall or door, the street beyond, the sky. Thomas refused to follow her gaze, instead watched her as if the strength of his stare might penetrate something, put him in her heart.

"No. You can't. You can't stay here."

Margaret began to cry. Irene touched her daughter's shoulder, less a gesture of comfort than of resignation.

"Why?" he demanded. "Why can't we?"

She looked at him, finally. Her lovely mouth parted then trembled shut for a moment. "You must be hungry," she said in a shaky voice. "I'll get you something to eat."

. . .

They had been with her for two days. She seemed happier, even laughing the way she used to whenever Margaret said or did something funny. "Oh! You remind me so much of Aunt Lena when we were little." They were playing old maid at the parlor table, and Margaret had just dropped her cards.

"I do?" Margaret seemed disappointed.

"Oh yes, she was always so impatient. So clumsy about certain things."

"I'm not clumsy." Margaret set the cards down.

Under the table Thomas gave her a mindful nudge.

"In a cute way," Irene tried to explain. "That's all I meant,

Margaret. Really. You're not clumsy in the way you do things. But . . . well, in the way you act sometimes, that's all I meant."

Margaret pushed back from the table. "I don't want to play anymore," she announced.

"In the way people think of you," Irene called after the footsteps hurrying up the narrow back stairs. "It's endearing," she said, looking now at Thomas. "I didn't mean anything bad by it. I didn't mean to hurt her." She quickly drank the rest of her tea. Margaret's footsteps clomped overhead. He was glad. Now it could be just him and his mother.

She had left them alone for an hour this morning while she ran errands. They were to sit quietly and not answer the door if anyone came. She had returned with beef from the butcher for the stew they had just eaten and molasses for the gingerbread cooling on the windowsill. She stood up with her cup and saucer. "I sent Aunt Lena a letter today," she said on her way into the tiny kitchen.

"You did?" He followed her to the doorway. The kitchen was little more than a pantry with a sink and stove. The icebox was in the back shed. The one bedroom, hers, was just off the tiny parlor. For the last two nights he and Margaret had slept in an iron bed in the windowless, steeply pitched attic room above.

"You have to go back. You can't stay here." As she spoke she kept busy, drying knives, forks, spoons with careful scrutiny of every blade, tine, and hollow, scrubbing with her towel. "It's not a good situation. I'm all by myself. It wouldn't work. I just couldn't do it."

"But we'd be good. I swear, I promise. We wouldn't get

in trouble and I . . . I could help. I could bring up the coal and run all the errands." He looked frantically about. "And sweep and clean, and I can mind Margaret until you get home from work. I did that all summer, and anyway we'd be in school so we wouldn't be that much of a bother."

She shook her head and continued wiping, their three glasses, three plates. Even these were too much bother for her, he thought.

"I can do that. I can wash the dishes and dry them and put them away. Here, I'll do that." He reached for her towel.

She turned away and buried her face in the towel, crying softly.

"Don't send us back. Please?"

"You don't understand," she finally gasped. "I can't. I just can't."

She was right. He didn't understand.

. . .

In the morning he and Margaret ran downstairs to warm themselves at the parlor stove. Refreshed by sleep Margaret had either forgotten or forgiven her mother's criticism. She was very happy. She wanted to play outside. Three girls lived in a brown house on the other end of Kressey Court. The middle one was about Margaret's age. Yesterday afternoon, from the window, she had watched them playing ball and jumping rope. This morning she intended to go out and introduce herself, she told Thomas. He reminded her that the girls would be going to school. Well, when they came home, she said.

Irene emerged from her bedroom wearing a green dress

with a wide lace collar and matching cuffs. It wasn't at all like dresses she used to wear, Thomas noted.

"Oh, Mommy, you look so pretty!" Margaret touched the lacy cuff. "Where are you going?" Margaret followed her into the kitchen, where Irene ladled oatmeal into bowls for them. "Are you going to work ?" Margaret persisted.

She wasn't going anywhere, she said. As a matter of fact someone was coming today. A friend of hers. Coming here.

Carrying the sugar bowl, Margaret followed her to the square table in the corner of the parlor. She wished she could get dressed up too, Margaret said. Would it be a tea party like Mommy had gone to once at Mrs. Farley's with the Grange ladies? No, Irene said. She poured warm milk over their cereal, then set the pitcher on the blue sideboard. The furniture, like the little cottage itself, was painted in vivid colors. The whimsy of green doors with yellow moldings, rose window casings, and violet sills was actually an economy of left-over paint, dregs of the many cans in the caretaker's shed, Irene had been quick to explain when Margaret declared this the prettiest place she had ever lived in. It seemed to Thomas that his mother was always pulling them back to earth.

It wasn't a tea party, Irene was saying. Just a visit, that was all. Mr. Dexter would be coming by in the afternoon. And when he did, the minute the doorbell rang, they were to run straight upstairs and stay there, quietly, without a sound until he was gone. Why, Margaret asked, disappointed. Thomas was relieved, but puzzled.

"Because. Because I said so," Irene told her.

"But why?" Margaret badgered. "Doesn't he like kids?"

"Because," Irene answered. "Mr. Dexter owns Kressey

Court. All these houses are his and he's agreed to let *me* stay here. Not my children."

"Why doesn't he want us here?" Margaret asked, getting on her mother's nerves once again, Thomas could tell, her snappish little voice persistent as ever. "He doesn't even know us!"

"Please, Margaret," Irene said distractedly. "Just eat."

"We don't break things. The whole time we were at the Farleys' we never broke anything. Did we?"

"Well, nothing important anyway." He wiggled his nose to remind her of Jesse-boy's battered nose.

"Nothing much he means." Margaret giggled.

"You make the best oatmeal," he told his mother before Margaret could say more.

While they ate, their mother moved about fretfully, straightening doilies, plucking infinitesimal motes of lint from the upholstery, raking her long fingers through the fringe to smooth the dog-eared carpet flat. She was very quiet. She had a lot on her mind. They too grew quiet and watchful. As the day went on the weight of Mr. Dexter's impending visit pressed as heavily upon them as her.

. . .

Before the doorbell was even rung, the clang of the iron gate announced the visitor.

"Upstairs! Go now! Hurry!" She shoved them up the steep, narrow stairs. "Sit quietly," she called then closed the door below.

Knees drawn to their chins, they sat on the bed. Margaret exhaled, expecting her breath to vaporize in the air the way it did in early morning, but the afternoon sun lay full on the eaves. Below them a man was talking at length. His voice droned like a faint rumble beneath the rough floorboards. If Irene did say anything it was too soft to hear. Every now and again they could make out a few words. Fingertips splayed against the floor, Thomas hung partway off the bed, listening. Mr. Dexter was telling about a party he had attended in Boston over the weekend. Apparently at his brother-in-law's.

". . . much too lavish though, considering the . . . rather amazing how desperate Archie is to keep up . . . even had his . . . kept thinking about you . . . got this for you . . ."

"Oh, Louie! Thank you!" Irene said, the details of her gratitude murmurous and indistinct.

"What's she saying?" Margaret pestered from above. Not tall enough to hang down to the floor, she had wearied of being waved off for quiet.

". . . don't have much time . . ." Mr. Dexter said.

Irene's voice answered, trailed off. A door closed.

"Did he leave?" Margaret whispered.

"Shh!"

"I don't hear anything."

"Shh!"

"Let's go down. C'mon!"

"No, listen."

"What's that?"

"Something, I don't know." He dangled over the musty mattress, listening, straining to hear the not unfamiliar rhythmic struggle that was more vibration now than sound to his blood-pulsing ears.

"Is that him? Is he laughing?" Margaret whispered.

"No."

Voices gone, all sound ceased. Something cold and

dagger-sharp hung in the air. If he moved it would destroy everything. There was only uneasiness, that moment of revelation when all is understood though nothing is known. Yes. Of course. But what? The violation was too vast. It changed everything.

. . .

"Forty-five, forty-six, forty-seven, forty-eight, forty-nine, fifty," Irene counted as she brushed her daughter's hair. The silver brush had been his gift, the etched mirror bearing Margaret's reflection part of the set. Irene's cheeks were flushed. She was happy, laughing easily at Margaret's imitation of old Bibeau bellowing at Gladys for being so homely she'd never find a man. "Poor Gladys," Irene sighed.

"She never even wears lipstick," Margaret said, gazing back at her mother.

Thomas knelt on the floor moving jigsaw puzzle pieces around. He was sure some were missing, but there was nothing else to play with. Now that Margaret had her mother, she had no need of toys or games. He felt excluded from their easy companionship.

"She's got hairs on her chin." Margaret shuddered. "And she even wears men's boots."

"Gladys was never very feminine. She just didn't care about those things," Irene sighed again.

"She's a good cook." Thomas sat back on his heels. "And she knows how to fish."

"Yes." Irene glanced at her son. "I'm sure she does."

"Old Bibeau told Daddy he should've married Gladys. *She* never would've run off, he said." Margaret's prattle was belied by the steadiness of her gaze.

Thomas leaned closer, peering at the pieces. The blues

and whites were all the sky, but there was no way of telling where the sky began and where it ended.

. . .

Early the next morning they went to the grocer's with their mother. Their appetites amazed her. She had forgotten how much food two growing children required, she said, uneasily counting the coins in her cloth purse. Thomas asked if she had enough. Enough to be concerned, she answered in her perplexing way where nothing was clear or tenable. There was still their five dollars, but to admit that might only buy them two tickets back home. Even Margaret was unaware of the bulge in his instep.

After enough days cooped up in the cottage together, Irene had finally relented. She let them go out to play. If anyone asked, they were to say only that they were visiting. Under no circumstances could they say they were her children. It wasn't allowed. Please, she said closing the door; they mustn't betray her.

It was very cold, but they were glad to be outside again. Neither one had mittens; Margaret had left hers in the crazy man's car. They walked through the patchy circle of dead weeds that made up the courtyard. In a U-shape around it, the houses stood close together, closer than any back home, all owned by the Dexter Mill Company. Three were rented by supervisors and foremen at the mill. A worker whose hand had been mangled in one of the mill's machines occupied a house. One stood empty. Set back and smaller than the others was their mother's cottage.

They had ventured as far as the busy street beyond. Here, people spoke a different language and lived in three-story tenements even closer together than the houses on Kressey

Court. Italians. Thomas nudged Margaret as two ancient women in long black dresses passed by. A basket of red and yellow peppers dangled from one woman's arm. Margaret asked Thomas if they were apples. Italian ones, he told her confidently.

Children began to pass them. School had let out. Thomas and Margaret turned, enjoying the steady stream around them. When they got to Kressey Court some of the children were already there. Two younger boys ran around the courtyard whacking shriveled pods off the milkweed stems with sticks. A cluster of girls watched Thomas and Margaret approach. The tallest girl was very skinny. The first to speak, she asked if they were from the cottage. Grinning, Margaret said they were. But they were just visiting, Thomas was quick to add. That's all, just visiting. Who? the girls asked in unison. That lady in there? the taller girl asked. Yes, they said with Margaret grinning, exhilarated as much by their rapt attention as by the secret they kept.

"Is she nice?" one asked with a wary glance at the cottage.

"Oh yes, very nice," Margaret said with Thomas nodding.

"We can't go over there," the smallest one said.

"Her name's Miss Talcott," another said.

"No, it's—" Thomas caught himself. "It's Irene."

The gray sky was lowering. All was drab and dingy, all but the pale blue cottage.

"The shady lady, that's what my father calls her," the youngest one said. The others were uneasy. They'd better go. They had to get home.

. . .

Mr. Dexter was a very nice man, she told them. She enjoyed talking about him. Thomas stiffened into silence whenever she did. Her cheeks pinkened and her eyes glowed just saying his name. Louie, she had called him that day, but to them he was Mr. Dexter. Mr. Dexter was letting her live here until something better came along. What was that? A better situation, she said. A job? Well, something that suited her more. What did she mean? She had first heard about the mill from that Mr. Hemmings. He'd passed himself off as one of the bosses, when he was only a salesman. That had been disappointing enough when she got there with just the few things she'd been able to fit into her little suitcase, but then she found out how difficult working in a mill could be. Too many rough people. It hadn't been a good situation. Mr. Dexter had come into the office one day when the head bookkeeper had been screaming at her. Swearing and saying the most vulgar things. She had made the mistakes, but only because she had misunderstood his accent. Ordering him to stop, Mr. Dexter took her aside and tried to calm her. She couldn't stop crying. She was sorry, but she wasn't used to their system, all the double entries and confusing postings. Or to such coarse people, she would later confide. Maybe she should go back home. Where she came from, people were plain and hardworking, but they showed respect for a woman. They knew how to treat a lady. The way she told it, it sounded like a fairy tale.

The gingerbread had never risen, but they ate it anyway. She made applesauce pudding so sour they curled up with stomachaches all through the night. Every day she hurried to the mailbox, but there was no letter from Lena. Mr. Dexter came again, midafternoon as before, his visit, this time, longer, harder for Margaret to endure in stillness on the attic bed. She whispered how bored she was, how she couldn't stand it a minute more. The silent ruckus over, the door opened, closed again. His voice droned below.

"I hate that smell," she whispered as the rich cigar smoke seeped through every crack and seam. "I'm going to sneeze," she warned and Thomas pushed a pillow into her face. She pinched his arm. Enraged, he pinched her back as hard as he could, angry with her and his mother, but she couldn't cry out because he pressed down on the pillow. Grunting, she kicked her legs and flailed her arms.

"I'm sorry," he hissed, lifting the edge of the pillow.

"I can't breathe," she gasped and tried to free herself. "You're smothering me!"

"Shh. Shh!" He lay next to her and begged her not to cry, to be quiet so Mr. Dexter wouldn't hear them. So they could stay. She wanted to stay, didn't she?

She covered her mouth and cried, sobbing into her hands. He stared up at the cold glints of sunlight through the gaps in the frosted roof boards.

12

MR. DEXTER VISITED TWO OR THREE AFTERNOONS A WEEK and never came weekends. On the sofa table next to his cut-glass brandy decanter was a green marble ashtray. Yesterday's half-smoked cigar was still in it. The colder the cottage grew, the worse the cigar smelled. Thomas offered to dump it out in the ash bin, but Irene said she'd take care of it in a while. Actually, she liked the smell, she admitted.

"It stinks." Margaret held her nose.

"That's because you're young." Irene moved her red checker forward. She had come home with the board yesterday. "You won't think so when you're older," she said with a little smile.

"Yes, I will." Margaret leaned over the table, watching.

Irene reached up and patted her cheek. "You'll see."

"See what?" Thomas made his move.

"Well, that things change. From when you're young, that is."

"Did you like the way cigars smelled when you were like me?" Margaret asked.

"But I wasn't like you, Margaret," Irene said absently.

"Yes, you were!" Margaret stood so quickly the board

shifted. She was crestfallen. "Everyone says so, that I look just like you."

"What I meant was in some ways we're very different. You've always been such a happy little girl, and . . . and I never was."

"I'm not happy!" Margaret protested.

"Yes, you are. You're so sweet and outgoing. People have always loved that about you, Margaret." Irene leaned back and held Margaret's hand.

"I just do that," Margaret said. "So people will like us."

Irene's mouth opened, but nothing came out for a moment. "People like you," she said weakly. "They like the both of you."

"No, they don't. They never want us around much. Like old Bibeau. He didn't like me too much, but he liked Thomas. And then some people like me, but they don't like him, so then I try and make them like me even more so we can stay."

"Oh, Margaret." Irene kept patting her hand. She shook her head, with a look of astonishment as if she'd had no idea Margaret could feel such things.

"Will you come back home with us? Please? Please, Mommy?"

Thomas nervously pushed his checker back and forth between two squares. So there it was. Right out there.

"I can't," she quietly answered.

"Why not? You don't even have a job. You just live here, that's all. We could go home and you could just live *there*. With us."

"I couldn't. No. I . . . I couldn't."

. . .

When they went to bed the rain was falling steadily, the close pattering on the roof a comfort, like rain on the tent when their father had been near. They were sound asleep. The ringing came from far, far away. Each stirred, then fell back to sleep. The wind was howling now. As the night had grown colder the rain had turned to wet, heavy flakes. Thomas's eyes opened with the banging. Outside, someone called loudly. He jumped up and started down the stairs. He pressed against the icy wall. His mother opened the front door.

Mr. Dexter sounded drunk. His voice was loud and slurred. His key had fallen in the snow. He had been at the club. But the roads were terrible. Glare ice. He couldn't drive any farther, so lucky girl, here he was. All hers, for the rest of the night. At bedtime his mother always left the door at the bottom of the steps open to let heat up. Thomas could hear every word. His mother tried to whisper, but Mr. Dexter demanded that she speak up; he couldn't hear a damn thing she was saying.

"But what about your wife? She'll be worried."

"No, she won't. She'll be glad!"

"But what will you tell her?"

"I'll tell her what I always tell her, and that's whatever the hell I wanna tell her."

Thomas crept down three more steps. The street lamp shone through the window. Mr. Dexter's coat and hat had been thrown over one of the small pink chairs. He had pulled off his tie and was unbuttoning his shirt. Thomas was surprised to see such a small, stoop-shouldered man. He had oiled black hair, a thin mustache, and he was the same height as Irene.

"Louie." Irene's arms were folded over her nightgown. "You have to go. What if your wife . . ."

"Oh! Oh!" He advanced on her, laughing. "I see. You're not happy to see me."

"No. I'm happy to see you. I'm just . . . I'm surprised, that's all."

"You didn't expect me, so maybe you've got another visitor. Who is it?" He threw open her bedroom door. "Who's in there? What son of a bitch has crawled into my—"

She watched from the doorway as he ripped the blankets from her bed. "Louie! Stop it! See! Of course there's no one here." She picked up his tie from the floor and carried it into him with his hat and coat. "You shouldn't be here like this."

"If it wasn't for me, *you* wouldn't be here!" he growled. "Maybe *you're* the one who should leave!"

"All I meant was . . . well, you're in a terrible state."

"A terrible state!" he bellowed. There was the sound of a slap. And then the bedroom door was quickly closed.

Thomas ran to the bottom of the stairs. It was a minute before he realized that it wasn't his mother crying, but Mr. Dexter. Between high, gasping sobs he begged Irene to forgive him. It would never happen again. Ever. He promised. Of course she forgave him, she assured him.

"I just wanted to be with you, to stay," he wept. "That's all I wanted."

"Yes, I know. And now you are. Oh, my dear, sweet Louie, now you are."

It seemed only moments before his heedless, fleshy snore exploded in the room. Thomas tiptoed back up to bed. "It was Mr. Dexter," he whispered, though Margaret lay so still with her back to him he thought she was asleep.

"I know," she whispered and curled tighter on the edge of the bed.

. . .

The next day they played outside. Mr. Dexter had left at dawn. The deep ruts of his spinning tires ran along the fence. Margaret and Thomas rolled snow until they had the base of their snowman. Margaret wore her mother's cloth gloves, but Thomas's hands were purple with cold. He kept stopping to blow them warm.

"Hey!" It was the tall, skinny girl. She wore a purple coat that hung over her shoes. With every step she had to lift the hem. She asked what they were doing.

"What's it look like we're doing?" Thomas said, shoulders hunched and shivering, fists deep in his pockets. Now, Margaret was rolling the chest.

"I'm just trying to make friends, that's all," the girl said with narrowing eyes.

"We're making a snowman." Margaret turned and smiled. "But there's not too much snow."

"Want me to help?"

"Sure!" Margaret said, drowning out her brother's no.

The girl helped Margaret roll the snow until it was big enough to set on the base. Her name was Clementine, she said as she and Margaret packed snow into all the crevices. Her hands were also bare. She had two older brothers and two younger brothers. Her father's hand had practically been cut off at work last year, so now he stayed home. Her mother worked. Six days a week. She cleaned a big house over in Dearborn. Mr. Pratt sold cars, Fords. The Pratt family was so rich they'd wear something one time and then throw it out just because they were sick of it. Like this coat she had on, it used to be Connie Pratt's, she said proudly, then scowled at the lack of response. Didn't they know who Connie Pratt was?

No, Margaret said. They didn't know anyone. They weren't from around here. They were from Vermont, she added. Clementine asked if they were going to live here now or if they were—

"Visiting," Thomas interrupted.

"But we're gonna stay," Margaret said in a forceful tone. "We're gonna live here." She would not look at her brother.

"So that lady, she's your mother?" Clementine's eyes were wide.

Margaret nodded.

"So where's your father?" Clementine asked.

"He's not here," Thomas said with a searing look meant to silence his sister.

"Did he die?" Clementine asked.

"No!" Margaret turned to Thomas, troubled now, as if it might be true and no one had told her.

"You're awful nosy, what do you care?" he snapped at the girl. He began to pack more snow around the base. Black smoke poured out from the distant factory stacks. The sooty haze hung over the rooftops.

"I was just asking, that's all." Now, Clementine pounded snow on the opposite side.

"Well, I didn't ask about your father, how his hand got cut, did I?" he said.

"Go ahead, ask me, I don't care."

"None of my business," he grunted, working on her side now.

Margaret's face was drawn with worry. Something far worse than jail had happened to her father and no one wanted to tell her—it would explain everything.

"It got caught in a big machine. Most of it got cut off, so the doctor had to finish it the rest of the way. He almost died," Clementine said. For a moment the only sound was the thump, thump, thump of their hands against the dense snow. "Mr. Dexter's really rich. That mill." She pointed toward the biggest chimney. It towered over all the others. "That's the Dexter Mill. They have three houses. They even have horses. Somewhere, I don't know where, but they have five kids—just like us," she added with pride of the connection. "Mrs. Dexter's sick though. My mother said rich ladies shouldn't have too many kids, they're just not strong enough."

Margaret headed toward the door. She said she was going to go in now, she was cold. Saying he was cold too, Thomas started to follow.

"What about the head?" Clementine asked.

"You can do it," he called from the open door.

Clementine hiked up her coat and hurried after him. "I'm cold too, can I come in?"

"No." He shut the door.

. . .

Word spread quickly. The children were conscious of being watched. The women moved from window to window, alert for signs of trouble, eager for it—a woman like that. They looked away when Irene passed them on the street. Clementine had become the object of much attention. Vying for secrets only she possessed, the older children courted her, their mothers' jaws agape with the fanciful reports: her husband was such a cruel man that the pretty lady in the gatekeeper's cottage had run away and then sent for her children later. Terrified of their father the poor little things were grateful for Mr. Dexter's protection. They said he was the kindest man in the whole world. The Kressey Court mothers rolled their eyes. They knew all about *that* kind of kindness.

Again, the doorbell was ringing. Clementine's ravenous eye scoped against the glass sidelight. Irene was hanging clothes on the little line behind the cottage. Still no letter had come from Lena. Every day Irene waited for the mail delivery before she did anything. Today when none came she hurried outside to get the clothes on the line before it snowed. The doorbell rang again.

"You're not supposed to play with her," Thomas warned. Margaret headed for the door anyway. They were tired of being cooped up inside. Mostly though, each was tired of being constantly with the other. He grabbed her arm and pulled her back.

"I just want to see!" She struggled to get free.

"No!" He pushed her against the loveseat, so hard it moved a little.

"You hurt me!" She seized the checkerboard and threw it, checkers flying as the corner struck his collarbone. The quick, sharp blow was nothing; it was her weakness, her need to be with people and please them, the constant betrayal that so enraged him now, especially with the perfidious Clementine so near a threat. He picked up the board and threw it hard. Hard as he could. Damn her for ducking, he thought as it crashed into the globed parlor lamp.

"You broke it!" Margaret cried as the painted splinters landed at her feet.

Clementine was gone, either as bearer of this fresh report or simply in frustration. The back door opened and closed.

"What have you done?" Irene gasped. "What in God's name have you done?" Sobbing, she dropped to her knees and made a pile of the lavender shards as if they were sacred relics. "Don't you understand? This isn't my lamp. It's not mine. This isn't my house. Nothing here is mine. Nothing! Do you understand? Do you?" she demanded from her knees, her eyes sharp with tears. Distorted by panic her face was no longer pretty, but long and somehow foolish-looking. Pity stirred in Thomas, uneasily, shamefully. What about them? *They* were hers, but saying it would only heighten her desperation.

. . .

The next morning Irene went off with two letters to mail. She returned quickly, happier than she'd been in days. That afternoon Mr. Dexter's long visit cheered her even more. He wasn't at all upset about the lamp, she reported later. In fact, another would be arriving soon from Hetter's Furniture Store. Of course, she had taken the blame, she said, as if they should be grateful for her sacrifice for weren't they all in this together, the three of them, children, existing on the man's whim. She had told Mr. Dexter she had knocked it over when she'd been cleaning. As before, they stayed upstairs, so still, so quietly on the thin mattress that every sound in the little cottage came to them. Now neither questioned the rhythmic ruckus, the weepy little cries, then at last his profoundly grateful moan. Margaret held to her side of the bed, rigid and, Thomas knew, breathless. Soon, the cigar was lit and sourness seeped into Thomas's throat. They were as much intruders here as at old Bibeau's. More so here, perhaps. At least there Gladys had wanted them to stay.

. . .

A week had passed without a visit from Mr. Dexter. Margaret asked if he wasn't going to come anymore. Oh no, Irene said, he was just away. Traveling. But his trip would be over soon. Tomorrow, as a matter of fact, she called in to them. "Cinnamon sugar," she announced, as she came from the kitchen, stirring the amber granules in a crystal bowl. Late afternoon tea and toast were what people did now, she was telling them. In the past they had not been allowed anything before dinner.

"Fancy people?" Margaret asked in a shiver of delight as Irene sprinkled the toast.

"Very fancy people!" Irene placed the toast in front of her. Margaret giggled and took a bite, craving the hesitant glow of her mother's attention far more than the sweet toast. Thomas ate his and said little. Even this teatime was a wan and hollow exercise. Margaret would do anything to make her mother love them while his mother's happiness had little at all to do with them.

"Use your napkin, Tom. You're making grease marks on the chair," Irene said.

"It's such a pretty chair. Is that Mr. Dexter's too?" Margaret asked and he scowled at her.

"Oh yes. He had it all fixed up like this."

They watched her smile, her grateful gaze around the room.

"Is Mr. Dexter nice?" Margaret asked a little sadly.

"Oh, very nice. He's very kind." She made a sweeping motion with her hand. "Well, as you can see. He's very thoughtful. When I first came here I didn't know anyone. Other than that awful Mr. Hemmings. And then when the job turned out to be so horrible, it was Mr. Dexter who told me not to worry. That I could stay here." She smiled a little. "I thought that was so kind of him."

"Why didn't you come home?" Thomas blurted.

Her eyes lifted warily. "I couldn't." That said, neither spoke. His anger built, boiling inside.

"Does Daddy know Mr. Dexter?" Margaret asked, and Thomas stared, incredulous.

"No. No, he doesn't." She reached down and plucked something from the carpet. A bit of toast crust. She pressed it onto the rim of her dish. "They haven't met."

The gate clanged outside and the mailbox lid squealed open then closed. Irene rose quickly. Every day the mailman had passed the cottage by.

"Aunt Lena's not going to take us, you know. She's drunk all the time," he said before she could get to the door.

"Thomas! That's not a very nice thing to say," Irene said.

"Well it's true. She hides the bottles in the hamper. And Uncle Max doesn't want us there either."

The minute she opened her mouth he regretted having launched this attack. "Well, I'm sorry," she said, opening the door, "but something has to be done." She hurried outside.

"Stop it! You're going to make her mad!" Margaret hissed.

Irene sat at the table with the sheet of paper shaking in her grasp. The square, almost reproachful script on the envelope was Gladys's, but the letter it held had been written by their father—34 Common Street was crossed out. Kressey Court had been penciled on the bottom of the envelope. She closed her eyes and took a deep breath that seemed to hold her. They watched her. In the afternoon sun the cut-glass lines of the decanter reflected on the opposite wall, glinting like fine rainbows.

"Is Daddy coming?" Margaret finally asked.

There was a weight of stillness in the room, and once again Margaret tried to plow through it. "He could live here. With us. There's slaughtering jobs. There must be. Right, Thomas? We saw some farms, remember? On the way here. We did."

Irene rose stiffly and went into her bedroom. They picked up the letter and read it.

Their father was still in jail. Uncle Max had gone there demanding that Henry do something. Why had his and Irene's children become their problem? Margaret and Thomas were no one's *problems,* Henry wrote that he had told Max. They were their parents' responsibility. He could not make restitution to Farley for the damaged barn door or the "stolen" saw and tire, so he had no choice but serve out the six weeks left of his sentence.

I know how hard it must be to work and take care of them both, but it will have to be that way for a while longer. I wish there was something I could do, but I can't. Even Gladys is trying to help, but she doesn't have enough money to lend me yet. They can both take pretty good care of each other. Tell them I said to help with the chores and they will. As soon as I can I will come and get them.

Your husband,

T. Henry Talcott

P.S. Or you can bring them back here if that's what you want to do. Irene—I hope that you are all right and doing fine. I mean that. I really do.

13

EVEN THOMAS THOUGHT THEY SHOULD BE GOING TO SCHOOL now that they were here for good. He didn't want to end up like Billy Pfeiffer, who'd been absent so long one winter he never came back. Billy Pfeiffer did all right, skinning raccoons and selling the pelts, but he couldn't read or write so everyone said he was plain stupid, like every other Pfeiffer.

Margaret had walked down the hill with Clementine one day to see her school, the Burleigh. The next day Margaret took Thomas. He didn't like the look of it at all. Brick with granite over the tall windows and wide oak doors, it was the biggest school he'd ever seen. That's probably where they'd go, she said on their way back. Clementine's teacher had a mustache. Believe it or not, but her name was Miss Beardsley. When she thought no one was looking she clipped her chin whiskers with tiny little scissors—Clementine had seen her. Miss Beardsley would probably be his teacher too, because he and Clementine were in the same grade. Sixth.

"She's fourteen!" He stopped in his tracks.

"I know," Margaret said, admitting Clementine's oddness with a shrug. But Clementine was her friend and as she had at first with Jesse-boy she could not just overlook strangeness, but had to champion it when no one else would. Margaret was fast becoming the most sought after playmate on Kressey Court. To her credit, she insisted Clementine be included. The annoying Clementine may have been the neighborhood's first access to the mysterious goings-on inside the little cottage, but now they had Margaret herself. The little girls loved her, but no more than their mothers, who also took pleasure in her pretty face and held up her sweet manner as an example for their own children. Margaret Talcott always said thank you. She left her wet shoes on their doormats and fussed over their babies. A lovely little girl. Not at all unfriendly like the brother and mother. But why wasn't such a smart child in school? Both children for that matter. Might it have something to do with Mr. Dexter? He still came by his few afternoons a week in his elegant topcoat and his gleaming green car. They watched eagerly through their window curtains. Imagine, with children in the house. What did he care with all his money about anything or anyone. But their own mother—no wonder she hurried down the street looking straight ahead in her smart new hat and fur collared coat, while her children wore the same clothes day in and day out. Couldn't she at least patch the boy's worn trouser knees or mend the little girl's torn sleeve?

So when *will* you be going to school, Mrs. Ronan from next door asked. Pretty soon, Margaret answered, ever adroit, intriguing them with detail while revealing nothing: as soon as the papers came from their last school. Well, it hadn't even been a school, not a real one like the Burleigh, but private in a way. They'd had their own teacher and there'd only been the three of them, her brother, herself. And Jesse-boy. Of course, he always had to be in his wheelchair. Everyone called him Jesse-boy, which was strange because he wasn't really a boy anymore. Not like Thomas, that is. And so off she went every day, outside to play, happy to have so many friends clamoring for her attention while all the while she managed to hold herself remote enough that there was nothing of her they could possess.

Thomas sulked inside, drawing floor plans of enormous mansions. In addition to the ordinary rooms for living, his homes had rooms devoted exclusively to the closeting of shoes, the maintenance of tools, the storage of books. Shoe-Room, he penciled in tiny letters, below it, the Book-Room. In this rendition the Tool-Room was on the third floor. He drew a tiny square to indicate the sink where the gore could be washed from his father's tools.

"Book-Room," Irene said, looking over his shoulder. "You mean the library, don't you?"

He didn't know what he meant.

"That's what it's called," she said, pulling on long gray leather gloves, another gift brought yesterday. "Mr. Dexter has a library. In his house. All the walls are lined with books. The shelves go right up to the ceiling. And the furniture's all red leather. Except for the reading table, of course. That has big brass lamps with green glass shades."

The pencil lead dug into the paper. It was the most she'd said in days. Her silence had reminded him of her last bleak months at home. Even Margaret's brightest efforts hadn't been able to pierce her melancholy. Until now.

"Were you there?" he made himself ask, both hating and having to know. "In the library?"

"Yes." She jammed one finger between the other to work the glove down as far as it would go. "Just once though."

"Oh."

"To see about a job. Mr. Dexter thought I might like working there. Keeping track of things for the family. Household accounts, things like that."

He waited. "Did you get the job?" he asked carefully. Just her speaking to him was wonderful, even if it had to be about that snake, Dexter. However, hearing that he had brought her into his home frightened Thomas. That would have been worse, having to share her not just with Mr. Dexter, but with his family. With five other children.

"No," she sighed and picked up her purse. "She didn't want me. His wife, that is."

Was she smiling? Yes. She was. With what? The irony of it? Or in some sense of triumph, that in the end, she'd still managed to be available to him. Her touch was light on his shoulder. "Just so you'll know, Thomas. I can't say this to Margaret. She's too young, she doesn't understand. But I had to leave. It wasn't right, I knew it wasn't. I knew how awful it would be for you and your sister, but I still had to. I was so afraid, but I knew if I stayed something terrible would happen."

Something terrible, him hating her, that's what she meant. That's what had driven her away. Every bad thing he'd ever done and said to her. To his sister, his father, everyone. He held his breath as she continued. "It was like . . . like dying inside."

"I'm sorry, Mommy," he whispered, but she didn't seem to hear, so determined was she to explain.

"Always pretending. Always wanting something else and

feeling so trapped. It really was. Oh, I shouldn't be telling you any of this. I'm sorry. But I just want you to know, not a day went by that I didn't think of you. Not a day. Not one single day." She squeezed his shoulder, then kissed the top of his head. He wanted to leap up and hug her, so that she would hold him back, but she was telling him that she was going to get her hair done. He was to find Margaret and tell her to come inside until she got back from the beauty parlor. It wouldn't take more than an hour or so.

. . .

"She said that?" Still in her coat and hat Margaret sat at his feet, hugging her knees. "That we're gonna stay here?"

"No, but that's what she meant. That she's tired of pretending."

"Of pretending what?"

"Tired of us not being with her." His mind raced through the magnitude of her few words. How annoying that Margaret, of all people, expected exact quotes, every word and nuance perfect. "She said she was always thinking of us, every day. The whole time."

Margaret's smile was raw with happiness. So they would be going to the Burleigh after all. See? Hadn't she told him? Hadn't she been right? Come on, admit it. That's when she'd known, when Daddy's letter came. She could just tell. That's why Mommy had been so quiet these last few days. She was thinking, making up her mind what to do. They'd miss Daddy, of course, poor Daddy, but even if they did go back, he'd still be in jail. This way they'd be with their mother. And pretty soon their father too. When he did get out, because he'd probably come right down here to see them. Yes, that'd be the first thing he'd do. And then he'd see Mommy and she'd see him and they'd both be in love all over again, forever and ever.

"Take off your coat."

"They will. I know they will. And you do too, Thomas, but you don't want to admit it, because I said it first."

He erased Book-Room and printed LIBRARY. He erased two doorways and three windows. Every bit of wall space would be for shelves. Floor to ceiling. Was his father thinking of him every day the way his mother had? Probably not, but that was okay. Someday he'd tell his father about choking on the cigarette Otis had given him. Someday when he was older. When he couldn't get in trouble. When maybe they could laugh about things.

Margaret lay on the loveseat reading a torn book Ann Ronan had let her borrow. Pages fell out as she turned them. She kept sticking them back in, then finally held up just the page to read it. Someday Margaret would have her own library, every shelf crowded with brand-new books, more than she could ever in a lifetime read. The gate clanged shut. He pushed his blueprint—he had written that above the drawing—to the edge of the table where his mother would see it when she came home. Her key turned in the lock. Margaret ran to meet her.

"Oh." She stood still, holding the door open. "I thought it was my mother," she said guiltily.

Louis Dexter looked at her, then in at Thomas. He carried a large bouquet of yellow roses. "I've come to see Miss Talcott. Is she here?"

"No," Margaret said.

"Do you know when she'll be back?"

Margaret shrugged. She looked back at her brother.

"Pretty soon," he said.

"Well, I might wait for her then. If you don't mind, that is."

Again, Margaret looked at her brother.

"Okay," he said.

"Good then!" Mr. Dexter came in. "I'll just sit down a minute. See if she comes. I'm Mr. Dexter," he said as he laid the roses on one side of the loveseat. He removed his hat and unbuttoned his coat, then sat with his hands on his knees, smiling at them.

Not knowing what to say, they lowered their gaze to the floor. When he spoke each looked at the other, in alarm. He asked their names. Margaret and Thomas, Thomas answered for both. He asked old they were. Twelve and eight, Thomas told him. Where did they live?

Belton, Vermont, Thomas said.

"Oh, of course. That's where Miss Talcott's from." He smiled. "And how long are you here for?"

"I don't know," Thomas said.

Mr. Dexter checked his watch. "Did Miss Talcott say when she'd be back?"

Too dry to speak, Thomas's mouth could only open. Now he shrugged.

"She went to the beauty parlor," Margaret said softly.

"Yes. Well, that'll probably take some time then, won't it?" He stood, holding his fine gray hat lightly by its crease. A diamond glinted in his wide gold wedding band. "A lady having her hair done, that's no brief excursion, now is it?" He went to the door then turned to say the flowers were for

Miss Talcott. "Tell her they're from a very fond admirer." He winked at Margaret.

If the gate had even creaked, no one had heard it, but suddenly the door opened and Irene rushed in, hair tightly waved, her face white with dread. What was he doing here? He knew she wouldn't be here. She'd told him she wouldn't. Why had he come? Why did he do this? Why?

To surprise her. See? The roses. It had been eight months. He was going to leave them inside for her to find. He was about to let himself in, but her young visitors had been kind enough to let him in. He touched her cheek and brought his face close to hers. "You look so tired. Very beautiful, but tired."

"Go upstairs! Now!" she told them.

"No," he called before they could leave. "Irene, don't be mad at them. They were very nice. But they're from Belton, Vermont, so of course they'd be lovely children." He nuzzled his forehead against hers. "Almost as lovely as you," he whispered.

"They're my children." She pulled back and stood rigidly apart from him. "They're mine."

He looked at them then, not with the patronizing amusement of moments before, but brokenly, with defeat.

"I'm sorry," she said.

Sorry for what, Thomas wondered as he ran up the stairs after Margaret. For not telling she had children or simply for having these children, poor ragamuffins that they were.

The door to the street closed. She came up a moment later. The powerful engine of his great car roared to life, then was as quickly lost in the distance. Still in her coat, she huddled on the edge of the metal bed with her face in her hands. Stayed there for a long time, but she did not cry. They felt no pity for her, only excitement for what would be theirs again. Her. Their mother.

. . .

In the days that followed, she moved quietly through the forced routine of their lives, but with a heaviness that allowed only the most necessary dialogue. She cooked for them though did not seem to eat herself. She hung their wet socks and underwear to dry at night by the glowing stove and in the morning reminded Thomas to get more coal from the bin, though he had already been downstairs before she was even up. He was awake long before sunrise. If his father had six weeks left in jail, then they might be together again by Christmas. It wasn't that long, but to Margaret it seemed forever. Now that Mr. Dexter was gone, she wanted them to go back home with their mother and if they couldn't afford the bus tickets right now, then why couldn't she at least go to school? Ann Ronan said she was going to stay back if she missed any more time. Thomas was constantly telling her to shut up. She was upsetting their mother.

Irene withdrew to her room for long periods of time. If she slept she seldom looked rested. Instead she was always agitated, bumping into the doorway, gasping when one of Margaret's chattery outbursts broke the silence. She startled easily, as if she were forgetting they were still here. One morning she wrote two more letters, then prepared to walk down the hill to mail them at the post office. Margaret asked to go too. There wouldn't be anyone to play with until the little girls came home from school. She was as sick of her brother as he was of her. Irene said she had other stops to make. It was too snowy, and Margaret would be tired. Margaret promised not to complain once, no matter how many places she had to go.

Irene was buckling her boots. The snow had started late last night. Thomas had just shoveled the front walk and their sidewalk, but the rest of the sidewalks and the road were already ankle deep.

"Please," Margaret begged. "I'll keep up. I promise I will."

"You don't have boots and you don't have leggings so stop, please stop asking me," she said angrily.

"I don't care about boots. I don't need leggings," Margaret persisted.

"Well you should care!" Irene snapped.

"We could probably get some from the church. Mrs. Ronan got Ann's there," Margaret said on her heels to the door. "I know where it is. St. Mary's, Mrs. Ronan told me."

Irene looked down, then bit her lip against whatever she had been about to say. "I may be a little late getting back," she said, then closed the door.

. . .

"Little beggars," the housekeeper muttered, leaving them in the vestibule.

"See!" Thomas said and Margaret covered her mouth, giggling. This was all her idea and they were actually doing it. He hadn't been able to talk or threaten her out of it. Rather than risk her going off alone, he had become her reluctant accomplice.

The high ceilings, the dark, polished wood, the warm, unnatural quiet was like the Farleys'. The priest seemed to float down the stairs. Tall and graceful in the flowing black cassock, he was more delicate than a man should be, Thomas thought. He knew from the housekeeper why they were here, the priest said. To get some boots and, if they had them, leggings, Margaret said, eager, gloating in her adventure, never happier than when she could be solving a problem, always trying to fill gaps, plug endless holes. Smile and be nice, friendly and sweet, it always worked. Leggings would be nice. Any kind would do. Then she could go sliding too. With Ann and her sister. On the sheets of tin Mr. Ronan had brought home. Her voice died out with the priest's silence.

"Talcott," he mused. "Are you in this parish, your family?"

Stricken, Margaret looked to her brother. The lark had taken a bewildering turn. Nice, friendly, and sweet weren't going to be enough.

"Um. I don't know. Maybe we are." Thomas glared at her. Here in the low light, by the lovely furnishings, she looked messy and uncared for, feral in her desperation.

"Are you Catholic?"

"Yes." At least his father was or had been, Thomas was pretty sure.

"Well what school do you go to?"

"We don't go to school. Not right now anyway. But we will. We're going to."

Warning them to hold tight to the railing, the priest led them down to the dusty cellar. Most of the winter clothes were gone now, he said, rooting around in the deep wooden bin in the corner. Let's see now, some old pieces of cloth. One sock. Here you go! Black rubber boots for Thomas; men's, but with rags stuffed in the toes, they should fit all right, he grunted, reaching back in. No boots or leggings, nothing for the little girl, his voice called hollowly from the box. What about these? He held up a big pair of boy's wool pants. There were patches on the knees.

"No, thank you," Margaret said. She cringed from the orangey tweed. They couldn't have been more horrible to her than if they contained a boy.

"Good heavy wool," the priest coaxed, holding them out. "They'll keep you warm." The priest persisted, assuring her they were quite good-looking, even rather jaunty with the red-patched knees.

"They'll be fine. Thank you." Thomas took them from him. He wanted to go. The priest was asking too many questions. About their mother, their father, again about school. Where did they live?

"Kressey Court," Thomas said, and with his first direct answer they were finally on their way.

The boots flopped through the falling snow. A coal truck sped by, splashing up a cold, drenching wave of gray slush. Whimpering, Margaret wiped her legs. "See," he gloated, holding out the pants. "You should've put them on."

She strode ahead.

"Your shoes're all wet and now your legs are too. What good's that?"

Walking faster, as fast as she could manage through the deepening snow, she would not answer him.

"There's nothing wrong with these pants. You're just spoiled, that's what's wrong." He huffed alongside her through the stinging cold. Two young men struggled down steep stairs under the weight of a wide oak wardrobe. A door flipped open and a silky red dress slid onto the snow.

A gray-haired woman came out of the tenement carrying two bulging valises. She slung the wet dress over her arm, then continued down the street after the men and her wardrobe, which seemed now in the distance to be moving of its own accord like an enormous wooden carapace, headed to a cheaper flat or else in with a relative, a son or daughter. Or maybe to see what the junk man might give for her last piece of furniture.

He ran to catch up with his sister, but it was hard with the big boots suctioning into the snow. "You better not fuss either when Mommy says to wear them." He grabbed her arm.

"Leave me alone!"

"No, because you're going to make her cry. You can't get her upset. You have to do what she says. You have to, Margaret. Please?"

. . .

A few days later it was early evening when Mr. Dexter came to the door. He asked Irene if she would go for a ride in his car. He was on his way home, but needed to talk to her. She told him she couldn't leave her children alone at night, but he was welcome to come in if he'd like. Whatever he said in a low voice made her turn from the door and tell them to go upstairs. Quickly!

Even with their ears pressed to the floorboards they couldn't hear much. Mr. Dexter did most of the talking, but his voice was guarded, his tone indistinct. From time to time their mother answered with a dismal sigh. "I can't . . . I've already tried . . . there's no one . . ."

Mr. Dexter's voice rose with impatience. But the wind

that had been blowing all day whistled through the eaves, obscuring his words.

"Of course I do! You know I do!" she cried out.

"No, because if you did, if you really did, you'd do something!" he said angrily. The door closed. His car started and then he was gone. Margaret rose giddily. She got as far as the door when their mother's deep, painful sobs pushed up against the floorboards. Thomas and Margaret sat on the bed, more helpless than if someone had been down there beating her. She moaned and gagged, then shrieked for help, for someone to please help her. They ran down the stairs.

"Mommy!" they cried.

"Go away," she groaned from her dark bed. "Just go away. Please, please just go away."

14

ALREADY WEARING HIS HAT, JACKET, AND BOOTS, THOMAS watched from the window. It was sunny, but frigid. The snow had melted days before, ridging the frozen ground like a scrub board. Christmas was only weeks away. He and Margaret were excited even though they knew there wouldn't be any presents. Probably not even a tree, he warned again, preparing not just his sister, but himself. At least they were with their mother. Still though, when he saw Mr. Ronan drag a scrawny tree out behind his house it was hard not to remember last Christmas, when they had all been together.

Baby James had been dead almost a year then and everyone had been happier. Or that's the way it had seemed. They had eaten dinner at old Bibeau's. As usual Gladys had done most of the cooking. His mother must have helped, even though he couldn't seem to picture her in any particular place or performing any specific chores. What he did remember was Gladys whipping cooked acorn squash with a wooden paddle while Margaret poured in melted butter and cream. His father and old Bibeau sat by the fire, talking. If his mother had been unusually quiet, he wouldn't have thought much of it. She couldn't stand the old man but that was the one day Henry insisted they spend with him. After all, old Bibeau had taken him in when no one else would. Christmas dinner with his family was a very small thank you, considering.

Now that Thomas thought back, he wondered if she'd known that very day that she was leaving. Had she already bought her bus ticket? Or had it really been just that terrible next morning telling her he hated her when what he'd really wanted to ask was "Why don't you love me anymore?" Why had she been so angry? It hadn't been anything, really. He and Margaret had been arguing. Or maybe he'd just been teasing her, but Margaret ran into the kitchen, whining. He remembered the way his mother stood there, through Margaret's complaints, hunched over the washtub, continuing to knead his father's work shirt up and down, up and down the scrub board so hard he heard her knuckles on the glass ridges. Margaret demanded she do something.

"Stop it! Stop it! Stop it! Do you hear me?" she had screamed, lunging at him, suds dripping from her hands as she hit him, slapping, punching, shaking him.

"I didn't do anything. What did I do?" he had cried, while Margaret begged her to stop.

"You're mean, mean, mean, just like your father. Just like him!" she had sobbed, kicking him as he cowered in the corner. "And I'm sick of it! Sick, sick, sick, sick to death of being alone and no one caring."

"I hate you! You're a terrible mother. And I hate you!" he had screamed and she finally stopped. Had she packed her bag then and brought them to Aunt Lena's?

"See them yet?" Margaret called from the table. She had

been cutting snowflakes out of newspaper. With no tree to hang them on, it seemed an empty task, but she said she didn't care. Maybe she'd just give them as Christmas presents. He didn't want one, thank you, he told her. Well, that was good, she answered, snipping into the tiny folds, because she wasn't making one for him, anyway.

"Here they come!" he called, and she ran in to see. The children from Kressey Court were coming home from school. He and Margaret watched them run past the cottage into their houses.

"Where's Mommy?" Margaret whined. They couldn't go outside until she came home from the store. Yesterday her errands had kept her away until it was too dark to go outside. As it was there was probably only an hour of daylight left.

Ann Ronan waved from the street and Margaret banged on the window, gesturing for her to come in. Ann shook her head; she couldn't. Her mother wouldn't let her. But the wide curve of the courtyard was neutral enough territory for any morally displaced children. Clementine had spotted Margaret in the window. She ran up the walk and banged on the door. "I'll play with you," she shouted through the glass to Margaret, who tried to say she couldn't. But then not wanting to hurt Clementine's feelings she opened the door. Clementine shoved her way inside.

"You can't come in here!" Thomas said.

"I already am!" she said. She moved quickly around the room, putting her hand into an empty blue vase, opening and closing a tortoiseshell box, smelling the marble ashtray. Everything she picked up, Thomas ordered her to put down. Just looking, she said. She held a pink porcelain seashell to her ear. He told her not to do that.

"Shut up! I'm tryna hear the waves."

"You can't. It's not real."

"It's a seashell," she scoffed, setting it down hard. "Hey, what're those?" She held up the newsprint snowflakes to peer through. Grateful to have Clementine away from her mother's precious things, Margaret folded paper into a smaller and smaller square. She showed Clementine how to cut a design into the paper. Clementine quickly tired of her own fumbling attempts. Instead she tried hanging the finished snowflakes in the window. She licked the back wet and pressed them against the glass. They kept falling to the floor. Thomas said she'd better go. His mother would be home soon. Clementine said he was just jealous because she was playing with Margaret and not with him. She decided that the snowflakes would stick with paste. They'd make some, she said, pulling the red flour tin from the shelf.

"Margaret!" Thomas warned, but his sister was helpless.

Clementine needed a pan, a spoon, she said, ordering Margaret around the little kitchen, now some water. She lifted the stove lid to draw the flame higher when Margaret could bear her polite cowardice no longer. They weren't supposed to cook, she said.

"I'm not cooking." Clementine clumsily spooned more flour into the pan. "I'm just making paste." She poured in more water from the metal cup Margaret had given her. "This way they'll stick." She bent close to stir the bubbling mixture. "A little more flour," she said. Only this time she tilted the tin over the pan. The rush of flour spilled into the pan, down on the stove top, onto Clementine's shoes, and all over the floor. A cloud of white dust floated in the air.

"Look what you did!" Thomas shouted. "Look at the mess! You're gonna be in trouble for this!"

Clementine ran to the door, slamming it behind her. Margaret was trying to sweep the mess on the floor into the dustpan. With the wet dishrag Thomas wiped away his and Clementine's trail of white footprints across the parlor rug. The bell rang. Sure it was Clementine again, he opened it in a rage.

"Well," said the tall priest. He had a bag in his arms. "So I did find the right house. And hello, Margaret," he said as she came out from the kitchen. Told their mother wasn't home, he said he'd only be a minute. He opened the bag to show them what he'd brought. For Thomas a red wool cap with furry fold-up ear flaps. A pair of red knitted mittens. And look at this, a perfectly good flannel shirt. Just this one little stain on the pocket, he said, trying to scrape it away with his fingernail. And for Margaret—from the second bag he pulled a pair of blue wool leggings—"girls'!" he announced, holding them up, the bib at his own chest. And girls' boots, he said, setting them down on the floor. A nice warm hat, white with mittens to match!

"Thank you," Margaret said, grinning.

"What's that smell?" The priest lifted his head and sniffed at the smoke pouring out from the kitchen. Not only had the glue concoction burned down to the bottom of the charred pan, but the flour on the stove top was burning. Margaret, who still held the broom, stood stunned for a moment, watching as the priest plunged the charred pan under the faucet. Using Thomas's rag, the priest was trying to wipe the smoking flour off the stove.

"What happened? What're you doing? Who are you?" Irene demanded from the doorway.

It was all Clementine's fault, they tried to explain as the priest introduced himself. Father Harrington. He'd just stopped by with warm clothes for the children when the fire broke out.

"The fire?" she gasped, her eyes already swollen raw. It hadn't been very long ago that she'd been crying, so now these tears poured out. It was all too much. And she couldn't do it any more. She just couldn't.

"We'd better get these windows open," the priest grunted as he forced up the balky sashes.

"I'm sorry, Mommy," Margaret wept to see her mother so bereft.

She couldn't look at them, couldn't even lift her head. "I can't," she sobbed from the chair. "I can't . . . I can't . . . I can't . . . I can't . . ."

"You can't what?" Every time the priest asked she groaned. He slid down on one knee to hear better. "Tell me, what is it you can't do? The smoke? Get the smell out? I'll help you. Is that it? Tell me. Tell me now." He touched her hand and she looked up, her once lovely face ravaged by such sorrow that her children stared down at the floor.

"This!" she said, turning her sore, wet gaze on him with as much anger as regret. "Any of it."

. . .

St. Elizabeth's. The first day there Thomas was shoved aside so hard he staggered into a door.

"Don't walk in front of me," growled his assailant, a wide-chested older boy in the same brown trousers and tan shirt they all wore.

Thomas watched him swagger down the corridor. Margaret was in the girls' half of the building. They would see each other at mealtime but not to talk. They would eat their meals in the same dining room, boys on one side, girls on the other, Sister Mary Sebastian had explained when the priest brought them. They were lucky children. As it was, St. Elizabeth's was bursting at the seams, but Father Harrington had persuaded the nun to take them in. Their mother was distraught. No job, no husband, the poor woman could barely take care of herself. Providence, Father Harrington said; something divine had brought him to that little cottage. In the nick of time. A fire. A mother on the verge of a complete breakdown. And now the benevolence of Louis Dexter.

Mr. Dexter had come to the house late in the night after Father Harrington left, promising to be back first thing in the morning. He said the priest had called him. They'd heard his voice veer between anger and exasperation. How dare she have a priest call in her behalf. What did she expect of him? What could he do; think about it, Irene, a man in his position. He had his own situation to consider. She should have been honest from the beginning—about her circumstances. And about the children. Of course it made a difference. How could it not? She was a married woman with children. Children the same age as his. He had his own family to consider, their well-being, their happiness. His wife wasn't a well woman. Such a scandal would destroy her.

Cigar smoke seeped into the cold attic room. It smelled of shame and regret. It always would.

Her flat voice rose with a relentless question, the words ineluctable in their unceasing demand.

"Yes! Yes!" Of course he cared for her.

Again, the same question, again and again, over and over, a dull chant for the dead.

All right! Yes! He did! He loved her! But there was nothing he could do about it, didn't she understand?

. . .

Mr. Dexter's donation to St. Elizabeth's, while small, was most remarkable considering that Mr. Dexter was Episcopalian. The children's mother had worked for him at one time, but the mill had been too rugged a place for a lady of her temperament. And so he had been helping her until she found a better situation for herself.

That first night in the orphanage Thomas lay awake for a long time. He couldn't fall asleep surrounded by so many other whispering, squirming boys. As the newest arrival he got one of the middle beds. The rows along the walls were the most desirable, Monty whispered from the next bed. Monty had just been warned by the nun not to wet his bed again. "Takes a while though. The best one's the corner one," Monty continued as soon as the nun was gone. "That's Robert Groomes's. He's been here the longest, that's why."

Thomas looked up. "How long?" he whispered, his head sinking into the pillow. It had been Groomes who had pushed him into the door.

"Since he was little. Ten years, I think."

"Ten years!"

"Yeah. Except for St. Leo's. He was there for a while too."

Thomas crossed his arms over his face. Ten years. It was like being in jail. Was his father feeling this same numbness? Or would he get used to it? Ten years. He'd be old by then. He'd be twenty-two; Margaret, eighteen. It was all her fault. Once again she'd messed everything up for them. So what if she had hurt Clementine's feelings. She never should have let her into the house. No one else on Kressey Court ever did. Margaret always let things get so terribly out of control that she'd just freeze and turn helpless. Poor Margaret. Father Harrington had to drag her away from her mother to get her into the car. Someone was crying. He lifted his arms to look.

"Shut up, Monty," someone said.

"It ain't me," Monty sniffled back.

"It is too, you crybaby."

"No, it's him. The new kid."

"Hey!" Thomas said. He sat up, but Monty's back was to him.

"It's always him," the voice said with a yawn.

. . .

Except for the fact that he ate and slept in the same building, it was almost like being in a real school again. The girls and boys weren't separated in class, but Margaret was four grades behind him. At recess they eyed each other across the play yard. Margaret was swinging one end of a jump rope. Her brown dress was like the other girls'. Too big, it hung unevenly below the hem of her coat in clumps above her ankles. Without her mother's care her thick hair was wild again.

"Hi, Margaret." He stood next to her.

"Hi." She kept swinging. The girl jumping was up to seventy-eight.

"Tomorrow's Saturday. Maybe Mommy'll come visit." He thought she nodded. She seemed to be in a daze. "Or maybe even Daddy." He whispered, telling her again how that had been one of the letters Irene had gone out to mail the day the paste burned. He hadn't actually seen it, but it made sense that she would have written, care of the sheriff, to Henry asking him to come for them as soon as he could. He said he wasn't sure who the other one had been to. "Couldn't be Aunt Lena though. Uncle Max said not to."

"Ninety-one, ninety-two," the eagerly waiting jumpers chanted. The next girl in made crazy faces, trying to make the jumper laugh and falter.

"Say something." He nudged Margaret's arm.

"What?" she said through her fixed stare.

"I don't know." Something, anything to make him feel better the way he was trying to cheer her up. Why was he always the one having to hold things together? He nudged her, harder this time. The rope bobbled and caught the jumper's ankle. "Hey!" she said.

"I saw that!" Sister Mary Joseph called. A short, bulky woman with girth and height almost the same in inches, she lifted long, heavy skirts and waddled toward him in a rattle of beads and jangling keys. Her cheeks bulged out from her stiff wimple. "That was a push. A deliberate push, young man!" Her hand clamped onto his shoulder.

"I bumped her. By accident!" He raised his eyebrows in a plea for Margaret's confirmation of this, but she was too afraid of the red-faced nun to help him.

"You were bothering her. I saw you."

"She's my sister."

"That only makes it worse, young man!" she panted, steering him back inside the building.

A double detention meant no playtime for the next two days. Instead, he would work in the kitchen peeling carrots and potatoes. He sat on a low stool turning the paring knife around the potato. He'd nicked his thumb. The cook was a fierce-eyed man with a cigarette always burning in the corner of his mouth. Two nuns also worked in the kitchen. The older one did all the baking, assisted by a much younger nun in glasses so thick her eyes looked wavy. The cook had just dragged another sack of potatoes over to Thomas. He picked up a peeled potato. "What the hell's this?" Ashes spilled with every word.

"I don't know. Blood?"

"Jesus Christ!" He threw it into the pail and grabbed Thomas's arm.

"Mr. Kent!" warned the older nun. She was dropping spoonfuls of raisin cookie dough onto long trays that the younger nun slid into the oven.

"He's bleeding all over the potatoes!" he said, flipping Thomas's arm away.

"Then he shouldn't be peeling them," the older nun said. "Just give him another job, Mr. Kent."

"I don't have another job, unless you want blood in the meat loaf too. I told you before this ain't no place for kids. I'm not a damn jailhouse guard, I'm a cook!" With that he hurled a pot cover, which clanged into the sink.

The younger nun hurried over to ask Thomas his name. "All right, Thomas, you come help me. But first let's take care of that cut." All the while Mr. Kent slammed down ladles and cans, banging his way about the kitchen, she washed Thomas's hand under warm water, then patted it dry. She asked how long he'd been here and where in the city he'd come from. Kressey Court, he said, explaining how he was really from Belton, Vermont. To get the gauze right on the cut she had to hold his hand so close he felt her breath on his palm. When she spoke she lisped through large, gapped teeth. Stray ends of red hair stuck out from her wimple. Her eyebrows and lashes were orangey red and magnified under her thick lenses. He couldn't stop looking at her. What seemed at first glance a rash was really freckles. More than he'd ever seen on a face. She cut a strip of cloth and wrapped it around gently. He knew better than mention Mr. Dexter, but he told her about his mother getting sick, for that was what the priest had said. He told her about the burned paste, the terminated bus ride with Margaret, Mr. Wentworth's sleepy classes in the Farleys' hot front parlor, Margaret's kitten scratching old Bibeau, scaring him half to death, lying in the tent at night while the spring peepers sang and raccoons prowled close by under stars so near they almost seemed to fizz.

"Well, it's been an adventure then, hasn't it?" She smiled and returned his hand, placing it in his lap because he had forgotten that it was his, so unaccustomed was he to the touch of another.

. . .

By the time his punishment was over, Margaret was very sick. She had come down with a fever in the middle of the night. She could barely walk, her joints ached so, and there was no food and little liquid her stomach would tolerate.

She had been carried next door to the infirmary, a smaller brick building with high-windowed, southerly oriented porches where the young convalescents lay drying out their lungs in the brief afternoon sun. She stayed there for three days. And for three days of recess her brother stood idly in the play yard. More than alone, he felt unconnected. Something might happen at any time. Groomes or any of the older boys might take a dislike to him and beat him, a violent gust of wind might pick him up and carry him even farther away from the few people who knew him. As if to brace himself, he stood with his back hard against the rough brick wall. At meals he ate nothing except for the sweet pastries, the cakes and cookies Sister Mary Christopher had slid into the oven and out, the only kitchen task her poor sight would allow. He longed to be back there. By the time he left she had known everything about him, even about his double-blade, nickel-plated Palomino jackknife and his father's arrest for trying to get back only what was his. Well, almost everything; he told her about Jesseboy, but not about the pictures or breaking his nose, or about Mr. Dexter's joyful yelps and the ruckus in the air, or about tipping the kitten overboard. To its death. Or about his mother leaving because she had hated him, and him, her; then, but not now, even though it didn't matter anymore. Nothing seemed to.

A week had passed. No visitors came, but few of the other children had visitors, so it didn't seem so bad. He saw Sister Mary Christopher and another nun walking through the play yard and was shocked to see her limp. He ran, waving, but by the time he got near she had disappeared inside the building. He felt bad that she had ignored him. He shouldn't have talked so much. She was probably afraid he'd start up again and she wouldn't be able to get rid of him.

"Hey, Talcott! Your sister's out of the infirmary!" Monty called after him. "I just saw her. She's back in the main house."

He wasn't supposed to, but he ran inside and up the noisy metal stairs. The door to the girls' side was locked, as always. He rang the bell, then knocked, rang the bell again, butting his toe against the brass foot plate. Sister Mary Marion finally opened the door, annoyed to find a boy here. She was the girls' principal. Yes, she said, Margaret had been brought back to her room. She was better, but still weak. Bed rest had been ordered. For at least a week, she told him. He asked if he could see her. Just for a minute. To say hello. No, she said. Margaret had to rest. The next day when he asked to see Margaret again, the same nun told him no again. He came the third day and asked if she was strong enough yet. A tall, imperious woman, Sister Mary Marion stared down at him, her height and piercing stare reminding him of Gladys. He could see his sister in five more days. But not a moment sooner. Did he understand that? Because if he did not, she would have Sister Mary Martin, the boys' principal, explain it to him. Yes, he did, he said, his voice raised in panic before the moving door could close. Margaret would get better faster if she could see him, he shouted. "She gets scared real easy, but if she—"

"Thomas!" Sister Mary Marion stepped outside. The heavy oak door closed behind her. "You have an unnatural need of your sister. You must learn to need no one but yourself. Someday soon you and your sister may be even more separated than the way you are here by a wall. Some of our children don't stay very long. They join other families. And if that happens, you'll have to get used to being on your own. You may have to let Margaret go, Thomas." She opened the door and stepped inside. "We all have to do it at some point in our lives." She said this softly, kindly, with concern in her small, pained smile. "It won't be so hard. Really."

. . .

He stood by the door as the girls filed through, their voices filling the play yard. He was looking for the girl with the rosy cheeks. She had been holding the jump rope with Margaret the last time he'd seen his sister. "Hey! Hey, you!" he called, catching up to her. "You know my sister, Margaret? Margaret Talcott."

She nodded, but wouldn't look up.

"Here. Give her this note." He held out the paper folded into a small tight square. "Please? It's from me."

"No. We can't pass notes. We're not supposed to."

"But I'm her brother. She's sick. It just says hi," he said, opening the note and holding it out. "See? Here. Read it."

"Hey, Tailcutter!" a voice called. It was Groomes. He had begun calling Thomas Tailcutter, which for some reason made everyone laugh. "Who's this, your little girlfriend?" He came surrounded by four boys, each a head shorter than him. The youngest was Monty. Humiliated, the girl fled. "Let me see!" Groomes snatched the note from him and read it aloud.

Dear Margaret,
I hope you are getting better. I tried to see you three times, but the sister said I couldn't. Please send a note back to me. I am very lonesome. I miss you very much.
Love,
Thomas

The four boys hooted with laughter, none louder than Monty.

"Give me that!" Thomas danced around Groomes, trying to grab the paper. Groomes held it over his head, now pretending to read more. "You are my dear darling and I want to kiss you and make—"

With an almost effortless lunge Thomas was on Groomes's back. Both arms were locked around the thick neck and beefy head. Swearing, Groomes spun around, trying to throw him loose, but Thomas held on until Groomes staggered then tripped. With Thomas still a weight on his back he landed on his hands and knees. From behind, Thomas began to pummel his head. A crowd of boys had gathered. Some, who had been bullied in the past by Groomes, shouted for Thomas to give it to him, to hit him, kill him.

"I will. I will," he grunted and punched the side of Groomes's head so hard pain shot up his arm.

Someone was pulling Thomas's arm. "No-good dirty bastard, you no-good dirty bastard," he was still sobbing as the two nuns yanked him to his feet. Groomes's eye was bleeding. He crouched with his face at his knees. He was sobbing too.

"You come with me, young man," the nun insisted, attempting to drag him from the play yard. He knew he should let her subdue him and go to his punishment, but he couldn't. He couldn't walk with her, couldn't be dragged into that enormous building again, so he pushed free of her. As hard as he could. She was a blur of black as she caught the railing.

. . .

There was talk of sending him to St. Leo's Home for Troubled Boys. Instead he was given another detention. In addition, he would take every meal at the sisters' long table and eat in silence. None of the nuns spoke to him. He was passed bread and butter, beets and potatoes, chicken in its perpetually dreary fricassee sauce, all without anyone looking at him. No one would believe that he hadn't struck the nun, only tried to get free of her. Sister Mary Christopher didn't believe him either. For two days she hadn't said a word beyond instructing him in his chores. Today they were alone in the kitchen. She had given him a bowl of butterscotch pudding. It was delicious, he said, scraping his spoon around the rim for the skim of pudding there. Would he like another, she asked, and he ate this one more slowly. She said she'd made the pudding herself. Yesterday, after Sister Mary Frances left the kitchen.

"So you can see good enough to cook?" He was surprised.

"I see well enough to do a lot of things." She stacked another dirty pan on the pile. "But I have to be careful." She laughed, and he smiled gratefully. "Or else I might burn the place down."

"So are you blind?" He turned on the water.

"Well I can see you." She stood close, but seemed to be looking at a spot above his head. "I can't make out the details, that's all."

"Oh." He began scrubbing a pan. "Well that's good," he said over the running water. "Were you born that way?"

"Now that's a personal question, isn't it?" She sounded surprised. Her hand passed lightly over the drainboard until it found her wide spatula he had washed. She dried it then hung it on the nail next to the oven. He watched her limp around the kitchen, hands grazing every surface, not searching as much as gauging, reaffirming where she stood or what she passed.

"I didn't hit that lady, that sister, you know."

"You better learn to control your temper." She brought him another pan to wash.

As he scrubbed he tried to explain how Groomes had grabbed the letter for his sister and read it out loud to everyone.

"But it wasn't Groomes you were really mad at, now was it?" She ran her finger along the bottom of the pan, checking for grease before she dried it.

"Sure it was him."

"No. It was really Sister Mary Marion you were hitting for not letting you see your sister. And that lady on the farm you told me about. And that terrible old man. And your mother, she's another one you'd like to sock, now wouldn't you?"

"No! I'd never do that."

"Yes you will." She wiped her hands, then flipped the towel over her shoulder. "Soon enough. That's where you're headed, you know. Probably even hit Margaret one of these days. If she gets you mad enough." She had been stacking the muffin tins and putting them on the wooden shelves. "If you haven't already hit her, that is," she said, turning. Her magnified, half-closed, dull eyes stared past him.

He scrubbed harder, resentment boiling. She couldn't even see or walk straight, what did she know about anything?

"You don't want to end up in jail like your father, do you?"

He spun around. "My father didn't hit anyone! He was just tryna get his things back, that's all!"

"And isn't that what you were trying to do too? Get what was yours back? Your note? Your sister?"

He wouldn't answer. He didn't have to. She wasn't even supposed to be talking to him.

"Thomas." She touched his shoulder, leaving her hand there. "I could see as well as you once. I didn't even limp. I could run and do everything the other children could. But then one day someone was mad. He wasn't even mad at me, but at something that had nothing to do with me. And right then I guess I screamed too loud or ran in too suddenly. Anyway I startled him, and he picked me up and threw me down the stairs."

"How old were you?"

"Four."

"Who did it?"

"That doesn't matter. He did what he did and nothing was ever the same again."

"So then when you got older and you . . . you . . . well, then you came here and you decided to be a nun." The question turned so convoluted because he had almost said, when you couldn't do anything else.

"They sent me here then. Right after. They were poor. And it was too hard to see me like that. Like this," she added with a light, little laugh.

"I'd hate it if I couldn't see too good! I don't know what I'd do!" he said angrily. He was beginning to understand how hard a world this was, how cruel people could be, not just old Bibeau, and the Farleys, and T. C. Whitby in Belton, Vermont, but people he hadn't even met yet.

15

MARGARET WAS BETTER. HE SAW HER PASSING IN THE CORridor or at meals in the far corner of the crowded dining room. She had lost weight. Her dress hung in deep folds over her bony frame. Sometime during her illness her thick hair had been cut into a bob, but badly. It stuck out like a fuzzy fur hat around her wan face.

It had been snowing for three days. Christmas was next week. Every classroom window was decorated with the snowflakes and striped candy canes the children spent the last hour of every school day cutting from paper and coloring. Margaret's snowflakes might be hanging in his mother's window. Maybe she'd saved them to hang on the Christmas tree. He was convinced they wouldn't be here for Christmas. She wouldn't let that happen. Even if she was still sick, she'd come for them. Or at least visit them. Maybe she hadn't because she wanted to surprise them on Christmas morning. He didn't care if there were no presents. Being with her would be the best present of all.

"Take your seats, children," Sister Mary Andrew called excitedly with a wave of her hand, passing them along, one after another into the auditorium. "Take your seats. Take your seats. Where you always sit. Come along. Let's not keep the nice ladies waiting now."

Little ones up front. Taller children behind. Boys on the left. Girls on the right. As always. Thomas strained in his seat for a glimpse of Margaret. He could just see the bushy top of her head. On the stage feet moved under the crimson curtain. High heels. Ankles. There were ladies up there. Real ones like his mother. COLLERTON LADIES AID SOCIETY, said the red and gold letters on the sign. The lights dimmed. His heart was racing. They had walked through a snowstorm last year to get to the Bibeaus' so she could ask Gladys for a ride into town. Aunt Lena was having a party and his father still wasn't home. His excuse would be that his truck had broken down in the middle of nowhere, but Irene said he had conveniently forgotten. His father hated parties, especially Aunt Lena's. They were loud, with Uncle Max telling dirty jokes and everyone drinking and smoking, even the ladies. By the time Gladys dropped them off, wet and shivering, the party was well under way.

"Look everyone! My baby sister's here! She made it! All the way in from the farm!" Aunt Lena called half drunkenly.

"I have to get out of there. I have to," his mother said in a low, strained voice.

"What, and leave handsome Henry?" Aunt Lena laughed, tripping a little as she tried to take off Margaret's coat. She hadn't undone the collar button. "You won't do that and you know it."

The curtain opened. The right side dragged, then stopped. One of the older boys hurried out from the wings and forced it back. Sister Mary Sebastian, the director, introduced the ladies and thanked them for not only entertaining the children every year but for all their hand-knit caps and mittens and scarves that were so greatly needed and deeply appreciated. The ladies in their blue choral robes smiled out at the children they could not see beyond the bright, dusty footlights. A silver-haired lady's head bobbed as she began to play the piano.

"Silent night, holy night. All is calm. All is bright. Round yon virgin, mother and child," they sang.

The children watched, listening intently. Of course his mother wasn't up there. She would never surprise them like that. She would just simply come. Even if it meant walking through a snowstorm to get to them.

"Sleep in heavenly pee-eace. Slee-eep in heavenly peace."

A great warmth swelled in his heart. He squinted until there were only blue shapes in the blur of lights. The words and the music ached inside of him. Any moment now his chest would burst wide open, with what, he did not know, but it was wonderful, even though it hurt.

. . .

The standoff between Thomas and Groomes had lasted this long because he had ignored the loud, lumbering bully. Groomes still called him Tailcutter, still jostled him in the cafeteria line, spilling his milk, but a new guidepost had taken hold. Thomas was afraid that if he got in another fight his punishment might be not seeing his mother on Christmas Day.

The color was back in Margaret's cheeks. She had a lot of friends. Now whenever he saw her she seemed in a hurry to be off. She was either arm in arm with one of the girls vying for her attention or excelling in yet another jump-rope contest, dodge ball, or Red Rover, Red Rover. Resenting her happiness, he watched her across the play yard. Nothing here was fun for him. It hadn't taken her long to forget about him and all they'd been through. Her turn came for High Water, Low Water. So far no one had jumped as high as Margaret. The girls holding the rope lifted it higher. Starting even farther back, Margaret ran and then right at the last minute sprang easily over the rope. Now it was lifted chest high. Some of the girls on the side covered their mouths. She walked back, then stood a moment, fists clenched, staring fiercely at the rope. In a movement so imperceptible he was sure no one else saw it, her head and upper torso rocked, readying herself. She burst forward. Certain she would fall this time, he squinted as the brown blur cleared the rope, then fell. The girls screamed and converged on her.

"Margaret Talcott! What on earth are you trying to prove?" a nun said, helping her up. Blood ran down her legs from her scraped knees. She was crying. He ran to help, but two girls were already on either side of her. He stood in their way. "I'll bring her."

"Back with the boys now," the nun said, waving him off.

"My friends'll bring me," Margaret said in a small, choked voice.

A chill passed through him. Never had she sounded so much like their mother.

"Move!" the girls said, then helped Margaret limp past him.

"Hey, look," Groomes called pointing as he sulked back. "Even the girls don't wanna play with Tailcutter. That's how queer he is." With Groomes following, baiting him all the way, Thomas walked the length of the play yard. When he came to the building he climbed to the top step then sat down, arms folded on his knees. "Whatcha crying for, Tailcutter? Girls hurt your feelings, you skinny crybaby," Groomes taunted from below. "C'mon down, crybaby. C'mon, I'll play with you."

Through his tears everything was distorted. Even Groomes wasn't Groomes anymore, but a ridiculous voice. And just as he had known Margaret would fall, he could feel his mother's longing. Right now, at this very moment she was thinking of him the way he was thinking of her. He knew she was because he could feel her ache inside. For a moment it was like being together.

. . .

"Please sit down, Thomas." Sister Mary Sebastian closed the door and folded the sides of her heavy skirt onto her lap so she could fit into her chair. She was a large woman with a long face, a pitted nose, and thick black eyebrows. Thomas couldn't help staring at the hairs on her chin. She leafed through the papers on her desk until she found one she wanted. As she read it his mind raced. This was either going to be very good or very bad. A visit to the director's office was serious business. He was either going home or being sent to St. Leo's Home for Troubled Boys. But he'd been on his very best behavior. Even this morning when he got out of bed and slipped his feet into shoes filled with ice cold water he had only dumped them out and ignored the snickering. Groomes's torments had accelerated. Yesterday an ice ball had hit Thomas between the shoulders, knocking the breath out of him for a few seconds. Groomes smirked as he packed another one between big striped Ladies Aid mittens.

"Your father," the nun said, setting the paper aside. She took off one pair of glasses, put on another. "You haven't heard from him since you've been here, is that correct?"

"No, ma'am."

The bushy eyebrows raised over the glasses.

"I mean, Sister."

"Have you heard from him?"

"No."

"We need to get in touch with your father, Thomas. Do you have an address? Is there some way we could write to him?"

"I don't know." He wasn't about to admit that his father was in jail and make it even easier for her to ship him off to St. Leo's.

"Do you know where he is?" Again she picked up the paper. "According to what your mother's written here, she has no idea where he went or what's become of him."

He shrugged. His mother was ashamed to admit it. So she *was* coming. She was ready for them to go back.

"And you don't either?"

"No." He couldn't help grinning, yet he was afraid he might cry.

"Is everything all right, Thomas?"

"I guess so," he said with another shrug.

"Have you been happy here?" This, he could tell, was a tricky question.

"Pretty much."

She smiled. "Well, it appears that everyone here is happy with you pretty much of the time too. Are you working on your temper?"

"I am. Yes, Sister."

She got up and told him he could go back downstairs now. She opened the door and the smell of cinnamon apples baking filled the room. It was almost dinner time. "You can come in now, Margaret," Sister Mary Sebastian said.

"Thomas," Margaret whispered, her face drained with fright. She hurried past him into the office.

Instead of going down to dinner he waited at the bottom of the stairs. Her visit was taking a lot longer than his had.

"Margaret!" he called when he saw her skinny ankles turn on the stairwell above. He ran up to meet her. "What did she want? Was it about Daddy?"

"Shh." She whispered, afraid of them being caught together. She started down the stairs. He grabbed her arm and demanded to know what Sister had said. "She wanted to know where Daddy is," she whispered.

"You didn't tell her, did you?"

She nodded.

"You said he was in jail?"

"She asked me. She said Mommy doesn't know. But we told her, didn't we?" She looked stricken. "Maybe she forgot."

"You know what that means, don't you?" He squeezed her arm.

"No, what?"

"That I'm going to St. Leo's and then you'll be here forever! Alone!" He didn't know what anything meant anymore, but he wanted to punish her for not protecting their father, and, at the same time, he was afraid to raise her hope to the wild level of his.

"She wanted to know about the Farleys."

"The Farleys! What'd you tell her about them for?"

"She knew about them. I didn't tell her."

"She ask about me hitting Jesse-boy?" He pressed her against the banister.

"No! It was just about them. Were they nice people and did they live in a nice house, things like that."

"Yeah?"

"I said they were rich."

"What's wrong with you? You shouldn't've said anything! You're so stupid! You mess everything up! Everything!"

She shoved him away. "I hate you, Thomas! I hate you so much! I'll be glad if you go to St. Leo's! I hope I never see you again!"

. . .

After dinner he waited by the dining room door. As always, Margaret emerged in a cluster of laughing girls. When he called to her, she didn't turn around.

"Hey, Tailcutter!" Groomes said as he left the dining room. "You forgot your books."

He hurried back and slid the pile of books out from under his chair. Late for study hall he ran down the corridor. The only seat left was next to Groomes, who scribbled studiously in his composition tablet. Their assignment for English was to write an essay telling what they were most grateful for. Thomas stared into the distance. There wasn't a thing to be grateful for. Even his shoes were still wet. His sister hated him. The food tonight had been awful by the time he got to it, cold peas and a mushy mix of potatoes and rubbery ham. Now that he thought of it, it was all his father's fault. If he'd been a smarter man, say like Mr. Farley, he would have made enough money for them to own a big house in town and his mother never would have left.

And he and Margaret wouldn't have ended up in a mess like this. He didn't like anyone here and no one liked him. Except maybe Sister Mary Christopher. He picked up his pencil, but what could he say about her? That she had listened to all his troubles, but then he was probably the only kid here that'd ever talked to her, which would only prove what an idiot he was when the essays were hung in the hallways for everyone to read. He could just hear Groomes's singsongy voice, *"Tailcutter's grateful for the wall-eyed, gimpy nun because she can't see how queer he really, really is!"*

"You'd better get busy, Thomas," Sister Mary Martin, the study hall monitor, warned as she came down the row.

"Hey, Monty! What did you write about?" he whispered when she had passed in a camphorous swish of black wool. The small boy's eyes widened and he burst out laughing.

"Thomas, stop talking and get started!" Sister Mary Martin called.

"Peas," Groomes whispered as Thomas picked up his tablet. "He wrote about peas."

The first two pages were stuck together with a thick green paste. So were the next, the next. Peas, smashed between every page. Around him everyone snickered.

The open tablet in hand, he sprang from his chair. He wanted to rub the pages in that big, fleshy face, but Groomes easily batted him away. Thomas lunged again, pulling him onto the floor. "No-good fat bastard," he grunted as they struggled to hit each other, wrestling between the toppled chair legs. Now Groomes straddled his chest, punching his face.

"Stop that! I said stop it!" Sister Mary Martin shouted with a loud smack to the back of Groomes's head. Groomes groaned. Thomas's nose was bleeding. Groomes started to get up, but Thomas rose quicker. He dove, his panting, sobbing frenzy of blows knocking Groomes into the overturned chairs. Now three nuns were trying to pull the boys apart. One held on to his shirt as he strained toward Groomes, Groomes who was the true cause of all his unhappiness.

"You've done it now, Thomas Talcott!" Sister Mary Martin said, shaking her finger at him. "Two weeks' detention! No party! No Christmas! Nothing!"

It wasn't the somber, gravelly-voiced nun his arm batted away, but that finger wagging back and forth in his face. Why was it there? Why was any of this happening?

"St. Leo's," it was declared as the nun lost her balance and staggered into the table. "That's where this one belongs."

. . .

Detention again. But it wasn't so bad because for two hours every afternoon he could be near Sister Mary Christopher. She had scolded him the first day, but now she seemed as pleased with his presence as he was with hers. Groomes, she confided, was a pathetic kid. Abandoned here as an infant, he had no known relatives. He was clever enough, but had no good sense about people. It was as much an ailment, she said, as bad eyes or crippled legs. He had long ago given up trying to be liked. "He has no friends," she said.

"Yes, he does," Thomas said.

"No. Just boys that're scared of him," she said.

After the pans were washed and put away and it was

time to leave the warm kitchen, she would turn her back just long enough for Thomas to fill his pockets with pilfered cookies. He usually shared them with his sister the next day in the play yard. And with her friend Katie. Katie had eyes as big and blue as Margaret's, bright, rosy cheeks, and soft, golden curls. Her smile made him smile. She called him Tommy and always grinned when she said it. Tonight, the cookies had been gingerbread boys. He could only fit one in each pocket. They were for Katie and Margaret.

"Wait!" Sister Mary Christopher was wrapping two gingerbread boys in butcher paper. "I want you to do me a favor. Here. Give one to Robert Groomes."

"No. He'll just start another fight."

"Thomas, you have to try very hard to get along with Robert. You may be here for a long time and you can't always be fighting with him."

"I'm not gonna be here long. I'll be going home pretty soon."

"What makes you think so?" She peered at him.

"Because." His brain reeled in a collision of all the questions he had been afraid to ask. His world existed in separate parts. His father. His mother. This place. Margaret. Himself. Moving any of the pieces was like a raft starting to break apart under him on fast-moving water. "Because it's Christmas. Almost." There. Of course. That was why.

She put her hands on his shoulders and brought her face close. Magnified, her distorted eyes seemed to be searching through a layer of ice. "It's beautiful here at Christmas. There's ham and turkey for dinner, and everyone gets a present. Every single child."

. . .

The next morning he ran through the play yard looking for Margaret. He waited, scowling through the snow glare until she'd had her turn in the game. Their breath billowing in the icy air, the girls linked arms and screamed, "Red Rover, Red Rover, send Margaret over!"

She ran, hard as she could, but couldn't break through. Margaret had gotten tough and the girls all knew it. That's why she had so many friends, he thought. Or maybe followers, like Groomes had. Maybe they were afraid of her.

"Here," he said when she finally trotted over. He gave her the gingerbread boy and she slipped it into her pocket. If anyone saw it, they'd be mobbed. He had already eaten Groomes's. He'd been going to give it to him, but then last night Groomes had put rocks under his sheet. He asked where Katie was. Why? Margaret smirked. Because he had one for her too, he said, feeling foolish. He liked Katie, didn't he, Margaret said; she could tell.

"No. I'm just trying to be nice to your friends, that's all."

"Why don't you have any friends? You're always alone," she said.

"Because I don't want friends. What's the point? Here, anyway."

Silent for a moment, Margaret looked around. Sister Mary Marion watched from the top step, arms folded in her full sleeves, the long black veil whipping up in the quick gusts. Margaret stepped closer. "I think we're going."

"Where?"

"Home."

"When?" Suddenly he wished he still had Groomes's gingerbread boy so he could smash it into bits and leave the crumbs on his pillow. Or in his footlocker. With rocks and water and peas. It wouldn't matter anymore.

Margaret wasn't sure, but this morning Sister Mary Sebastian had called her into the office again. This time the nun had done most of the talking. She said Margaret's mother was a very nice woman. She'd had a hard life, but had done her best in these difficult times to raise such fine children as the two of them were. Unfortunately, Margaret's father still wasn't able to take care of them. Her mother was very concerned that his circumstances had had a terrible effect on the children, especially Margaret.

"What's that mean?" he interrupted.

"Probably because I cry sometimes," Margaret said quickly.

"Sometimes!"

Margaret shrugged. Because that wasn't the most important part. Because then Sister Mary Sebastian asked Margaret if she understood that her mother only wanted her to be happy. Margaret grinned at him.

"What's that mean?" He frowned to hide his own exhilaration.

"That she's taking us back!"

"How do you know?"

"There's going to be a meeting tomorrow. In her office. She wants me to be very polite, she said. Someone's going to be there, she said."

"Yeah, your teacher probably." Margaret hadn't been doing well in school.

"No. Because I'm taking my bath tonight. Don't you see?"

He stared blankly at her. It was a moment before he comprehended. Baths were taken on Saturday nights. Never during the week. This was Wednesday. "Yeah. They're gonna clean you up before they send you to St. Leo's," he said, and tears filled her eyes.

"I'm just kidding. Here." He gave her the second gingerbread boy. What did it matter? After tomorrow, he'd never see Katie again either. "St. Leo's is for boys. Not girls."

"I know!" she wept.

"Well, so stop blubbering then!"

"I will!" she cried and ran off, sobbing.

All through the day, then into the night he waited to be called to the office, to his bath. Maybe they figured it was more important for a girl to look nice. Yeah. A boy had to take care of himself. That's just the way it was. At bedtime he washed his face, ears, and neck with great care. He scrubbed his teeth so hard his gums bled. And when he climbed into his salt-sprinkled sheets, he rolled out and brushed them clean with the flat of his hand, not only impervious, but superior now to the wave of snickering and pillowed squeals that rose around him. He almost felt bad for them. His misery had become their greatest happiness. That's what happened to kids when nobody loved them, he thought as he fell asleep.

It was two days before Christmas. The tall tree in the dining room was covered with decorations the children had made these last few weeks. His call to the office came right after breakfast. Sister Mary Martin stopped him as he left the dining room. Sister Mary Sebastian wanted to see him at nine o'clock.

"Should I bring my clothes?" He couldn't stop grinning.

"What you're wearing is fine, Thomas," she said, then continued her brisk way down the hallway.

But it wasn't. These clothes belonged to the orphanage.

He didn't want to go home in this awful tan shirt and brown pants. He didn't even want his mother to see him dressed like this. It mattered how he looked. She'd always been careful about things like that. So fussy that after she left he'd liked not having to care if things matched, stripes, checks, colors. But now it would matter again. And he wanted it to, desperately.

He and Margaret waited on the slat-backed wooden chairs outside the office. Instead of her uniform Margaret wore a pink and blue dress he'd never seen before. There was a pink ribbon in her smoothed-down hair. Patent leather shoes. Frilly white socks. They had made her look real nice, he thought, but she didn't look as happy as he felt. Even in these dull clothes. Every now and again voices could be heard from inside. He would look at his sister and she would stare down at her shoes, trying to listen. Sister Mary Sebastian's authoritative voice was the easiest to identify. The other two, a man and a woman's, were low, muffled, as if they were revealing secrets. Which they probably were. After all that had happened. Sister Mary Sebastian probably had to be sure their mother and father were going to be all right together. That they could manage the kids and get along okay. Last week a little kid named Bernie Steele had been sent home with his mother and uncle only to come back three days later with awful bruises on his face and a long gash down the back of his head. His uncle wasn't really his uncle after all. Monty said the uncle wanted him to do bad things, but Bernie wouldn't. Bernie was still in the infirmary.

The door opened and Thomas jumped to his feet, grinning.

"It'll be just a minute, Thomas," Sister Mary Sebastian said. "I need to see Margaret first."

Margaret stayed in there a while. That was okay. Made sense. After all, Margaret had been such a crybaby, needing her mother so bad. They knew he could take the waiting and she couldn't. His father wasn't saying much. Mostly it was still Sister Mary Sebastian. Every now and then his mother would agree to whatever was being said. "Yes . . . of course . . . we know that . . . she's such a dear child . . ."

He leaned toward the door. His mother wouldn't talk like that. Not usually. Never. Maybe she had missed them so much, she was saying things she couldn't tell them before. He wondered what she'd tell Sister Mary Sebastian when it was his turn. Usually she'd get real quiet when he came near her. He'd long ago given up trying to hold her hand. She didn't like it. "You're just like your father!" she'd said their last day in the cottage. He'd smiled until he saw the look on her face. Fear almost. As if she were afraid of her own son.

His head shot up. His father was saying something about his jackknife, but he couldn't make it out. He didn't sound mad though. Thomas remembered the day his father had thrown the rusted jackknife into the pond. And how much he had hated his father for doing that. How much he'd hated not losing the jackknife, but his father's rage and pain. He'd tried to act pleased when Gladys gave him the brand-new one on his birthday. But he hadn't really felt it, because he didn't care anymore. It didn't matter. It couldn't. Nothing could matter that much ever again. His father had scolded him all the way home in the truck that night, calling him an ungrateful whelp. He hadn't been able to tell his father it wasn't the jackknife he'd been disappointed in. It was his mother. For not coming on his birthday.

". . . a good companion," his father was saying. "Very polite." He leaned closer. The voice was different. High and nasally. "Believe me, if we could, Margaret, we would . . ."

The door opened. "Thomas." Sister Mary Sebastian steered him inside. He could barely hear her. His eardrums were going to burst. Margaret's head was down, though she watched him with raw, swollen eyes. She was hugging a beautiful new doll. The doll's dress matched hers.

Mr. and Mrs. Farley sat facing the desk. They were all dressed up. The short black veil on Mrs. Farley's red hat puffed up over her pudgy nose with every breath. Mr. Farley wore a gray suit and a blue tie with big white polka dots. He balanced a briefcase on his knees. Neither one looked at Thomas as he sat down beside Margaret. An empty chair stood between the children and the Farleys.

"Say hello, now, Thomas."

"Hello, Sister," he mumbled.

"I meant to Mr. and Mrs. Farley, Thomas."

He glanced at them. "Hello."

Mrs. Farley managed a pained tweak of a smile. Mr. Farley nodded.

"Mr. and Mrs. Farley have come a long way. And for a very good reason. They're very kind people."

"Thank you," Mrs. Farley said primly. She couldn't keep her eyes off Margaret who absently stroked the doll's long blonde curls.

"I must tell you," Sister Mary Sebastian said to the Farleys. "We don't often have such happy endings, especially with the differences in religion. But because Mrs. Talcott is so agreeable to this arrangement, so very anxious, actually, it's certainly not in my authority to present an obstacle." Frowning a little, she adjusted her glasses. "Though I must say, I think Mrs. Talcott was most relieved to hear that the child will be raised in the Catholic faith."

The child. Were they getting rid of Jesse-boy? Was he coming here? What did his mother care if Jesse-boy was Catholic or Protestant?

"Well, we know because our own faith is so important to us," Mr. Farley sniveled. "But in the end, we're all Christians, aren't we?"

Sister Mary Sebastian gave such a patronizing smile, even Thomas could tell she thought he was a fool. Of course hers was the one true religion. But if Mr. Farley didn't care what religion his own son was raised in, why should she? Still, though, this was confusing; the tension in the air, the stiffness. Everyone sat quietly for a few moments.

"Well," Sister Mary Sebastian said. She checked her watch. "Mrs. Talcott's late. I'm sure she said ten though."

"Yes," Mrs. Farley said. "Ten, that's what she said."

"Probably the weather. Last night's sleet turned everything to ice." She glanced over at the tall window. "The streets must be terrible." In front of her were two stacks of papers. She took a paper from one and read it.

"Yes. That's why we got such an early start," Mr. Farley said.

"The roads were terrible," Mrs. Farley said. She had begun to pick at her nails. The sound used to bother Thomas, but now he almost felt bad for her.

"It was mighty slow going," Mr. Farley said.

"We left at three in the morning," Mrs. Farley said. "Just to be on the safe side."

Nodding, Sister picked up the next paper and read that.

"Everything should be there," Mrs. Farley said, and her husband agreed.

Thomas kept trying to get Margaret to look at him. He was smiling. Their mother *was* coming. Maybe the Farleys were going to give them all a ride back to Vermont after they dropped off Jesse-boy. This would be the perfect place for him. Groomes would make his miserable life even worse.

Margaret kept her head down. Her shoulders trembled the way they did when she was trying hard not to cry. He glanced around. No one was looking at him. They probably blamed him for having to get rid of Jesse-boy. After he'd hit him and he and Margaret had run away, they must have realized what a disgusting dirty boy of a son they had.

Mrs. Farley cleared her throat. "Fred," she said in a low voice. "The kaleidoscope."

"Oh, yes. Got it right here." Mr. Farley opened the briefcase and removed a red kaleidoscope. "For you!" He held it out to Thomas.

Thomas thanked him and put it to his eye. Tilting his head all the way back, he aimed it at the bright hanging globe, turning the end slowly. With each flash of the intricate prisms the silence in the room heightened.

"We thought he'd like it," Mrs. Farley was telling the nun. "Our Jesse-boy used to love those," she added, and Margaret gave a little gasp. "Oh, you poor, little thing." Mrs. Farley reached across the empty chair and patted her leg.

"We should've thought. You'd like one too, wouldn't you? Well, don't you worry. We will. First thing we'll do when we get back, is bring you down to Whitby's and let you pick out the one you like best. There's some a lot nicer than that. Right, Fred?"

"Yes. There are, and we'll do that. This afternoon." He checked his watch. "If we get back in time."

"And if not, first thing in the morning then. Right, Fred?"

"First thing!" he agreed.

Margaret whimpered and laid her brow on the doll's head. Sister Mary Sebastian had been watching her. "Try to be happy, dear. It'll be fine. You'll see," she said. "And you already know the Farley family. Some children leave here with perfect strangers."

"Yes, dear. We'll take such good care of you." Mrs. Farley patted Margaret's leg again. "You know we will, now, don't you?"

"Why? What do you mean?" Thomas asked, of no one in particular. And no one answered.

Sister Mary Sebastian removed her glasses, put on another pair. "Why don't we begin?" she said to the Farleys. "You can start reading through these papers. And then when Mrs. Talcott comes everyone can sign." She handed a sheaf of papers to Mr. Farley and one to his wife.

Thomas gripped the edge of Sister's desk. "My mother's taking us back, isn't she?"

The Farleys busied themselves, reading. Mrs. Farley's lips moved from line to line. Sister Mary Sebastian folded her arms into her sleeves. "Perhaps we'd better start explaining things to Thomas," she said to them, though she looked right at him now. "I'd been hoping to do it with your mother here, but we're running late, and I know Mr. and Mrs. Farley have to get back as soon as they can."

"Yes," Mrs. Farley said. "Poor Jesse-boy. His cold was deep in his chest. But Otis and his wife are there. They're so good with him. You remember Otis," she said to Margaret now, telling her how Otis and his wife were expecting a baby in the spring. "Won't that be nice? Jesse-boy's so excited. A brand-new baby to look forward to." She couldn't wait, she added with an eager shiver.

Mr. Farley told Sister Mary Sebastian his wife loved babies. Yes, Mrs. Farley agreed. The papers in her hand shook. Baby anythings. And Jesse-boy was the same way, wasn't he, Fred? Oh, yes, kittens, lambs, calves. Puppies. Ducklings, she added almost feebly.

"Yes," Sister Mary Sebastian said with a glance at the brown metal clock on the wall. Ten thirty-five. Sister was a very busy woman. Behind her the crucifix seemed to grow from the top of her head. Christ's eyes were closed, his head sagged to one side, chin slumped at his shoulder in defeat. "Now Thomas, as I was saying, you're certainly old enough to understand what's going on here. In fact, I'm sure you already do."

Margaret was crying. Mrs. Farley opened her purse and offered a lacy handkerchief. But Margaret couldn't see it through her tears.

"Thomas is a very bright boy," Sister Mary Sebastian told Mrs. Farley as if this one last plea might work.

"Oh, yes. He is. We know that," Mrs. Farley said, trying to minister to Margaret, who shrank away from her.

"No!" Margaret burst out. "I don't want to go. I want to stay with Thomas."

"You have to, dear," Sister Mary Sebastian said.

"No, she doesn't," Thomas said. "Not if she doesn't want to. She can stay with me. She's supposed to. I'm her brother!"

"Now, Thomas, listen," Sister Mary Sebastian said. "Listen to me. I know this is hard. I know it's painful to have to be separated from your sister, but right now Mr. and Mrs. Farley can only take one child. Maybe sometime in the future they can take you too—we've certainly discussed it—but for now, with their son doing so poorly, they can only take Margaret."

"No! Don't make her go there. Please!" he begged the nun, who'd obviously been through this enough times to have her speeches and heart well-prepared. "She hates it there!"

"See! I knew he'd do this," Mrs. Farley told her husband. "He's a very selfish boy. And he wasn't very nice at all to our son last time," she informed Sister Mary Sebastian in a tremulous voice. "And . . . well . . . for other certain reasons I'd rather not speak of here. Especially in front of this poor little girl." She was sniffling.

"I'm not going!" Margaret sobbed. "I won't go there!"

Thomas reached for his sister's hand, but she shrank from him too.

"You have to, dear," Sister Mary Sebastian said again softly. "It's already been decided. It's what your mother wants. She'll be here any minute now, and she'll tell you the same thing. She wants you to have a good life. And so do the Farleys. They've driven all the way down here to bring you back for Christmas. And for their son's birthday. Just think, you'll be with your lovely new family for Christmas. And I know, Thomas," she said, looking over her glasses, with stern emphasis on each word, "that you'll be happy if your sister's happy."

"She won't be with *them*! They're the ones that caused all the trouble in the first place. That's why my father can't take care of us. Because they made him go to jail!"

"Now you just hold on there, young man," Mr. Farley said. "Your father stole something from me. He broke the law and he was punished. And just so you'll know, he's not in jail. He got out a week ago. But he's not sitting in this chair, now is he? No, because he's not a fit father—"

"Even his wife says the same thing," Mrs. Farley told the nun over her husband's angry voice.

"—which is why you're on the road you're on, young man, beating a poor boy who can't even defend himself, with a knife no less, then setting my barn on fire besides. Burned the whole back wall and half the roof," he told the nun. "Here, see for yourself." He unfolded a stained, wrinkled paper and handed it to her. She looked at the paper, then as quickly, folded it. "That's the sort of boy we're dealing with. Rough and depraved! Not worth a tinker's damn! Just like the—"

"Fred! Please don't," Mrs. Farley gasped. "The mother will be here soon. Let her deal with him."

Sister Mary Sebastian looked hard at Thomas, not shocked so much as warning him to toe the line here.

"No, because this is what we don't want Margaret exposed to anymore. She's just too dear a child," Mr. Farley was telling Sister Mary Sebastian. "And she means so much to our son."

"Yes, she's such a comfort." Mrs. Farley patted her eyes with the handkerchief.

"They get along so well," Mr. Farley added.

"But that's not true, Mr. Farley," came Margaret's small voice. "Thomas didn't draw that picture. Jesse-boy did. He showed me it and that's why Thomas hit him."

"Margaret, that's a terrible thing to say. Jesse-boy would never do something like that. And you know that." Mr. Farley's lean face strained purple.

"Well, he did. And *she* knows because he did it before too. Lots of times, and she caught him. And she cried so he promised her he'd never do it again. But he did. Only that time Thomas hit him."

Mr. Farley stared at his wife. She smiled blankly, placidly back. "Nonsense. Of course not," he said to Sister Mary Sebastian. "The boy's an invalid, right, Phyllis? He's lucky he can breathe some days."

"Poor thing." Tears leaked from Mrs. Farley's closed eyes.

From the hallway came a noise, voices: the room seemed to shudder as if a hard wind had suddenly struck the outer walls. "No, no, you can't," a woman protested. "You just wait outside. Wait! Wait! Do you hear me, sir? Sir! Sir!" she was demanding when the door was thrown open.

There he stood in soiled dark clothes, the coarse cloth stiff with sweat, grease, and blood, stained and still flecked from yesterday's butchering, because with the call he had risen from a dead man's dreamless sleep, buttoning his shirt as he ran to meet the car, sure this was a nightmare, had to be, because of all the hard luck and loss in his life, this was the most incomprehensible, that she would do such a thing, give away their children, her own flesh and blood. Her life and future. And his.

"She's not right, not thinking straight at least," Gladys had said from behind the wheel.

"But even a sick animal doesn't abandon its young!" he had roared back, then said the same to her, Irene, when they finally got there.

She kept trying to shush him, worried her neighbors might hear, "So please, please whisper," she begged while he told her flat-out what he'd held inside for so long, all the pain and anger, and the wanting, the ache of how much they loved her—especially the boy and girl. He could not say their names, for weeks had not, because their absence made his failure too real.

Now, with the badgering nun still at his heels, he looked around, frantic, wild-eyed, afraid almost, as if in the fury and rejection he'd lost everything, didn't know where he was, maybe didn't even know them, his children.

They jumped up and ran at him. And then he did something Thomas had never seen before. He knelt down and held out his long, hard arms and held them so tightly it hurt. They pressed close, breathing in his tobaccoey reek and the harsh smell of blood.

"Excuse me, sir." Sister Mary Sebastian loomed over them. "You can't just barge in here like—"

"I'm their father. These are my children. And I'm taking them home with me," he said, from his knees, as afraid to let them go as they were of being released.

"Where? To live in your truck?" Mrs. Farley cried out shrilly. "He doesn't have a home," she told Sister Mary Sebastian. "That's why we're here. Her own mother wants us to take her."

"My wife's got no say in this," Henry said, rising over the children. He held them in front of him, arms pinned over their shoulders. "And she knows it. That's why she didn't come."

"Oh why, because you threatened her?" Mrs. Farley turned to the nun. "She's probably afraid. He's a very violent man."

Henry Talcott stared at the round little woman. Thomas pressed harder against him, as if to hold back his father's rage.

"Watch yourself there, Henry," Mr. Farley warned, pointing. "Don't you make a wrong move now or you'll regret it. I promise you."

"The only thing I regret is never telling you what a lying, cheating, spineless son of a bitch you are, Farley." He took a deep breath. "Guess I just did, didn't I?"

"How can you talk like that in front of these children?" Mrs. Farley gasped. "See?" she said to the nun. "This is all this poor girl has. A father who curses like that. And a mother who doesn't care or even want them!"

"No," Henry Talcott said. "That's not true. It's me she doesn't care about anymore. And it's not that she doesn't want them. She just knows how much I do."

16

GLADYS WAS WAITING IN THE CAR. SHE HAD DRIVEN HENRY down in Dr. Creel's car. In the middle of the night the old doctor had been called to Jesse-boy's bedside. Otis's wife said the boy was so excited over Margaret's coming that he'd gotten his asthma so worked up he couldn't catch his breath. Gladys told Henry, then brought him to Farley's house, where he demanded that Otis tell him exactly where the Farleys had gone. Otis hadn't known for sure, just that it was an orphanage. And that the little girl's mother was signing her over for the Farleys to adopt. Next, Henry stood in the sleet banging on Lena's door. It was still dark, and scared as she was of Henry, she was even more afraid of being saddled with her sister's kids again. She refused to tell him anything. From there Gladys drove Henry down to Collerton. He went to the rooming house, the only address he knew. It was with even greater delight that the gloating rooming-house lady directed the children's father to the pale blue cottage on Kressey Court.

Gladys drove them back to Vermont. Margaret slept up front in her father's arms. Thomas had the whole backseat to himself, with the doctor's black watch plaid Pendleton lap blanket covering him. "You all right back there?" Gladys would call every now and again in her rough voice, as if all that was after them, all that mattered was the cold wind blowing at the iced-up glass. Didn't she know how alone he felt back there? He was safe now, and still alone. But maybe that was the price a boy had to pay for growing up before he was ready. Before he wanted to.

Years later, he would realize watching his own children, then his children's children, that it wasn't just him, but everyone it happened to. Because that's what growing up is. That's what it feels like. Like being alone. And strong. Even when you don't want to be, or think you can't. You just suddenly are. And that was how Margaret would describe it also, years later at his seventieth birthday party. "To my wonderful brother," she said, her champagne glass raised. "He always took care of his little sister. And oh God, I was such a selfish little thing. But then one day I had to be strong too. Just like you, Thomas. But it was easy, because you showed me how."

. . .

How many of us are there now? Too many to count, it seems some days. Gladys and Dad never did get officially married. I found out years later when I was looking for their marriage certificate one day at city hall. No such document existed, I was informed.

Our lives together began with us living in Dr. Creel's three spare rooms upstairs. Too old to be climbing the stairs every night, Dr. Creel slept down in the little parlor next to his office. Gladys did all the nursing and records; though not much bookkeeping, Dr. Creel would complain. Because there's none to do, she would snap right back. Most of his patients couldn't pay, so he'd overcharge the few who could. This didn't settle well with the more affluent patients. Oftentimes the aging doctor fell asleep at a sickbed in the wee hours of the morning. So when a new younger physician moved into a fancy office downtown, more and more of Dr. Creel's patients switched over.

Gladys and my father had two boys two years apart, Honus and Henry Jr. Gladys named Honus after her father. It was the first I knew old Bibeau ever had a real name. He died a year after we got back from seeing our mother. Died in his sleep and did one good thing in his mean life, left his house and the acre it stood on to Gladys. We moved back there and, no matter how hard things got (which was hard for a long time after), my father would never take out another loan from anyone for anything for the rest of his life. If we didn't have the money we went without. And if it was really needed we saved up first.

No one ever knew Honus and Henry Jr. were born illegitimate because when Dr. Creel delivered them he checked the box for Married. Didn't matter to him. (Or maybe he just never knew. Nobody else did.) My father and mother never did get divorced. Strange in a way, and yet what was there to be divorced from? I suppose in his mind it ended the day she left, but just as he couldn't tell us that or why until that snowy morning in the orphanage office, so perhaps he could not bring himself to make official an act, a state of being he never wanted. Not in his whole life, I think. Not ever. Sometimes, especially when Margaret was a grown woman, I'd see it in his face, how much he loved her. And for the stunning image she had become of her mother.

Such beauty. In my mother's case was it a curse? A waste?

I think so, but I can't be sure because I never saw my mother again. Or wanted to. I only know what Margaret has told me about her.

Margaret stopped off in Collerton once with her new husband on her way home from her honeymoon in Boston. She told my mother it was a spur-of-the moment decision, though knowing my sister, I doubt it. She called first, from a pay phone around the corner from the cottage. (Lena had probably given Margaret the number. Lena would pester Margaret for years, for rides, money, attention, and Margaret was always kind.) She described the silence at the end of the line when she said her name. A silence that felt, when she closed her eyes, like being back in the tent. Alone. And covered with bee stings.

Margaret. Her mother repeated the name as if trying to place her in the murky context of someone she used to be. Margaret Talcott. Your daughter, she made my sister say. And hearing that, I hated her for the first time. For that unjustifiable cruelty. Because *that* Margaret was not just her daughter, her lost child to forget, but still my dear little sister. *That* Margaret would always be more mine than hers. Recovering quickly, she invited Margaret and Brad to come by in the morning. Ten thirty would be good. Margaret explained that they were on their way home and could only come now. Brad had to be back at his base in the morning.

"Well, it'll have to be now then, won't it?" she said, trying to sound pleasant though not eager.

It was still that same little cottage. Only to Margaret's adult eyes it seemed even smaller, tiny. More like a dollhouse with everything in place, a bouquet of fading yellow roses the only jarring note. Brown petals lay on the table-top. One stem was bare, the water brackish and cloudy. Irene poured Brad a brandy and said she was delighted her daughter had married an Army man, adding that her father had been in the Army. Margaret wasn't sure who she meant, Henry or Grandfather Jalley. The brandy and my mother's charm warmed shy Brad into talking more than Margaret had ever seen before. When my mother went into the kitchen to get more iced tea for herself and Margaret, Margaret read the card that was stuck in the withered roses.

"Thinking of you" was all it said. The rest of the visit was pleasant, however awkward for all that went unsaid, all the questions my mother never asked, the names she never spoke. Mine. I asked, and Margaret hesitated, but as always, she was truthful and said, "No, but she only did when I brought someone up. She'd ask how they were doing and—"

"But you never brought me up, right?" I said, feeling the old edge, the cold, hard barrier rising.

"Of course I did. But she just listened."

"She never asked anything, not one thing about me?"

"She's a very unhappy woman, Tom. I could tell. She has a job at a department store. And she's got beautiful clothes and nice furniture, but she's all alone and she regrets what she did. What she gave up."

"She told you that?"

"No, but I could tell. I could see it in her eyes. Even Brad, he said the same thing. She's got the saddest eyes."

"Yeah, probably because you stayed more than five minutes."

"No, Tom, really! If you saw her you'd know what I mean."

"Well that ain't gonna happen," I laughed, but Margaret continued. She was positive my mother was all alone in life. When Margaret had asked (as only Margaret would dare) how Mr. Dexter was doing, my mother said he'd died a few years before. In an automobile accident. We both recalled the stormy night he'd come banging on the cottage door.

"That's why I think it must have been Dad who sent the roses. And that's why she couldn't throw them out."

"In a million years he wouldn't do that," I assured her. "And besides he doesn't know the first thing about sending flowers to someone." The poor man barely knew how to make a long distance telephone call. But Margaret was convinced. She said there was something strange about those dead flowers in that perfect little cottage. It was almost as if she couldn't enjoy them or throw them out.

"So I think he did. Just like I've always thought he still loves her," she said.

"That's ridiculous! He loves Gladys," I said, surprised at how angry I felt.

"I know, but sometimes when Dad looks at me I know what he's thinking. He's thinking of Mom."

Yes. For how could any of us not? How do you forget your mother? Even if you make that conscious effort, there is still the longing, the almost primitive need. In the marrow, the blood, the genes. What is so very amazing then is how she could walk out on her children and then betray them.

So, no, I never saw her again. When each of my own children were born I was angry and hurt all over again because she had deprived them of their grandmother, even though they loved Gladys, who was surely more fun, hiking and camping and fishing with them, than my mother ever would have been.

Years later, when our mother died, my sister begged me to go to the funeral with her. Margaret's own children refused to attend the services for a woman who had abandoned their mother. There was no wake, just the funeral mass in a cavernous, nearly empty stone church. We walked the casket down the aisle. We had discussed it in the car on our way to Collerton. Irony or not, we would take, as once before, the little we could of her presence, her body if not her soul. In the second pew sat a few wizened women who had worked with my mother at the department store. They leaned forward, surprised, probably thinking we were some bequest-driven niece or nephew who'd never bothered visiting the poor old woman when she was alive. At the back of the church was a dapper, nervous-looking old man. After the service, he left quickly before the casket came up the aisle. Was he another married suitor? I wondered if there had been many more after Mr. Dexter, each as devoted and as furtive in departure. She must have been a breathtaking companion—for men who couldn't stay too long or give too much.

When we went to the cottage afterward to go through her few possessions, another vase of yellow roses stood on the kitchen table.

"Thinking of you," Margaret read the card aloud. "So it couldn't have been Daddy." Henry Talcott had died ten years before. "I wonder when they came. Oh look." She picked up the envelope. "Here's the date. Five days ago. August twenty-first. Now what's August? Your birthday. Oh

Tom," she cried, throwing her arms around me. "Oh my poor Tommy. You sent them. And the others too. You did that, didn't you? It was your birthday and you . . . you wanted her to know you were thinking of her."

Margaret had herself a good cry. And I let it go at that. But the selfish truth was, for at least one day a year, I had found a way of making my mother remember me, think about me, and maybe even miss me as much as I have always missed her.

Even as an old man now there are still moments when I feel that twelve-year-old boy's emptiness deep in my heart. Part of me will always be that distrustful child, alone, afraid, and sometimes angry for no reason that I can explain. I long ago gave up judging her. I will never know what inexorable needs must have driven her from us. Perhaps it is self-delusion but I have always chosen to believe that her decision was a painful one. I can only pity her for all the love and living she left behind. Children, grandchildren she never knew, now, great-grandchildren.

Margaret got my father to talk about it only once. She said it was late in the day and they were sitting on old Bibeau's porch watching the streaks of color fade behind the trees with the setting sun. My father enjoyed seeing the new houses built across the road on Farley's pastures. Mr. Farley had died some years before. He'd been bringing a lost calf out of the woods when he collapsed and died of a stroke not far from our old tent site. A year or two later Mrs. Farley and Jesse-boy moved to Arizona where, according to letters he sent Margaret through the years, unanswered letters, he has become a watercolorist of some local renown.

Whenever the contractor wasn't on the site my father

would walk over and talk to the carpenters while they worked. One hot day he brought ice-cold bottles of Gladys's root beer and her ham salad and a jar of homemade piccalilli. Gladys said it reminded her of old times, how much he loved sitting around and shooting the breeze at the end of a long day. He was always a better talker with men, she said. With women he'd freeze up. Margaret being the exception, she added. My father had cancer then, but only he and Gladys knew. Six more months, the doctor said. He lasted a year, long enough to see Henry Jr. marry one of the Tillotson girls. It was a big fancy church wedding and the older sister played the organ.

But that day on the porch Margaret didn't know he was dying, only that he looked old, and frail, and more tired than she could remember. In the warmth of the porch and his nearness she told him all the things I never did, what a wonderful man, a wonderful father he'd been. And how hard it must have been, working night and day while he tried to hold on to his children. And probably his sanity, she added. "Not many men would've done what you did, Daddy," she told him, then took his hand in hers. He didn't grip back, she said, but let her hold it while they sat in the quiet dusk. He was trembling. Finally, an awful sob wrenched up from his chest.

"It's a terrible thing letting your kids down. Failing them. And that's what always hurt most of all. That I couldn't keep her for you. I couldn't hold on to her."

"She didn't want to stay. It wasn't your fault. Just like it wasn't my fault or Tom's."

"I begged her to come back. I want you to know that. I did. I said I'd quit butchering. I'd get a job in town, anything she wanted I'd do. And if she liked it better there in a big city like Collerton, well, that was fine too, I'd move in there with her. That very day. The next week, whatever she wanted. I promised her I'd never let anything bad as Jamie's dying happen to her again, ever. And all she said was, 'I can't. I just can't,' shivering, like it almost sickened her, the thought of it. Of me. Even Gladys tried. She went in with me that morning. Your mother just sat there, shivering and staring down at her hands the whole time Gladys told her how much I loved her. How I loved her more than any other woman I'd ever known. And by that she meant herself, of course. And I was so broken up then, I never even thought how she felt. Gladys, I mean. I just hope she knows. I've tried to make it up to her. She's been a good wife."

"And a good mother," Margaret said.

A wonderful mother.

With gratitude to Kathryn Court, my editor, and Jean V. Naggar, my agent, for the clarity of their vision and their kindness through these many years.

For more from Mary McGarry Morris, look for the 

A Hole in the Universe
"There are few contemporary authors whose work can absorb readers so fully and with such immediacy that the line between character and reader begins to seem dangerously thin. Among these few is the brilliant Mary McGarry Morris." —*Los Angeles Times*

After spending twenty years in jail for a senseless murder committed in his youth, Gordon Loomis returns home to a changed world.
ISBN 0-14-303472-3

Fiona Range
"Morris is a master storyteller . . . *Fiona Range* is a wealth of passion and heartbreak." —*USA Today*

Fiona Range is a beautiful, volatile and smart-tongued woman who has developed a high threshold for emotional pain. But her strength is put to the test when she meets Patrick Grady, a man who may or may not be her missing father.
ISBN 0-14-00184-4

Songs in Ordinary Time
"A gritty, beautifully crafted novel rich in wisdom and suspense . . . secures Morris's status as one of our finest American writers."
—*The Miami Herald*

It is the summer of 1960 in Atkinson, Vermont, and Marie Fermoyle's ambition for her three teenage children make her easy prey for a mysterious con man with a deadly secret.
ISBN 0-14-024482-4

A Dangerous Woman
"At once thrilling and deeply affecting. . . . Should burnish Ms. Morris's reputation as one of the most skillful writers at work in America today."
—Michiko Kakutani, *The New York Times*

Martha Horgan, like most women, craves love, independence, and companionship, but her relentless honesty makes her painfully vulnerable to those around her.
ISBN 0-14-027211-9

Vanished
"Astonishing. Morris's book should be judged on its own merits, and against the work of our most highly practiced and accomplished novelists."
—*Vogue*

Aubrey Wallace is the kind of man nobody notices. Dotty Johnson is a woman that no one can ignore. When a child disappears from a Massachusetts town, together they find themselves in danger.
ISBN 0-14-027210-0

FOR THE BEST IN PAPERBACKS, LOOK FOR THE